Half a King

Joe Abercrombie

D1352369

CORK CITY LIBRARY
WITHDRAWN
FROM STOCK

W F HOWES LTD

This large print edition published in 2015 by
W F Howes Ltd
Unit 4, Rearsby Business Park, Gaddesby Lane,
Rearsby, Leicester LE7 4YH

1 3 5 7 9 10 8 6 4 2

First published in the United Kingdom in 2014
by HarperCollins*Publishers*

Copyright © Joe Abercrombie, 2014

The right of Joe Abercrombie to be identified as
the author of this work has been asserted by him
in accordance with the Copyright, Designs and
Patents Act, 1988.

All rights reserved

A CIP catalogue record for this book is available
from the British Library

ISBN 978 1 47129 478 5

Typeset by Palimpsest Book Production Limited,
Falkirk, Stirlingshire

Printed and bound in Great Britain
by TJ International Ltd, Padstow, Cornwall

MIX
Paper from
responsible sources
FSC
www.fsc.org   FSC® C013056

For Grace

Better gear
Than good sense
A traveller cannot carry

From Hávamál, the Speech of the High One

PART I

THE BLACK CHAIR

THE GREATER GOOD

There was a harsh gale blowing on the night Yarvi learned he was a king. Or half a king, at least.

A seeking wind, the Gettlanders called it, for it found out every chink and keyhole, moaning Mother Sea's dead chill into every dwelling, no matter how high the fires were banked or how close the folk were huddled.

It tore at the shutters in the narrow windows of Mother Gundring's chambers and rattled even the iron-bound door in its frame. It taunted the flames in the firepit and they spat and crackled in their anger, casting clawing shadows from the dried herbs hanging, throwing flickering light upon the root that Mother Gundring held up in her knobbled fingers.

'And this?'

It looked like nothing so much as a clod of dirt, but Yarvi had learned better. 'Black-tongue root.'

'And why might a minister reach for it, my prince?'

'A minister hopes they won't have to. Boiled in water it can't be seen or tasted, but is a most deadly poison.'

3

Mother Gundring tossed the root aside. 'Ministers must sometimes reach for dark things.'

'Ministers must find the lesser evil,' said Yarvi.

'And weigh the greater good. Five right from five.' Mother Gundring gave a single approving nod and Yarvi flushed with pride. The approval of Gettland's minister was not easily won. 'And the riddles on the test will be easier.'

'The test.' Yarvi rubbed nervously at the crooked palm of his bad hand with the thumb of his good.

'You will pass.'

'You can't be sure.'

'It is a minister's place always to doubt—'

'But always to seem certain,' he finished for her.

'See? I know you.' That was true. No one knew him better, even in his own family. Especially in his own family. 'I have never had a sharper pupil. You will pass at the first asking.'

'And I'll be Prince Yarvi no more.' All he felt at that thought was relief. 'I'll have no family and no birthright.'

'You will be Brother Yarvi, and your family will be the Ministry.' The firelight found the creases about Mother Gundring's eyes as she smiled. 'Your birthright will be the plants and the books and the soft word spoken. You will remember and advise, heal and speak truth, know the secret ways and smooth the path for Father Peace in every tongue. As I have tried to do. There is no nobler work, whatever nonsense the muscle-smothered fools spout in the training square.'

'The muscle-smothered fools are harder to ignore when you're in the square with them.'

'Huh.' She curled her tongue and spat into the fire. 'Once you pass the test you only need go there to tend a broken head when the play gets too rough. One day you will carry my staff.' She nodded towards the tapering length of studded and slotted elf-metal which leaned against the wall. 'One day you will sit beside the Black Chair, and be Father Yarvi.'

'Father Yarvi.' He squirmed on his stool at that thought. 'I lack the wisdom.' He meant he lacked the courage, but lacked the courage to admit it.

'Wisdom can be learned, my prince.'

He held his left hand, such as it was, up to the light. 'And hands? Can you teach those?'

'You may lack a hand, but the gods have given you rarer gifts.'

He snorted. 'My fine singing voice, you mean?'

'Why not? And a quick mind, and empathy, and strength. Only the kind of strength that makes a great minister, rather than a great king. You have been touched by Father Peace, Yarvi. Always remember: strong men are many, wise men are few.'

'No doubt why women make better ministers.'

'And better tea, in general.' Gundring slurped from the cup he brought her every evening, and nodded approval again. 'But the making of tea is another of your mighty talents.'

'Hero's work indeed. Will you give me less flattery when I've turned from prince into minister?'

'You will get such flattery as you deserve, and my foot in your arse the rest of the time.'

Yarvi sighed. 'Some things never change.'

'Now to history.' Mother Gundring slid one of the books from its shelf, stones set into the gilded spine winking red and green.

'Now? I have to be up with Mother Sun to feed your doves. I was hoping to get some sleep before—'

'I'll let you sleep when you've passed the test.'

'No you won't.'

'You're right, I won't.' She licked one finger, ancient paper crackling as she turned the pages. 'Tell me, my prince, into how many splinters did the elves break God?'

'Four hundred and nine. The four hundred Small Gods, the six Tall Gods, the first man and woman, and Death, who guards the Last Door. But isn't this more the business of a prayer-weaver than a minister?'

Mother Gundring clicked her tongue. 'All knowledge is the business of the minister, for only what is known can be controlled. Name the six Tall Gods.'

'Mother Sea and Father Earth, Mother Sun and Father Moon, Mother War and—'

The door banged wide and that seeking wind tore through the chamber. The flames in the firepit jumped as Yarvi did, dancing distorted in the hundred hundred jars and bottles on the shelves. A figure blundered up the steps, setting the bunches of plants swinging like hanged men behind him.

It was Yarvi's Uncle Odem, hair plastered to his

pale face with the rain and his chest heaving. He stared at Yarvi, eyes wide, and opened his mouth but made no sound. One needed no gift of empathy to see he was weighed down by heavy news.

'What is it?' croaked Yarvi, his throat tight with fear.

His uncle dropped to his knees, hands on the greasy straw. He bowed his head, and spoke two words, low and raw.

'My king.'

And Yarvi knew his father and brother were dead.

DUTY

They hardly looked dead.

Only very white, laid out on those chill slabs in that chill room with shrouds drawn up to their armpits and naked swords gleaming on their chests. Yarvi kept expecting his brother's mouth to twitch in sleep. His father's eyes to open, to meet his with that familiar scorn. But they did not. They never would again.

Death had opened the Last Door for them, and from that portal none return.

'How did it happen?' Yarvi heard his mother saying from the doorway. Her voice was steady as ever.

'Treachery, my queen,' murmured his Uncle Odem.

'I am queen no more.'

'Of course . . . I am sorry, Laithlin.'

Yarvi reached out and gently touched his father's shoulder. So cold. He wondered when he last touched his father. Had he ever? He remembered well enough the last time they had spoken any words that mattered. Months before.

A man swings the scythe and the axe, his father

had said. *A man pulls the oar and makes fast the knot. Most of all a man holds the shield. A man holds the line. A man stands by his shoulder-man. What kind of man can do none of these things?*

I didn't ask for half a hand, Yarvi had said, trapped where he so often found himself, on the barren ground between shame and fury.

I didn't ask for half a son.

And now King Uthrik was dead, and his King's Circle, hastily resized, was a weight on Yarvi's brow. A weight far heavier than that thin band of gold deserved to be.

'I asked you how they died,' his mother was saying.

'They went to speak peace with Grom-gil-Gorm.'

'There can be no peace with the damn Vanstermen,' came the deep voice of Hurik, his mother's Chosen Shield.

'There must be vengeance,' said Yarvi's mother.

His uncle tried to calm the storm. 'Surely time to grieve, first. The High King has forbidden open war until—'

'Vengeance!' Her voice was sharp as broken glass. 'Quick as lightning, hot as fire.'

Yarvi's eyes crawled to his brother's corpse. There was quick and hot, or had been. Strong-jawed, thick-necked, already the makings of a dark beard like their father's. As unlike Yarvi as it was possible to be. His brother had loved him, he supposed. A bruising love where every pat was just

9

this side of a slap. The love one has for something always beneath you.

'Vengeance,' growled Hurik. 'The Vanstermen must be made to pay.'

'Damn the Vanstermen,' said Yarvi's mother. 'Our own people must be made to serve. They must be shown their new king has iron in him. Once they are happy on their knees you can make Mother Sea rise with your tears.'

Yarvi's uncle gave a heavy sigh. 'Vengeance, then. But is he ready, Laithlin? He has never been a fighter—'

'He must fight, ready or not!' snapped his mother. People had always talked around Yarvi as though he was deaf as well as crippled. It seemed his sudden rise to power had not cured them of the habit. 'Make preparations for a great raid.'

'Where shall we attack?' asked Hurik.

'All that matters is that we attack. Leave us.'

Yarvi heard the door closing and his mother's footsteps, soft across the cold floor.

'Stop crying,' she said. It was only then that Yarvi realized his eyes were swimming, and he wiped them, and sniffed, and was ashamed. Always he was ashamed

She gripped him by the shoulders. 'Stand tall, Yarvi.'

'I'm sorry,' he said, trying to puff out his chest the way his brother might have. Always he was sorry.

'You are a king, now.' She twisted his crooked

cloak-buckle into place, tried to tame his pale blonde hair, close-clipped but always wild, and finally laid cool fingertips against his cheek. 'You must never be sorry. You must wear your father's sword, and lead a raid against the Vanstermen.'

Yarvi swallowed. The idea of going on a raid had always filled him with dread. To lead one?

Odem must have seen his horror. 'I will be your shoulder-man, my king, always beside you, my shield at the ready. However I can help you, I will.'

'My thanks,' mumbled Yarvi. All the help he wanted was to be sent to Skekenhouse to take the Minister's Test, to sit in the shadows rather than be thrust into the light. But that hope was dust now. Like badly-mixed mortar, his hopes were prone to crumble.

'You must make Grom-gil-Gorm suffer for this,' said his mother. 'Then you must marry your cousin.'

He could only stare into her iron-grey eyes. Stare a little upward as she was still taller than he. 'What?'

The soft touch became an irresistible grip about his jaw. 'Listen to me, Yarvi, and listen well. You are the king. This may not be what either of us wanted, but this is what we have. You hold all our hopes now, and you hold them at the brink of a precipice. You are not respected. You have few allies. You must bind our family together by marrying Odem's daughter Isriun, just as your brother was to do. We have spoken of it. It is agreed.'

Uncle Odem was quick to balance ice with

11

warmth. 'Nothing would please me more than to stand as your marriage-father, my king, and see our families forever joined.'

Isriun's feelings were not mentioned, Yarvi noticed. No more than his. 'But . . .'

His mother's brow hardened. Her eyes narrowed. He had seen heroes tremble beneath that look, and Yarvi was no hero. 'I was betrothed to your Uncle Uthil, whose sword-work the warriors still whisper of. Your Uncle Uthil, who should have been king.' Her voice cracked as though the words were painful. 'When Mother Sea swallowed him and they raised his empty howe above the shore, I married your father in his place. I put aside my feelings and did my duty. So must you.'

Yarvi's eyes slid back to his brother's handsome corpse, wondering that she could plan so calmly with her dead husband and son laid out within arm's reach. 'You don't weep for them?'

A sudden spasm gripped his mother's face, all her carefully arranged beauty splitting, lips curling from her teeth and her eyes screwing up and the cords in her neck standing stark. For a terrible moment Yarvi did not know if she would beat him or break down in wailing sobs and could not say which scared him more. Then she took a ragged breath, pushed one loose strand of golden hair into its proper place, and was herself again.

'One of us at least must be a man.' And with that kingly gift she turned and swept from the room.

Yarvi clenched his fists. Or he clenched one, and

squeezed the other thumb against the twisted stub of his one finger.

'Thanks for the encouragement, Mother.'

Always he was angry. As soon as it was too late to do him any good.

He heard his uncle step close, speaking with the soft voice one might use on a skittish foal. 'You know your mother loves you.'

'Do I?'

'She has to be strong. For you. For the land. For your father.'

Yarvi looked from his father's body to his uncle's face. So like, yet so unlike. 'Thank the gods you're here,' he said, the words rough in his throat. At least there was one member of his family who cared for him.

'I am sorry, Yarvi. I truly am.' Odem put his hand on Yarvi's shoulder, a glimmer of tears in his eyes. 'But Laithlin is right. We must do what is best for Gettland. We must put our feelings aside.'

Yarvi heaved up a sigh. 'I know.'

His feelings had been put aside ever since he could remember.

A WAY TO WIN

'Keimdal, you will spar with the king.'

Yarvi had to smother a fool's giggle when he heard the master-at-arms apply the word to him. Probably the four score young warriors gathered opposite were all stifling their own laughter. Certainly they would be once they saw their new king fight. No doubt, by then, laughter would be the last thing on Yarvi's mind.

They were his subjects now, of course. His servants. His men, all sworn to die upon his whim. Yet they felt even more a row of scornful enemies than when he had faced them as a boy.

He still felt like a boy. More like a boy than ever.

'It will be my honour.' Keimdal did not look especially honoured as he stepped from his fellows and out into the training square, moving as easily in a coat of mail as a maiden in her shift. He took up a shield and wooden practice sword and made the air whistle with some fearsome swipes. He might have been less than a year older than Yarvi but he looked five: half a head taller, far thicker in the chest and shoulder and already boasting red stubble on his heavy jaw.

'Are you ready, my king?' muttered Odem in Yarvi's ear.

'Clearly not,' hissed Yarvi, but there was no escape. The King of Gettland must be a doting son to Mother War, however ill-suited he might be. He had to prove to the older warriors ranged around the square that he could be more than a one-handed embarrassment. He had to find a way to win. *There is always a way*, his mother used to tell him.

But despite his undoubted gifts of a quick mind, empathy, and a fine singing voice, he could not think of one.

Today the training square had been marked out on the beach, eight strides of sand on a side and a spear driven into the ground at each corner. Every day they found different ground for it – rocks, woods, bogs, Thorlby's narrow streets, even in the river – for a man of Gettland must be equally ready to fight wherever he stands. Or equally unready, in Yarvi's case.

But the battles around the Shattered Sea were fought most often on its ragged shore, so on the shore they practised most often, and Yarvi had taken enough mouthfuls of sand in his time to beach a longship. As Mother Sun sank behind the hills the veterans would be sparring up to their knees in the brine. But now the tide was out across flats streaked with mirror-puddles, and the only dampness came from the hard spray on the salt wind, and the sweat leaking from Yarvi at the unfamiliar weight of his mail.

Gods, how he hated his mail. How he hated Hunnan, the master-at-arms who had been for so many years his chief tormentor. How he loathed swords and shields, and detested the training square, and despised the warriors who made it their home. And most of all how he hated his own bad joke of a hand, which meant he could never be one of them.

'Watch your footing, my king,' murmured Odem.

'My footing won't be my problem,' snapped Yarvi. 'I have two feet, at least.'

For three years he had scarcely touched a sword, spending every waking hour in Mother Gundring's chambers, studying the uses of plants and the tongues of far-off places. Learning the names of the Small Gods and taking such very special care over his penmanship. While he had been learning how to mend wounds these boys – these men, he realized with a sour taste in his mouth – had put all their efforts into learning how to make them.

Odem gave him a reassuring clap on the shoulder which nearly knocked him over. 'Keep your shield up. Wait for your chance.'

Yarvi snorted. If they waited for his chance they would be here until the tide drowned them all. His shield was lashed tight about his withered forearm with a sorry mass of strapping, and he clung to the handle with his thumb and one stub of finger, arm already burning to the shoulder from the effort of letting the damn thing dangle.

'Our king has been away from the square for

16

some time,' called Master Hunnan, and worked his mouth as though the words were bitter. 'Go gently today.'

'I'll try not to hurt him too badly!' shouted Yarvi.

There was some laughter, but he thought it had an edge of scorn. Jokes are a poor substitute in a fight for strong sinews and a shield-hand. He looked into Keimdal's eyes, and saw his easy confidence, and tried to tell himself that strong men are many and wise men few. Even in his own skull the thought rang hollow.

Master Hunnan did not smile. No joke was funny, no child lovable, no woman beautiful enough to bend those iron lips. He only gave Yarvi that same long stare he always used to have, as full of quiet contempt for him whether prince or king. 'Begin!' he barked.

If quickness was a mercy, it was a merciful bout indeed.

The first blow crashed on Yarvi's shield, tore the handle from his feeble grip so that the rim caught him in the mouth and sent him stumbling. He managed by some shred of instinct to parry the next so that it glanced from his shoulder and numbed his arm, but he never even saw the third, only felt the sharp pain as his ankle was swept from under him and he crashed down on his back, all his breath wheezing out like the air from a split bellows.

He lay blinking for a moment. They still told tales of his Uncle Uthil's matchless performances in the square. It seemed his own might live just as long in the memory. Alas, for very different reasons.

Keimdal thrust his wooden sword into the sand and offered his hand. 'My king.' Far better disguised than it used to be, but Yarvi thought there was a mocking curl to the corner of his mouth.

'You've got better,' Yarvi forced through his clenched teeth, twisting his crippled hand free of the useless shield-straps so Keimdal had no choice but to grasp it to pull him to his feet.

'As have you, my king.' Yarvi could see Keimdal's disgust as he touched the twisted thing, and made sure to give him a parting tickle with the stub of his finger. A petty gesture, perhaps, but the weak must thrive on small revenges.

'I've got worse,' muttered Yarvi as Keimdal walked back to his peers. 'If you can believe it.'

He caught sight of a girl's face among the younger students. Thirteen years old, maybe, fierce-eyed, dark hair flicking around her sharp cheeks. Probably Yarvi should have been grateful Hunnan had not picked her to give him his beating. Perhaps that would be next in the procession of humiliations.

The master-at-arms gave a scornful shake of his head as he turned away and the anger surged up in Yarvi, bitter as a winter tide. His brother might have inherited all their father's strength, but he had got his full share of the rage.

'Shall we have another bout?' he snapped across the square.

18

Keimdal's brows went up, then he shrugged his broad shoulders and hefted his sword and shield. 'If you command.'

'Oh, I do.'

A grumbling passed around the older men and Hunnan frowned even harder. Must they endure more of this demeaning farce? If their king was embarrassed they were embarrassed, and in Yarvi they could see embarrassments enough to crowd the rest of their days.

He felt his uncle gently take his arm. 'My king,' he murmured, soft and soothing. Always he was soft and soothing as a breeze on a summer day. 'Perhaps you should not exert yourself too much—'

'You're right, of course,' said Yarvi. *A fool is his anger's slave,* Mother Gundring once told him. *The wise man's anger is his tool.* 'Hurik. You stand for me.'

There was a silence as all eyes turned to the queen's Chosen Shield, sitting huge and silent on the carved stool that marked him out among Gettland's most honoured warriors, the great scar down his cheek becoming a white streak where it touched his beard.

'My king,' he rumbled as he stood and worked one arm through the tangled strapping of the fallen shield. Yarvi handed him his training sword. It looked like a toy in Hurik's great, scarred fist. You could hear his footsteps as he took his place opposite Keimdal, suddenly looking very much his sixteen years. Hurik crouched, twisting his boots into the sand, then bared his teeth and made a fighting growl, deep and throbbing, louder and louder until the square seemed to shake with it, and Yarvi saw Keimdal's eyes wide with doubt and fear, just as he had always dreamed of seeing them.

'Begin,' he said.

This bout was over quicker even than the last, but no one could have called it merciful.

To give Keimdal his due, he leapt in bravely enough, but Hurik caught the blow on his sword, wooden blades scraping, then darted in quick as a snake despite his size and kicked Keimdal's feet away. The lad whooped as he fell, but only until Hurik's shield rim caught him above the eye with a hollow ping and knocked him half senseless. Hurik frowned as he stepped forward, planted his boot on Keimdal's sword hand and ground it under his heel. Keimdal groaned, one half of his grimace plastered with sand, the other blood-streaked from the gash on his forehead.

The girls might not have agreed, but Yarvi thought he had never looked better.

He swept the warriors with a glare, then. The kind his mother gave a slave who displeased her. 'One to me,' he said, and he stepped over Keimdal's fallen sword as he strode from the square, choosing a path that forced Master Hunnan to shuffle awkwardly aside.

'That was ungenerous, my king,' said Uncle Odem, falling into step at his shoulder. 'But not unfunny.'

'I'm glad I made you laugh,' grunted Yarvi.

'Much more than that, you made me proud.'

Yarvi glanced sideways and saw his uncle looking back, calm and even. Always he was calm and even as fresh-fallen snow.

'Glorious victories make fine songs, Yarvi, but inglorious ones are no worse once the bards are done with them. Glorious defeats, meanwhile, are just defeats.'

'On the battlefield there are no rules,' said Yarvi, remembering something his father told him once when he was drunk and bored with shouting at his dogs.

'Exactly.' Odem put his strong hand on Yarvi's shoulder, and Yarvi wondered how much happier his life might have been had his uncle been his father. 'A king must win. The rest is dust.'

BETWEEN GODS AND MEN

'Mother Sun and Father Moon, shine your gold and silver lights upon . . . this union between Yarvi, son of Laithlin, and Isriun, daughter of Odem . . .'

The towering statues of the six Tall Gods glowered down with pitiless garnet eyes. Above them, in niches ringing the dome of the ceiling, the amber figures of the small gods gleamed. All judging Yarvi's worth and no doubt finding him as horribly wanting as he did himself.

He curled up his withered hand and tried to work it further into his sleeve. Everyone in the Godshall knew well enough what he had on the end of his arm. Or what he hadn't.

Yet still he tried to hide it.

'Mother Sea and Father Earth, grant them your harvests and your bounty, send them good weather-luck and good weaponluck . . .'

In the centre of the hall the Black Chair stood upon its dais. It was an elf-relic from the time before the Breaking of God, forged by unknown arts from a single piece of black metal, impossibly delicate and impossibly strong, and countless years had left not a single scratch upon it.

Seat of kings, between gods and men. Far too high for such a wretched thing as Yarvi to sit in. He felt unworthy even to look upon it.

'Mother War and Father Peace, grant them the strength to face whatever Fate brings . . .'

He had expected to be a minister. To give up wife and children with hardly a thought. Kissing the aged cheek of Grandmother Wexen when he passed the test was the closest he had hoped to come to romance. Now he was to share his life, such as it was, with a girl he hardly knew.

Isriun's palm was clammy against his, sacred cloth wrapped about their clasped hands to make a clumsy bundle. They gripped each other, and were tied together, and pressed together by the wishes of their parents, and bound together by the needs of Gettland, and still it felt as if there was an unbridgeable chasm between them.

'Oh, He Who Sprouts the Seed, grant them healthy issue . . .'

Yarvi knew what every guest was thinking. *Not crippled issue. Not one-handed issue.* He stole a glance sideways at this small, slight, yellow-haired girl who should have been his brother's wife. She looked scared and slightly sick. But who wouldn't, being forced to marry half a man?

This was everyone's second best. A day of celebration mourned by all. A tragic compromise.

'Oh, She Who Guards the Locks, keep safe their household . . .'

Only Brinyolf the Prayer-Weaver was enjoying himself. He had spun one ponderous blessing for Isriun at her betrothal to Yarvi's brother and now – to his delight if not hers – got the chance to construct a second. His voice droned on, exhorting Tall Gods and Small Gods to grant fertility in their fields, and obedience in their slaves, and no one would have been surprised by a plea for regularity in their bowels next. Yarvi hunched his shoulders, swamped by one of the heavy furs his father used to wear, dreading the magnitude of Brinyolf's blessing at the wedding itself.

'Oh, She of the Ewer, pour prosperity upon this royal couple, upon their parents and their subjects, and upon all of Gettland!'

The prayer-weaver stepped back, smug as a new parent, his chin vanishing into the roll of fat beneath it.

'I shall be brief,' said Mother Gundring, with the slightest knowing glance at Yarvi. He spluttered on a stifled laugh, then caught his mother's eye upon him, cold as the winter sea, and had no need to stifle another.

'A kingdom stands upon two pillars,' spoke the old minister. 'We already have a strong king.' No one laughed. Admirable self control. 'Soon, gods willing, we will have a strong queen also.' Yarvi saw Isriun's pale throat flutter as she swallowed.

Mother Gundring beckoned forward Yarvi's

mother and his Uncle Odem, the one person who looked happy to be in attendance, to give their blessing by placing their hands upon the bundle. Then with an effort she lifted high her staff, tubes and rods of the same elf-metal as the Black Chair gleaming, and called out, 'They are promised!'

So it was done. Isriun was not asked for an opinion on the matter, and neither was Yarvi. It seemed there was little interest in the opinions of kings. Certainly not of this one. The audience, a hundred strong or more, served up restrained applause. The men – heads of some of Gettland's greatest families, sword-hilts and cloak-buckles set with gold – beat approval on broad chests with heavy fists. On the other side of the hall the women – hair glistening with fresh oil and their household keys hung on best jewel-lustred chains – tapped fingers politely in their scented palms.

Mother Gundring unwrapped the sacred cloth and Yarvi snatched free his good hand, sticky-pink and tingling. His uncle seized him by the shoulders and said into his ear, 'Well done!', though Yarvi had done nothing but stand there and sing some promises he hardly understood.

The guests filed out, and Brinyolf closed the doors of the hall with an echoing clap, leaving Yarvi and Isriun alone with the gods, the Black Chair, the weight of their uncertain future, and an ocean of awkward silence.

Isriun rubbed gently at the hand that had held Yarvi's, and looked at the floor. He looked at the floor too, not that there was anything so very interesting down there. He cleared his throat. He shifted his sword-belt. It still hung strangely on him. He felt as if it always would. 'I'm sorry,' he said, at last.

She looked up, one eye shining in the heavy darkness. 'Why are you sorry?' Then she remembered to add uncertainly, 'my king?'

He almost said *That you'll have half a man for a husband*, but settled for, 'That you're passed around my family like a feast-day cup.'

'On feast-day, everyone's happy to get the cup.' She gave a bitter little smile. 'I'm the one who should be sorry. Imagine me a queen.' And she snorted as though there never was a more foolish joke.

'Imagine me a king.'

'You are a king.'

He blinked at that. He had been so fixed on his shortcomings it had never occurred she might be fixed on her own. That thought, as the misery of others often can, made him feel just a little better.

'You manage your father's household.' He looked down at the golden key hanging on her chest. 'That's no small task.'

'But a queen manages the business of a country! Everyone says your mother has a high art at it. Laithlin, the Golden Queen!' She spoke the name like a magic spell. 'They say she's owed a thousand thousand favours, that a debt to her is a matter for pride. They say her word is valued higher than gold among merchants, because gold may go down in worth but her word never does. They say some traders of the far north have given up praying to the gods and worship her instead.' She spoke faster and faster, and chewed at her nails, and tugged at one thin hand with the other, eyes opening very wide. 'There's a rumour she lays silver eggs.'

Yarvi had to laugh. 'I'm reasonably sure that one's false.'

'But she's raised granaries and had channels dug and brought more earth under the plough so there'll never again be a famine that forces folk to draw lots to see who must find new homes across the sea.' Isriun's shoulders drifted up as she spoke until they were hunched about her ears. 'And people flock to Thorlby from across the world to trade, so the city's tripled in size and split its walls and your mother's built new walls and split them again.'

'True, but—'

'I've heard she has a mighty scheme to stamp every coin of one weight, and these coins will pass through all the lands about the Shattered Sea, so that every trade will be made with her face, and make her richer even than the High King in Skekenhouse! How will . . . ?' Isriun's shoulders slumped and she flicked at the key on her chest and set it swinging by its chain. 'How can the likes of *me*—'

'There's always a way.' Yarvi caught Isriun's hand in his before she could get her vanishing nails to her teeth again. 'My mother will help you. She's your aunt, isn't she?'

'*She'll* help *me*?' Instead of pulling her hand away she drew him closer by it. 'Your father may have been a great warrior but I rather think he was your less fearsome parent.'

Yarvi smiled, but he did not deny it. 'You were luckier. My uncle's always as calm as still water.'

Isriun glanced nervously towards the door. 'You don't know my father like I do.'

'Then . . . I'll help you.' He had held her hand half the morning and it could have been a dead fish in his clammy palm. Now it felt like something else entirely – strong, and cool, and very much alive. 'Isn't that the point of a marriage?'

'Not just that.' She seemed suddenly very close, taper-light reflected in the corners of her eyes, teeth shining between parted lips.

There was a smell to her, not sweet and not sour, he could not name it. Faint, but it made his heart jump.

He did not know if he should close his eyes, then she did, so he did, and their noses bumped awkwardly.

Her breath tickled at his cheek and made his skin flush hot. Frighteningly hot.

Her lips just barely brushed his and he broke away with all the dignity of a startled rabbit, caught his leg on his sword and nearly fell over it.

'Sorry,' she said, shrinking back and staring at the floor.

'It's me who should be sorry.' For a king Yarvi spent a great deal of his time apologizing. 'I'm the sorriest man in Gettland. No doubt my brother gave you a better kiss. More practice . . . I suppose.'

'All your brother did was talk about the battles he'd win,' she muttered at her feet.

'No danger of that with me.' He could not have said why he did it – to shock her, or as revenge for the failed kiss, or simply to be honest – but he held up his crooked hand, shaking his sleeve free so it was between them in all its ugliness.

He expected her to flinch, to pale, to step away, but she only looked thoughtfully at it. 'Does it hurt?'

'Not really . . . sometimes.'

She reached out, then, sliding her fingers around his knobbled knuckles and pressing at the crooked palm with her thumb while the breath stopped in his throat. No one had ever touched that hand as if it was just a hand. A piece of flesh with feelings like any other.

'I heard you beat Keimdal in the square even so,' she said.

'I only gave the order. I learned a long time ago that I'm not much good at fair fights.'

'A warrior fights,' she said, looking him in the eye. 'A king commands.' And with a grin she drew him up the dais. He went uneasily, for even though this was his hall, with every step he felt more like a trespasser.

'The Black Chair,' he muttered as they reached it.

'Your chair,' said Isriun, and to his horror she

OAK CITY LIBRARY

reached out and swept her fingertips down the perfect metal of the arm with a hiss that made Yarvi's skin prickle. 'Hard to believe it's the oldest thing here. Made by the hands of elves before the Breaking of the World.'

'You're interested in the elves?' he squeaked, terrified she might make him touch it or, more awful yet, sit in it, and desperate for a distraction.

'I've read every book Mother Gundring has about them,' she said.

Yarvi blinked. 'You read?'

'I once trained to be a minister. I was Mother Gundring's apprentice, before you. Bound for a life of books, and plants, and soft words spoken.'

'She never said so.' It seemed they had more in common than he had imagined.

'I was promised to your brother, and that was the end of it. We must do what's best for Gettland.'

They gave much the same sigh at much the same time. 'So everyone tells me,' said Yarvi. 'We've both lost the Ministry.'

'But gained each other. And we've gained this.' Her eyes shone as she gave the perfect curve of the Black Chair's arm one last stroke. 'No mean wedding present.' Her light fingertips slipped from the metal and onto the back of his hand, and he found that he very much liked having them there. 'We were meant to discuss when we'll be married.'

'As soon as I get back,' he said, voice slightly hoarse.

She gave his withered hand one last squeeze then

let it fall. 'I'll expect a better kiss after your victory, my king.'

As he watched her walk away Yarvi was almost glad neither one of them had joined the Ministry. 'I'll try not to trip over my sword!' he called as she reached the doorway.

She smiled at him over her shoulder as she slipped through, the daylight setting a glow in her hair. Then the doors shut softly behind her. Leaving Yarvi marooned on the dais, in the midst of all that silent space, his doubts suddenly looming even higher than the Tall Gods above. It took a fearsome effort to turn his head back towards the Black Chair.

Could he truly sit in it, between gods and men? He, who could hardly bring himself to touch it with his crippled joke of a hand? He made himself reach out, his breath coming shallow. Made himself lay his one trembling fingertip upon the metal.

Very cold and very hard. Just as a king must be.

Just as Yarvi's father used to be, sitting there with the King's Circle on his furrowed brow. His scarred hands gripping the arms, the pommel of his sword never far out of reach. The sword that hung at Yarvi's belt now, dragging at him with its unfamiliar weight.

I didn't ask for half a son.

And Yarvi shrank from the empty chair with even less dignity than when his father still sat in it. Not towards the doors of the Godshall and the waiting crowd beyond, but away towards the statue of Father Peace, pressing himself to the stone and working his fingers into the crack beside the giant leg of the patron god of ministers. In silence the hidden door sprang open, and like a thief fleeing the scene of his crime Yarvi slipped into the blackness beyond.

The citadel was full of secret ways, but nowhere so riddled as the Godshall. Passages passed under its floor, inside its walls, within its very dome. Ministers of old had used them to show the will of the gods with the odd little miracle – feathers fluttering down, or smoke rising behind the statues. Once blood had been dripped on Gettland's reluctant warriors as the king called for war.

The passageways were dark and full of sounds, but Yarvi had no fear of them. These tunnels had long been his domain. He had hidden from his father's blazing anger in the darkness. From his brother's crushing love. From his mother's chill disappointment. He could find his way from one end of the citadel to the other without once stepping into the light.

Here he knew all the ways, as any good minister should.

Here he was safe.

DOVES

The dovecote was perched in the top of one of the citadel's highest towers, streaked inside and out with centuries of droppings, and through its many windows a chill wind blew.

As Mother Gundring's apprentice, feeding the doves had been Yarvi's task. Feeding them, and teaching them the messages they were to speak, and watching them clatter into the sky to take news, and offers, and threats to other ministers about the Shattered Sea.

From the many cages ranked around the walls they looked down on him now, the doves, and one great bronze-feathered eagle which must have brought a message from the High King in Skekenhouse. The one person in the lands around the Shattered Sea who had the right to make requests of Yarvi now. Yet here he sat against the dropping-speckled wall, picking at the nail on his shrivelled hand, buried beneath a howe of demands he could never fulfil.

He had always been weak, but he never felt truly powerless until they made him a king.

He heard shuffling feet on the steps and Mother

33

Gundring ducked through the low doorway, breathing hard.

'I thought you'd never get here,' said Yarvi.

'My king,' replied the old minister once she had the breath. 'You were expected before the Godshall.'

'Aren't the tunnels meant for a king's escape?'

'From armed enemies. From your family, your subjects, not to mention your bride-to-be, less so.' She peered up at the domed ceiling, at the gods painted there as birds, taking to a brilliant sky. 'Were you planning to fly away?'

'To Catalia, perhaps, or the land of the Alyuks, or up the Divine River to Kalyiv.' Yarvi shrugged. 'But I don't have two good hands, never mind two good wings.'

Mother Gundring nodded. 'In the end, we must all be what we are.'

'And what am I?'

'The King of Gettland.'

He swallowed then, knowing how disappointed she must be. How disappointed he was himself. In the songs great kings rarely crawled off to hide from their own people. He caught sight of the eagle as he looked away, huge and serene in its cage.

'Grandmother Wexen has sent a message?'

'A message,' echoed one of the doves in its scratching mockery of a voice. 'A message. A message.'

Mother Gundring frowned up at the eagle, still as a stuffed trophy. 'It came from Skekenhouse five days ago. Grandmother Wexen sent to ask when you would arrive for your test.'

Yarvi remembered the one time he had seen the First of Ministers, a few years before when the High King had visited Thorlby. The High King had seemed a grim and grasping old man, offended by everything. Yarvi's mother had been obliged to soothe him when someone did not bow in quite the manner he liked. Yarvi's brother had laughed that such a feeble little wisp-haired man should rule the Shattered Sea, but his laughter died when he saw the number of warriors that followed him. Yarvi's father had raged because the High King took gifts and gave none. Mother Gundring had clicked her tongue and said, *The wealthier a man is, the more he craves wealth.*

Grandmother Wexen had scarcely left her proper place at the High King's side, ever smiling like a kindly grandparent. When Yarvi knelt before her she had looked at his crippled hand, and leaned down to murmur, *My prince, have you considered joining the Ministry?* And for a moment he had seen a hungry brightness in her eye which scared him more than all the High King's frowning warriors.

'So much interest from the First of Ministers?' he muttered, swallowing an aftertaste of that day's fear.

Mother Gundring shrugged. 'It is rare to have a prince of royal blood join the Ministry.'

'No doubt she'll be as disappointed as everyone else that I've taken the Black Chair instead.'

'Grandmother Wexen is wise enough to make the best of what the gods serve her. As must we all.'

Yarvi's eyes slid across the rest of the cages, seeking a distraction. Pitiless though they were, the eyes of the birds were easier to bear than those of his disappointed subjects.

'Which dove brought the message from Grom-gil-Gorm?'

'I sent it back to Vansterland. To his minister, Mother Scaer, carrying your father's agreement to a parley.'

'Where was the meeting to be?'

'On the border, near the town of Amwend. Your father never reached the place.'

'He was ambushed in Gettland?'

'So it appears.'

'It does not seem like my father, to be so keen to end a war.'

'War,' croaked one of the doves. 'End a war.'

Mother Gundring frowned at the grey-spattered floor. 'I counselled him to go. The High King has asked for all swords to be sheathed until his new temple to the One God is completed. I never suspected even a savage like Grom-gil-Gorm would betray the sacred word given.' She made a fist, as though she would strike herself, then slowly let it uncurl. 'It is a minister's task to smooth the way for Father Peace.'

'But had my father no men with him? Had he—'

'My king.' Mother Gundring looked at him from under her brows. 'We must go down.'

Yarvi swallowed, his stomach seeming to jump

up his throat and wash his mouth with sour spit. 'I'm not ready.'

'No one ever is. Your father was not.'

Yarvi made a sound then, half a laugh, half a sob, and wiped tears on the back of his crooked hand. 'Did my father weep after he was betrothed to my mother?'

'In fact, he did,' said Mother Gundring. 'For several years. She, on the other hand . . .'

And Yarvi gurgled up a laugh despite himself. 'My mother's even meaner with her tears than her gold.' He looked up at the woman who had been his teacher, would now be his minister, that face full of kindly lines, the bright eyes filled with concern, and found he had whispered, 'You've been like a mother to me.'

'And you like a son to me. I am sorry, Yarvi. I am sorry for everything but . . . this is the greater good.'

'The lesser evil.' Yarvi fussed at his stub of a finger, and blinked up at the birds. The many doves, and the one great eagle. 'Who will feed them now?'

'I will find someone.' And Mother Gundring offered her bony hand to help him up. 'My king.'

PROMISES

It was a great affair.

Many powerful families in the far reaches of Gettland would be angered that news of King Uthrik's death had barely reached them before he was burned, denying them the chance to have their importance noted at an event that would live so long in the memory.

No doubt the all-powerful High King on his high chair in Skekenhouse, not to mention the all-knowing Grandmother Wexen at his elbow, would be far from delighted that they received no invitation, as Mother Gundring was keen to point out. But Yarvi's mother forced through her clenched teeth, 'Their anger is dust to me.' Laithlin might have been queen no longer but no other word would fit her, and Hurik still hovered huge and silent at her shoulder, sworn forever to her service. Once she spoke it was a thing already done.

The procession passed from the Godshall through the yard of the citadel, grass littered with the sites of Yarvi's many failures, under the limbs of the great cedar his brother used to mock him for being unable to climb.

Yarvi went at the fore, of course, his mother overshadowing him in every sense at his shoulder and Mother Gundring struggling to keep up behind, bent over her staff. Uncle Odem led the king's household, warriors and women in their best. Slaves came behind, collars rattling and their eyes on the ground where they belonged.

Yarvi glanced up nervously as they passed through the one entrance tunnel, saw the bottom edge of the Screaming Gate gleam in the darkness, ready to drop and seal the citadel against any enemy. It was said to have been let fall only once, and that long before he was born, but still he swallowed as he always did when he passed beneath it. A mountain's weight of polished copper hanging by a single pin tended to rattle the nerves.

Especially when you were about to burn half your family.

'You're doing well,' Yarvi's uncle whispered in his ear.

'I am walking.'

'You are walking like a king.'

'I am a king and I am walking. How could it be otherwise?'

Odem smiled at that. 'Well said. My king.'

Over his uncle's shoulder Yarvi caught Isriun smiling at him too, the torch she carried setting a gleam to her eyes and the chain about her neck. Soon the key to the treasury of Gettland would hang upon it, and she would be queen. *His* queen, and the thought gave him hope amidst his fears like a spark in the darkness.

They all carried torches, a snake of lights through the gathering gloom, though the wind had snatched out half the flames by the time the procession passed through the city's gates and onto the bare hillside.

The king's own ship, the best in Thorlby's crowded harbour, twenty oars upon a side and its high prow and tail carved as finely as anything in the Godshall, was dragged by honoured warriors to the chosen place among the dunes, keel grinding out a snaking trench in the sand. The same ship in which King Uthrik had sailed across the Shattered Sea on his famous raid to Sagenmark. The same ship which had wallowed low in the water with slaves and plunder when he returned in triumph.

On its deck they laid the pale bodies of the king and his heir upon a bier of fine swords, for Uthrik's fame as a warrior had stood second only to his dead brother Uthil's. All Yarvi could think was how that showed great warriors die no better than other men.

And usually sooner.

Rich offerings were placed about the dead in the manner the prayer-weaver judged the gods would most appreciate. Weapons and armour the king had won in battle. Armrings of gold, coins of silver. Treasures heaped glittering. Yarvi put a jewelled cup in his brother's fists, and his mother put a cloak of white fur over the dead king's shoulders, and placed one hand upon his chest, and stood looking down, her jaw clenched tight, until Yarvi said, 'Mother?'

She turned without a word and led him to the chairs on the hillside, the sea wind catching the brown grass and setting it thrashing about their feet. Yarvi squirmed for a comfortable position in that hard, high seat, his mother motionless on his right with Hurik a huge shadow behind her, Mother Gundring perched on a stool at his left hand, her staff clutched in one bony fist, the twisted elf-metal alive with reflected flames from the rustling torches.

Yarvi sat between his two mothers. One who believed in him. One who had given birth to him.

Mother Gundring leaned close then and said softly, 'I am sorry, my king. This is not what I wanted for you.'

Yarvi could show no weakness now. 'We must make the best of what the gods serve us,' he said. 'Even kings.'

'Especially kings,' grated out his mother, and gave the signal.

Two dozen horses were led onto the ship, hooves clattering at the timbers, and slaughtered so their blood washed the deck. All agreed Death would show King Uthrik and his son through the Last Door with respect, and they would be acknowledged great among the dead.

Uncle Odem stepped out before the ranks of battle-ready warriors massed upon the sand, a torch in one hand. With his silvered mail and winged helm and red cloak snapping he looked like a son, and brother, and uncle of kings indeed. He nodded solemnly to Yarvi, and Yarvi nodded back, and he felt his mother clutch his right hand and squeeze it hard.

Odem set the torch to the pitch-soaked kindling. The flames licked about the ship and in a moment it was all ablaze, a sorrowful moan drawn from the crowds – from the honoured and wealthy upon the high terraces before the walls of Thorlby, the crafters and merchants below them, the foreigners and peasants below them, the beggars and slaves scattered in whatever crevices the wind allowed them, each person in the place the gods had reckoned proper.

And Yarvi had to swallow, because he realized of a sudden that his father would never come back and he truly would have to be king, from now until he was burned himself.

He sat there, cold and sickly, a drawn sword across his knees, as Father Moon showed himself and his children the stars came out, and the flames of the burning ship, and the burning goods, and his burning family lit up the faces of the hundred hundred mourners. As scattered lights showed in the stone buildings of the city, and the wattle hovels huddled outside the walls, and in the towers of the citadel upon the hill. His citadel, although to him it had always had the look of a prison.

It took a hero's struggle to stay awake. He had

barely slept last night, or any night since they put the King's Circle on him. The shadows in the cold depths of his father's yawning bedchamber seemed crowded with fears, and by ancient tradition there was no door he could bolt since the King of Gettland is one with the land and the people and must hide nothing from them.

Secrets, and bedroom doors, were luxuries reserved for luckier folk than kings.

A queue of proud men in their war-gear and proud women with keys polished, some of them sore trouble to King Uthrik while he lived, filed past Yarvi and his mother to wring their hands, and press gaudy grave gifts on them, and speak in swollen terms of the dead lord's high deeds. They lamented that Gettland would never see his like again, then remembered themselves and bowed and mouthed 'my king' while behind their smiles no doubt they wondered how it might be made to profit them to have this one-handed weakling in the Black Chair.

Only the occasional hiss passed between Yarvi and his mother. 'Sit up. You are a king. Do not apologize. You are a king. Straighten your cloak-buckle. You are a king. You *are* a king. You are a *king*.' As if she was trying to convince him, and herself, and the world of it against all the evidence.

Surely the Shattered Sea had never seen so cunning a merchant, but he doubted even she could sell this.

They sat until the flames sank to a flickering,

and the dragon-carved keel sagged into whirling embers, and the first muddy smear of dawn touched the clouds, glittering on the copper dome of the Godshall and setting the sea-birds calling. Then his mother clapped her hands and the slaves with clinking collar-chains began to dig the earth over the still-smouldering pyre, raising a great howe that would stand tall beside that of Yarvi's uncle Uthil, swallowed in a storm, and his grandfather Brevaer, and his great-grandfather Angulf Clovenfoot. On down the coast marched the grassy humps until they were lost among the dunes, diminishing into the fog of time before She Who Writes entrusted woman with the gift of letters, and ministers trapped the names of the dead in their high books.

Then Mother Sun showed her blinding face and put fire upon the water. The tide would soon be draining, carrying with it the many ships drawn up upon the sand, sharp-tailed so they could slip away as swiftly as they arrived, ready to sweep the warriors to Vansterland to rip their vengeance from Grom-gil-Gorm.

Uncle Odem climbed the hill with fist firm on sword's hilt and his easy smile traded for a warrior's frown.

'It is time,' he said.

So Yarvi stood, and stepped past his uncle, and held high his borrowed sword, swallowing his fears and roaring into the wind as loud as he could. 'I, Yarvi, son of Uthrik and Laithlin, King of Gettland, swear an oath! I swear a sun-oath and a moon-oath.

I swear it before She Who Judges, and He Who Remembers, and She Who Makes Fast the Knot. Let my brother and my father and my ancestors buried here bear witness. Let He Who Watches and She Who Writes bear witness. Let all of you bear witness. Let it be a chain upon me and a goad within me. I will be revenged upon the killers of my father and my brother. This I swear!'

The gathered warriors clashed the bearded heads of their axes against their helms, and their fists against their painted shields, and their boots against Father Earth in grim approval.

Yarvi's uncle frowned. 'That is a heavy oath, my king.'

'I may be half a man,' said Yarvi, struggling to get his sword back into its sheepskin-lined sheath. 'But I can swear a whole oath. The men appreciated it, at least.'

'These are men of Gettland,' said Hurik. 'They appreciate deeds.'

'I thought it was a fine oath.' Isriun stood near, yellow hair streaming in the wind. 'A kingly oath.'

Yarvi found he was very glad to see her there. He wished no one else had been, then he could have kissed her again, and probably made a better effort at it. But all he could do was smile, and half-raise his half-hand in an awkward farewell.

There would be time for kisses when they next met.

'My king.' It seemed Mother Gundring's eyes, forever dry in any smoke or dust or weather, held

45

tears. 'May the gods send you fine weatherluck, and even better weaponluck.'

'Don't worry, my minister,' he said, 'there's always the chance I'll survive.'

His true mother shed no tears. All she did was fasten his twisted cloak-buckle yet again and say, 'Stand like a king, Yarvi. Speak like a king. Fight like a king.'

'I am a king,' he said, however much of a lie it felt, and he forced through his tightened throat, 'I'll make you proud,' even though he had never known how.

But he looked back, as he walked with his uncle's gently steering hand upon his shoulder, the warriors forming snakes of glimmering steel as they filed towards the water, and he saw his mother clutch Hurik by his mail and drag him close, strong man though he was.

'Watch over my son, Hurik,' he heard her say in a choking voice. 'He is all I have.'

Then the Golden Queen was gone with her guards and attendants and her many slaves towards the city, and Yarvi was striding through the colourless dawn towards the ships, their masts a swaying forest against the bruising sky. Trying to walk the way his father used to, eager for the fight, even though he was weak-kneed, and sore-throated, and red-eyed, and his heart was crowded with doubts. He could still smell the smoke.

He left Father Peace to weep among the ashes, and hastened to the iron embrace of Mother War.

MAN'S WORK

Each wave born of Mother Sea would lift him, roll him, tug his sodden clothes, make him twitch and stir as if struggling to rise. Each wave hissed back out would drag the body down the beach and leave it grounded, tangled hair stuck with froth and sand, limp as the knots of seaweed on the shingle.

Yarvi stared at him, wondering who he was. Or had been. Boy or man? Had he died running or fought bravely?

What was the difference now?

The keel ground against sand, the deck shuddered, Yarvi stumbled and had to clutch at Hurik's arm to steady himself. With a clunk and clatter the men unshipped their oars, unhooked their shields, and sprang over the ship's sides into the surf, sullen at being last to land, too late for any glory or plunder worth the taking. Crewing the king's ship would have been a high honour in King Uthrik's reign.

No honour at all in King Yarvi's.

Some men took the prow-rope and hauled the ship past the floating corpse and higher up the beach,

47

others unslung their weapons and hurried towards the town of Amwend. It was already burning.

Yarvi chewed at his lip as he made ready to clamber over the side with some shred of kingly composure, but the handle of his gilded shield twisted in his weakling's grip, tangled with his cloak and nearly dumped him face-first in the brine.

'Gods damn this thing!' Yarvi tugged the straps loose, dragged the shield from his withered arm and flung it away among the sea-chests the men sat on while they rowed.

'My king,' said Keimdal. 'You should keep your shield. It's not safe—'

'You've fought me. You know what my shield's worth. If someone comes at me I can't stop with sword alone I'm better off running. I'll run faster without my shield.'

'But, my king—'

'He is king,' rumbled Hurik, pushing his thick fingers through his white-streaked beard. 'If he says we all put aside our shields, it must be so.'

'Those with two good hands are welcome to theirs,' said Yarvi, slithering into the surf, cursing as another cold wave soaked him to the waist.

Where sand gave way to grass some new-made slaves were roped together, waiting to be herded aboard one of the ships. They were hunched and soot-smeared, wide eyes full of fear or pain or disbelief at what had surged from the sea and stolen their lives. Beside them, a group of Yarvi's warriors diced for their clothes.

'Your Uncle Odem asks for you, my king,' said one, then got up frowning and kicked a sobbing old man onto his face.

'Where?' asked Yarvi, his tongue sticking in his mouth, it was suddenly so dry.

'On top of the holdfast.' The man pointed up towards a drystone tower on a sheer rock above the town, waves angry about its base on one side, a frothing inlet on the other.

'They didn't close the gates?' asked Keimdal.

'They did, but three of the headman's sons were left in the town, and Odem slit one's throat and said he'd kill the next if the gate wasn't opened.'

'It was,' said one of the other warriors, then chuckled as his number came up. 'New socks!'

Yarvi blinked. He had never thought of his smiling uncle as a ruthless man. But Odem had sprouted from the same seed as Yarvi's father, whose rages he still carried the marks of, and their drowned brother Uthil, at the memory of whose peerless swordsmanship old warriors in the training square still came over dewy-eyed. Sometimes calm waters hide fierce currents, after all.

'A curse on you!'

A woman had tottered from the line of slaves as far as the ropes would allow, bloody hair plastered against one side of her face.

'Bastard king of a bastard country, may Mother Sea swallow—'

One of the warriors cuffed her to the ground.

'Cut her tongue out,' said another, jerking her back by her hair while a third drew a knife.

'No!' shouted Yarvi. The men frowned at him. If their king's honour was questioned so was theirs, and mercy would not do as an explanation. 'She'll fetch a better price with her tongue.' And Yarvi turned away, shoulders chafing under the weight of his mail, and struggled on towards the holdfast.

'You are your mother's son, my king,' said Hurik.

'Who else's would I be?'

His father's eyes and his brother's used to glow as they told tales of past raids, of great deeds done and grand prizes taken, while Yarvi lurked in the shadows at the foot of the table and wished he could have taken a man's part in the man's work. But here was the truth of it, and a place on a raid did not seem enviable now.

The fighting was over, if there had been any worthy of the name, but still it seemed Yarvi laboured through a nightmare, sweating in his mail and chewing at the inside of his mouth and startling at sounds. Screams and laughter, figures darting through the wriggling haze of fires, smoke scratching at his throat. Crows pecked and circled and cawed their triumph. Theirs was the victory, most of all. Mother War, Mother of Crows, who gathers the dead and makes the open hand a fist, would dance today, while Father Peace hid his face and wept. Here, near the shiftless border between Vansterland and Gettland, Father Peace wept often.

The tower of the holdfast loomed black above them, the noise of waves crashing on both sides of its foundations loud below.

'Stop,' said Yarvi, breathing hard, head spinning, face tickling with sweat. 'Help me out of my mail.'

'My king,' frothed Keimdal, 'I must object!'

'Object if you please. Then do as I tell you.'

'It's my duty to keep you safe—'

'Then imagine your dishonour when I die of too much sweating halfway up this tower! Undo the buckles, Hurik.'

'My king.' They stripped his mail shirt off and Hurik threw it over one great shoulder.

'Lead on,' Yarvi snapped at Keimdal, struggling to fasten his father's clumsy golden cloak-buckle with his useless lump of a hand, too big and too heavy for him by far and the hinge all stiff as—

He was stopped dead by the sight that greeted them beyond the open gates.

'Here is a harvest,' said Hurik.

The narrow space in front of the tower was scattered with bodies. So many that Yarvi had to search for patches of ground between to put his feet. There were women there, and children. Flies buzzed, and he felt the sickness rising, and fought it down.

He was a king, after all, and a king rejoices in the corpses of his enemies.

One of his uncle's warriors sat beside the entrance to the tower, cleaning his axe as calmly as he might have beside the training square at home.

'Where is Odem?' Yarvi muttered at him.

The man gave a squint-eyed grin and pointed upwards. 'Above, my king.'

Yarvi ducked past, breath echoing in the stairway, feet scraping on the stones, swallowing his surging spit.

On the battlefield, his father used to say, *there are no rules.*

Up, and up in the fizzing darkness, Hurik and Keimdal toiling behind him. He paused at a narrow window to feel the wind on his burning face, saw water crash on rock at the bottom of a sheer drop and pushed down his fear.

Stand like a king, his mother had told him. *Speak like a king. Fight like a king.*

There was a platform at the top, propped on timbers, a wooden parapet about the edge no taller than Yarvi's thigh. Low enough to bring the giddy sickness flooding back when he saw how high they had climbed, Father Earth and Mother Sea spread out small around them, the forests of Vansterland stretching off into the haze of distance.

Yarvi's Uncle Odem stood calmly watching Amwend burn, columns of smoke smudging the slate-grey sky, the tiny warriors bent to the business of destruction, the little ships lined up where surf met shingle to collect the bloody harvest. A dozen of his most seasoned men were around him, and kneeling in their midst a prisoner in a fine yellow robe, bound and gagged, his face swollen with bruises and his long hair clotted with blood.

'A good day's work!' called Odem, smiling at Yarvi over his shoulder. 'We have taken two hundred slaves, and livestock, and plunder, and burned one of Grom-gil-Gorm's towns.'

'What of Gorm himself?' asked Yarvi, trying to catch his breath after the climb and – since standing and fighting had never been his strengths – at least speak like a king.

Odem sucked sourly at his teeth. 'The Breaker of Swords will be on his way, eh, Hurik?'

'Doubtless.' Hurik stepped from the stairway and straightened to all his considerable height. 'Battle draws that old bear surely as it draws the flies.'

'We must round up the men and be back at sea within the hour,' said Odem.

'We're leaving?' asked Keimdal. 'Already?'

Yarvi found he was angry. Tired, and sick, and angry at his own weakness and his uncle's ruthless-ness and the world that was this way. 'Is this our vengeance, Odem?' He waved his good hand towards the burning town. 'On women and children and old farmers?'

His uncle's voice was gentle, as it always was. Gentle as spring rain. 'Vengeance is taken piece by piece. But you need not worry about that now.'

'Did I not swear an oath?' growled Yarvi. For the last two days he had been prickling whenever someone used the words *my king*. Now he found he prickled even more when they did not.

'You swore. I heard it, and thought it too heavy an oath for you to carry.' Odem gestured at the kneeling prisoner, grunting into his gag. 'But he will free you of its weight.'

'Who is he?'

'The headman of Amwend. He is the one who killed you.'

Yarvi blinked. 'What?'

'I tried to stop him. But the coward had a hidden blade.' Odem held up his hand and there was a dagger in it. A long dagger with a pommel of black jet. In spite of the heat of the climb Yarvi felt suddenly very cold, from the soles of his feet to the roots of his hair.

'It shall be my greatest regret that I moved too late to save my much-loved nephew.' And carelessly as cutting a joint of meat Odem stabbed the headman between his neck and his shoulder and kicked him onto his face, blood welling across the rooftop.

'What do you mean?' Yarvi's words came shrill and broken and he was suddenly aware how many of his uncle's men were about him, all armed, all armoured.

As Odem stepped calmly, so calmly towards him he stepped back, stepped back on shaky knees to nowhere but the low parapet and the high drop beyond.

'I remember the night you were born.' His uncle's voice was cold and level as ice on a winter lake. 'Your father raged at the gods over that thing you have for a hand. You've always made me, smile, though. You would have been a fine jester.' Odem raised his brows, and sighed. 'But is my daughter really to have a one-handed weakling for a husband? Is Gettland really to have half a king? A crippled puppet dangling on his mother's string? No, nephew, I . . . think . . . *not*.'

Keimdal snatched Yarvi's arm and dragged him back, metal scraping as he drew his sword. 'Get behind me, my—'

Blood spattered in Yarvi's face and half-blinded him. Keimdal fell to his knees, spitting and gurgling, clutching at his throat, black leaking between his fingers. Yarvi stared sideways and saw Hurik frowning back, a drawn knife in his hand, the blade slick with Keimdal's blood. He let Yarvi's mail drop jingling to the floor.

'We must do what is best for Gettland,' said Odem. 'Kill him.'

Yarvi tottered away, his jaw dropping wide, and Hurik caught a fistful of his cloak.

With a ping his father's heavy golden buckle sprang open. Suddenly released, Yarvi reeled back.

The parapet caught him hard in the knees and, breath whooping, he tumbled over it.

Rock and water and sky spun about him, and down plummeted the King of Gettland, and down, and the water struck him as a hammer strikes iron.

And Mother Sea took him in her cold embrace.

THE ENEMY

Yarvi came to himself in the darkness, smothered by rushing bubbles, and he writhed and thrashed and twisted with the simple need to stay alive.

The gods must yet have had some use for him, for when it seemed his ribs would burst and he must breathe in whether it was sea or sky, his head broke from the water. Spray blinded him, and he coughed and kicked, was sucked under, tossed and tumbled by the current.

A surging wave flung him onto rock, and he clutched at shredding barnacle and green-slick weed, just long enough to find another breath. He fought with the buckle, freed himself of the drowning embrace of his sword-belt, legs burning as he struggled at the merciless sea, kicking free of his leaden boots.

He gathered all his strength and as the swell lifted him he hauled himself up, trembling with effort, onto a narrow ledge of stone washed by the salt spray, speckled with jellies and sharp-shelled limpets.

No doubt he was lucky still to be alive, but Yarvi did not feel lucky.

He was in the inlet on the north side of the holdfast, a narrow space walled in by jagged rocks into which the foaming waves angrily surged, chewing at the stone, slopping and clapping and flinging glittering spray. He scraped the wet hair from his eyes, spat salt, his throat raw, good hand and bad grazed and stinging.

His foolhardy decision to strip off his mail had saved his life, but the padded jacket underneath was bloated with seawater and he pawed at the straps, finally shrugged it free and hunched shivering.

'D'you see him?' he heard, the voice coming from so close above that he shrank against the slick rock, biting his tongue.

'Got to be dead.' Another voice. 'Dashed on the rocks. Mother Sea has him for sure.'

'Odem wants his body.'

'Odem can fish for it, then.'

A third voice now. 'Or Hurik can. He let the cripple fall.'

'And which'll you be telling first to swim, Odem or Hurik?'

Laughter at that. 'Gorm's on his way. We've no time to dredge for one-handed corpses.'

'Back to the ships, and tell King Odem his nephew adorns the deep . . .' And the voices faded towards the beach.

King Odem. His own uncle, who he had loved like a father, always there with a soothing word and an understanding smile and a steering hand on

Yarvi's shoulder. His own blood! Yarvi was clinging with his good hand but the bad one he bunched into a trembling fist, his father's anger stealing up on him so strong he could hardly breathe for it. But his mother had always said, *never worry about what has been done, only about what will be.*

His mother.

He gave a needy sob at the thought of her. The Golden Queen always knew what should be done. But how to reach her? The ships of Gettland were already leaving. The Vanstermen would soon arrive. All Yarvi could do was wait for dark. Find some way back over the border and south to Thorlby.

There is always a way.

If he had to walk a hundred miles through the forest without boots he would do it. He would be revenged on his bastard uncle, and on that traitor Hurik, and he would take back the Black Chair. He swore it, over and over, as Mother Sun hid her face behind the rocks and the shadows lengthened.

He had not reckoned on that most ruthless of revengers, though, the tide. Soon the icy waves washed the shelf on which he clung. Over his bare feet rose the cold water, over his ankles, over his knees, and before long the sea was surging into that narrow space even more fiercely than before. He would have liked to weigh his choices, but for that you need more than one.

So he climbed. Shivering and weary, aching and

cold, weeping and cursing the name of Odem with every slippery foot or handhold. It was an awful risk, but better than throwing himself on the mercy of Mother Sea for, as every sailor knows, she has none.

With a last effort he hauled himself over the brink and lay for a moment in the scrub, catching his breath. He groaned as he rolled over, began to stand.

Something cracked him on the side of the head, tore a cry from him and filled his skull with light. The land reeled and struck him on the side. He crawled up groggy, drooling blood.

'A Gettland dog, judging by his hair.' And he squealed as he was dragged up by it.

'A pup, at least.' A boot caught Yarvi's arse and dumped him on his face. He scrambled a pace or two and was kicked down again. Two men were herding him. Two mailed men with spears. Vanstermen, no doubt, though apart from the long braids about their hard faces they looked little different to the warriors who had frowned at him in the training square.

To the unarmed, armed men all look the same.

'Up,' said one, rolling him over with another kick.

'Then stop kicking me down,' he gasped.

They gave him a spear butt on the other side of his face for that, and he resolved to make no more jokes. One of them hauled him up by the collar of his torn shirt and half-dragged him, half-marched him on.

59

There were warriors everywhere, some on horseback. Peasants too, perhaps townsfolk who had fled at the sight of ships, returned to the ruins of their homes, soot-smeared and tear-streaked, to dig through the wreckage. Bodies were laid out for burning: their shrouds flapped and tugged in the sea wind.

But Yarvi needed all his pity for himself.

'Kneel, dog.' He was sent sprawling once more and this time saw no pressing need to rise, moaning with each breath and his battered mouth one great throb.

'What do you bring me?' came a clear voice, high and wandering, as if it sang a song.

'A Gettlander. He climbed from the sea beside the holdfast, my king.'

'The Mother of Waters washes up strange bounty. Look upon me, sea creature.'

Yarvi slowly, fearfully, painfully raised his head and saw two great boots capped with scuffed steel. Then baggy trousers, striped red and white. Then a heavy belt with a golden buckle, the hilts of a great sword and four knives. Then mail of steel with zigzag lines of gold forged in. Then a white fur about great shoulders, the wolf's head still on, garnets set into its empty eyes. Upon it, a chain of jumbled lumps of gold and silver, precious stones winking: pommels twisted from the swords of fallen enemies, so many that the chain was looped three times about a trunk of a neck and still hung low. Finally, so high above

60

Yarvi that the man stood a giant, a craggy face, lop-sided as a wind-blown tree, long hair and beard hanging wild and streaked with silver-grey, but about the twisted mouth and eyes a smile. The smile of a man who studies beetles, wondering which to squash.

'Who are you, person?' asked the giant.

'A cook's boy.' The words were clumsy in Yarvi's bloodied mouth, and he tried to work his crippled hand into his damp shirt sleeve so it could not betray him. 'I fell into the sea.' *A good liar weaves as much truth into the cloth as they can,* Mother Gundring once told him.

'Shall we play a guessing game?' the giant asked, winding a strand of his long hair around and around one finger. 'Of what my name might be?'

Yarvi swallowed. He did not need to guess. 'You are Grom-gil-Gorm, Breaker of Swords and Maker of Orphans, King of the Vanstermen.'

'You win!' Gorm clapped his massive hands. 'Though what you win remains to be seen. I *am* King of the Vanstermen. Lately including these ill-doomed wretches that your countrymen of Gettland have so freely robbed, butchered, and stolen as slaves, against the wishes of the High King in Skekenhouse, who has asked that swords stay sheathed. He loves to spoil our fun, but there it is.' Gorm's eyes wandered over the scene of ruin. 'Does this strike you as just, cook's boy?'

'No,' croaked Yarvi, and he did not have to lie.

A woman stepped up beside the king. Her hair

61

was shaved to black-and-grey stubble, her long, white arms covered from shoulder to finger with blue designs. Some Yarvi recognized from his studies: charts for the reckoning of the future in the stars, circles within circles in which the relationships of the small gods were plotted, runes that told of times and distances and amounts permitted and forbidden. About one forearm five elf-bangles were stacked, relics of great age and value, gold and steel and bright glass flashing, talismans worked with symbols whose meanings were drowned in the depths of time.

And Yarvi knew this must be Mother Scaer, Gorm's minister. She who sent the dove to Mother Gundring, luring Yarvi's father to his death with promises of peace.

'What King of Gettland ordered such slaughter?' she asked, her voice every bit as harsh as a dove's.

'Odem.' And Yarvi realized with some pain it was the truth.

Her lip wrinkled as if at a sour taste. 'So the fox killed his brother the wolf.'

'Treacherous beasties.' Gorm sighed, turning a pommel absently around and around on his chain. 'It was sure to come. As surely as Mother Sun follows Father Moon across the sky.'

'You killed King Uthrik,' Yarvi found he'd spat from his bloody mouth.

'Do they say so?' Gorm raised his great arms, the weapons at his belt shifting. 'Then why do I not boast of it? Why are my skalds not setting the story to song? Would my triumph not make a merry tune?' He laughed, and let his arms drop. 'My hands are bloody to the shoulder, cook's boy, for of all things blood pleases me the most. But, sad to say, not all men that die are killed by me.'

One of the daggers had eased forward in his belt, its horn handle pointing toward Yarvi. He could have snatched it. Had he been his father, or his brother, or brave Keimdal who died trying to protect his king, he might have lunged for that blade, sunk it into Grom-gil-Gorm's belly and fulfilled his solemn oath for vengeance.

'Do you want this bauble?' Gorm drew the knife now, and held it out to Yarvi by the bright blade. 'Then take it. But you should know that Mother War breathed upon me in my crib. It has been foreseen that no man can kill me.'

How huge he seemed, against the white sky, hair blowing, and mail shining, and the warm smile on his battle-weathered face. Had Yarvi sworn vengeance against this giant? He, half-man, with his one thin, white hand? He would have laughed at the arrogance of it were he not shivering with cold and fear.

'He should be pegged on the beach and his guts unwound for the crows,' said Gorm's minister, her blue eyes fixed on Yarvi.

'So you always say, Mother Scaer.' Gorm slid the knife back into his belt. 'But the crows never thank me. This is just a little boy. It is hardly as if this outrage was his idea.' Truer than he knew.

'Unlike the noble King Odem, I do not need to swell myself with the killing of weak things.'

'What of justice?' The minister frowned over at the shrouded bodies, muscles working on the sides of her shaven head. 'The low folk are hungry for vengeance.'

Gorm pushed out his lips and made a farting sound. 'It is the lot of low folk to be hungry. Have you learned nothing from the Golden Queen of Gettland, wise and beautiful Laithlin? Why kill what you can sell? Collar him and put him with the others.'

Yarvi squawked as one of the men dragged him up while another snapped a collar of rough iron around his neck.

'If you change your mind about the knife,' Gorm called after him, smiling all the while, 'you can seek me out. Fare you well, ex-cook's boy!'

'Wait!' hissed Yarvi, realizing what was to come, mind racing for some trick to put it off. 'Wait!'

'For what?' asked Mother Scaer. 'Stop his bleating.'

A kick in the stomach left him breathless. They forced him limp upon an old stump, and while one held him gasping the other brought the pin, yellow-hot from the forge, and worked it through the clasp of his collar with pincers. The first struck it with a hammer to squash it fast but he bungled the task, caught the pin a glancing blow and scattered molten iron across Yarvi's neck.

He had never known pain like it, and he shrieked

like a boiling kettle and sobbed and blubbered and writhed on the block, and one of them took him by his shirt and flung him in a fetid pool so the iron hissed cold.

'One less cook's boy.' Mother Scaer's face was pale as milk and smooth as marble and her eyes were blue as the winter sky and had no pity in them. 'One more slave.'

PART II

THE SOUTH WIND

CHEAPEST OFFERINGS

Yarvi squatted in the stinking darkness, fingering the raw burns on his neck and the fresh scabs on his rough-shaved scalp, sweating by day and shivering by night, listening to the groans and whimpers and unanswered prayers in a dozen languages. From the broken throats of the human refuse around him. From his own loudest of all.

Upstairs the best wares were kept clean and well fed, lined up on the street in polished thrall-collars where they might draw in the business. In the back of the shop the less strong or skilled or beautiful were chained to rails and beaten until they smiled for a buyer. Down here in the darkness and the filth were kept the old, sick, simple and crippled, left to squabble over scraps like pigs.

Here in the sprawling slave-market of Vulsgard, capital of Vansterland, everyone had their price, and money was not wasted on those who would fetch no money. A simple sum of costs and profits, shorn of sentiment. Here you could learn what you were truly worth, and Yarvi learned what he had long suspected.

He was close to worthless.

At first his mind spilled over with plans and stratagems and fantasies for his revenge. He was plagued by a million things he could have done differently. But not by one he could do now. If he screamed out that he was the rightful King of Gettland, who would believe it? He had scarcely believed it himself. And if he found a way to make them believe? Their business was to sell people. They would ransom him, of course. Would King Odem smile to have his missing nephew back under his tender care? No doubt. A smile calm and even as fresh-fallen snow.

So Yarvi squatted in that unbearable squalor, and found it was amazing what a man could get used to.

By the second day he scarcely noticed the stink.

By the third he huddled up gratefully to the warmth of his gods-forsaken companions in the chill of the night.

By the fourth he was rooting through the filth as eagerly as any of them when they were tossed the slops at feeding time.

By the fifth he could hardly remember the faces of those he knew best. His mother and Mother Gundring became confused, his treacherous uncle and his dead father melted together, Hurik no longer could be told from Keimdal, Isriun faded to ghost.

Strange, how quickly a king could become an animal. Or half a king half an animal. Perhaps even those we raise highest never get that far above the mud.

It was not long after sunrise on his seventh day in that man-made hell, the calls of the merchant in dead men's armour next door just starting to challenge the squawking of the sea-birds, that Yarvi heard the voice outside.

'We're looking for men as can pull an oar,' it said, deep and steady. The voice of a man used to straight talk and blunt dealing.

'Nine pairs of hands.' A softer, subtler voice followed the first. 'The trembles has left some gaps on our benches.'

'Of course, my friends!' The voice of the shop's owner – Yarvi's owner, now – slick and sticky as warm honey. 'Behold Namev the Shend, a champion of his people taken in battle! See how tall he stands? Observe those shoulders. He could pull your ship alone. You will find no higher quality—'

A hog snort from the first customer. 'If we was after quality we'd be at the other end of the street.'

'You don't grease an axle with the best oil,' came the second voice.

Footsteps from above, and dust sifting down, and shadows shifting in the chinks of light between the boards over Yarvi's head. The slaves around him stiffened, quieting their breathing so they could listen. The shop-owner's voice filtered muffled to their ears, a little less honey on it now.

'Here are six healthy Inglings. They speak little of the Tongue but understand the whip well enough.

Fine choices for hard labour and at an excellent price—'

'You don't grease an axle with good dripping either,' said the second voice.

'Show us to the pitch and pig fat, flesh-dealer,' growled the first.

The damp hinges grated as the door at the top of the steps was opened, the slaves all cringing on instinct into a feeble huddle at the light, Yarvi along with them. He might have been new to slavery, but at cringing he had long experience. With many curses and blows of his stick the flesh-dealer dragged them into a wobbling, wheezing line, chains rattling out a miserable music.

'Keep that hand out of sight,' he hissed, and Yarvi twisted it up into the rags of his sleeve. All his ambition then was to be bought, and owned, and taken from this stinking hell into the sight of Mother Sun.

The two customers picked their way down the steps. The first was balding and burly, with a whip coiled at his studded belt and a way of glaring from under knotted brows that proclaimed him a bad man to fool with. The second was much younger, long, lean and handsome with a sparse growth of beard and a bitter twist to his thin lips. Yarvi caught the gleam of a collar at his throat. A slave himself, then, though judging by his clothes a favoured one.

The flesh-dealer bowed, and gestured with his stick towards the line. 'My cheapest offerings.' He did not bother to add a flourish. Fine words in that place would have been absurd.

'These are some wretched leavings,' said the slave, nose wrinkled against the stench.

His thick-set companion was not deterred. He drew the slave into a huddle with one muscled arm, speaking softly to him in Haleen. 'We want rowers, not kings.' It was a language used in Sagenmark and among the islands, but Yarvi had trained as a minister, and knew most tongues spoken around the Shattered Sea.

'The captain's no fool, Trigg,' the handsome slave was saying, fussing nervously with his collar. 'What if she realizes we've duped her?'

'We'll say this was the best on offer.' Trigg's flat eyes scanned the dismal gathering. 'Then you'll give her a new bottle and she'll forget all about it. Or don't you need the silver, Ankran?'

'You know I do.' Ankran shrugged off Trigg's arm, mouth further twisted with distaste. Scarcely bothering to look them over, he dragged slaves from the line. 'This . . . this . . . this . . .' His hand hovered near Yarvi, began to drift on—

'I can row, sir.' It was as big a lie as Yarvi had told in all his life. 'I was a fisher's apprentice.'

In the end Ankran picked out nine. Among them were a blind Throvenlander who had been sold by his father instead of their cow, an old Islander with a crooked back, and a lame Vansterman who could barely restrain his coughing for long enough to be paid for.

Oh, and Yarvi, rightful King of Gettland.

The argument over price was poisonous, but in the end Trigg and Ankran reached an understanding with the flesh-dealer. A trickle of shining hacksilver went into the merchant's hands, and a little back into the purse, and the greater share was split between the pockets of the buyers and, as far as Yarvi could tell, thereby stolen from their captain.

By his calculation he was sold for less than the cost of a good sheep.

He made no complaint at the price.

ONE FAMILY

The *South Wind* listed in its dock, looking like anything but a warm breeze.

Compared to the swift, slender ships of Gettland it was a wallowing monster, low to the water and fat at the waist, green weed and barnacle coating its ill-tended timbers, with two stubby masts and two dozen great oars on a side, slit-windowed castles hunched at blunt prow and stern.

'Welcome home,' said Trigg, shoving Yarvi between a pair of frowning guards and towards the gangplank.

A dark-skinned young woman sat on the roof of the aftcastle, one leg swinging as she watched the new slaves shuffle across. 'This the best you could do?' she asked with scarcely the hint of an accent, and sprang easily down. She had a thrall-collar of her own, but made from twisted wire, and her chain was loose and light, part coiled about her arm as though it was an ornament she had chosen to wear. A slave even more favoured than Ankran, then.

She checked in the mouth of the coughing

Vansterman and clicked her tongue, poked at the Shend's crooked back and blew out her cheeks in disgust. 'The captain won't think much of these slops.'

'And where is our illustrious leader?' Ankran had the air of already knowing the answer.

'Asleep.'

'Asleep drunk?'

She considered that, mouth moving faintly as though she was working at a sum. 'Not sober.'

'You worry about the course, Sumael,' grunted Trigg, shoving Yarvi's companions on again. 'The rowers are my business.'

Sumael narrowed her dark eyes at Yarvi as he shuffled past. She had a scar and a notch in her top lip where a little triangle of white tooth showed, and he found himself wondering what southern land she was born in and how she had come here, whether she was older or younger than him, hard to tell with her hair chopped short—

She darted out a quick arm and caught his wrist, twisting it up so his hand came free of his torn sleeve.

'This one has a crippled hand.' No mockery, merely a statement of fact, as though she had found a lame cow in a herd. 'There's only one finger on it.' Yarvi tried to pull free but she was stronger than she looked. 'And that seems a poor one.'

'That damn flesh-dealer!' Ankran elbowed past to grab Yarvi's wrist and twist it about to look. 'You said you could row!'

Yarvi could only shrug and mutter, 'I didn't say well.'

'It's almost as if you can't trust anyone,' said Sumael, one black eyebrow high. 'How will he row with one hand?'

'He'll have to find a way,' said Trigg, stepping up to her. 'We've got nine spaces and nine slaves.' He loomed over Sumael and spoke with his blunt nose no more than a finger's width from her pointed one. 'Unless you fancy a turn on the benches?'

She licked at that notch in her lip, and eased carefully backward. 'I'll worry about the course, shall I?'

'Good idea. Chain the cripple on Jaud's oar.'

They dragged Yarvi along a raised gangway down the middle of the deck, past benches on either side, three men to each huge oar, all shaven-headed, all lean, all collared, watching him with their own mixtures of pity, self-pity, boredom and contempt.

A man was hunched on hands and knees, scrubbing at the deck-boards, face hidden by a shag of matted hair and colourless beard, so beggarly he made the most wretched of the oarsmen look like princes. One of the guards aimed the sort of careless kick at him you might at a stray dog and sent him crawling away, dragging a great weight of heavy chain after him. The ship did not seem well supplied in general but of chain there was no shortage.

They flung Yarvi down with unnecessary violence

between two other slaves, by no means an encouraging pair. At the end of the oar was a hulking southerner with a thick fold of muscle where his neck should have been, head tipped back so he could watch the sea-birds circling. Closest to the rowlock was a dour old man, short and stocky, his sinewy forearms thick with grey hair, his cheeks full of broken veins from a life in the weather, picking at the calluses on his broad palms.

'Gods damn it,' grunted this older one, shaking his head as the guards chained Yarvi to the bench beside him, 'we've a cripple at our oar.'

'You prayed for help, didn't you?' said the southerner, without looking around. 'Here is help.'

'I prayed for help with two hands.'

'Be thankful for half of what you prayed for,' said Yarvi. 'Believe me, I prayed for none of this.'

The big man's mouth curled up a little as he looked at Yarvi sidelong. 'When you have a load to lift, you're better lifting than weeping. I am Jaud. Your sour oarmate is Rulf.'

'My name's Yorv,' said Yarvi, having turned his story over in advance. *Keep your lies as carefully as your winter grain*, Mother Gundring would have said. 'I was a cook's boy—'

With a practised roll of the tongue and twitch of the head the old man spat over the ship's side. 'You're nothing now, and that's all. Forget everything but the next stroke. That makes it a little easier.'

Jaud heaved up a sigh. 'Don't let Rulf grind the

laughter out of you. He's sour as lemons, but a good man to have at your back.' He puffed out his cheeks. 'Though, one must admit, since he's chained to your side, that will never happen.'

Yarvi gave a sorry little chuckle, maybe his first since he was made a slave. Maybe his first since he was made a king. But he didn't laugh long.

The door of the aftcastle banged wide and a woman swaggered into the light, raised both arms with a flourish and shrieked, 'I am awake!'

She was very tall, sharp-featured as a hawk with a pale scar across one dark cheek and her hair pinned up in a tangle. Her clothes were a gaudy patchwork of a dozen cultures' most impractical attire – a silken shirt with frayed embroidery flapping at the sleeves, a silvery fur coat ruffled by the breeze, a fingerless glove on one hand and the other crusted with rings, a crystal-studded belt the gilt end of which flapped about the grip of a curved sword slung absurdly low.

She kicked aside the nearest oarsman so she could prop one sharp-toed boot on his bench and grinned down the ship, gold glinting among her teeth.

Right away the slaves, the guards, the sailors began to clap. The only ones who did not join them were Sumael, her tongue wedged in her cheek on the roof of the aftcastle, the beggar whose scrubbing block was still scrape-scraping on the gangway, and Yarvi, ex-King of Gettland.

'Damn this bitch,' Rulf forced through a fixed grin while he applauded.

'You'd better clap,' murmured Jaud.

Yarvi held up his hands. 'I'm worse equipped for that than rowing.'

'Little ones, little ones!' called the woman, ring-covered fist pressed to her chest with emotion, 'you do me too much honour! Don't let that stop you trying, though. To those who have recently joined us, I am Ebdel Aric Shadikshirram, your captain and care-giver. You may well have heard of me, for my name is famous throughout the Shattered Sea and far beyond, yea unto the very walls of the First of Cities and so on.'

Her fame had not reached Yarvi, but Mother Gundring always used to say *the wise speaker learns first when to stay silent.*

'I could regale you with rousing tales of my colourful past,' she went on, toying with an earring of gold and feathers that dangled down well past her shoulder. 'How I commanded the victorious fleet of the empress at the Battle of Fulku, was for some time a favoured lover of Duke Mikedas himself but refused to become his wife, scattered the blockade at Inchim, sailed through the greatest tempest since the Breaking of God, landed a whale, and blah blah blah, but why?' She affectionately patted the cheek of the nearest slave, hard enough for the slapping to be clearly heard. 'Let us simply say this ship is now the world to you, and on this ship I am great and you are lowly.'

'We're great,' echoed Trigg, sweeping the benches with his frown, 'you're lowly.'

'Fine profits today, in spite of the sad need to replace a few of your brethren.' The many buckles on the captain's boots jingled as she swaggered between the benches. 'You will all have a mouthful of bread and wine tonight.' Scattered cheers at this spectacular show of generosity. 'Though you belong to me—'

Trigg noisily cleared his throat.

'—and the other shareholders in our brave vessel—'

Trigg nodded cautious approval.

'—still I like to think of us all as one family!' The captain gathered the whole ship in her outstretched arms, huge sleeves streaming in the breeze as though she were some rare and enormous sea-bird taking flight. 'I, the indulgent grandparent, Trigg and his guards the kindly uncles, you the troublesome brood. United against merciless Mother Sea, ever the sailor's most bitter enemy! You are lucky little children, for mercy, charity and kindness have always been my great weaknesses.' Rulf hawked up phlegm in disgust at that. 'Most of you will see the good sense in being obedient offspring, but . . . perhaps . . .' and Shadikshirram's smile collapsed to leave her dark face a caricature of hurt, 'there is some malcontent among you thinking of going their own way.'

Trigg gave a disapproving growl.

'Of turning his back upon his loving family. Of abandoning his brothers and sisters. Of *leaving* our loyal fellowship at some harbour or other.' The captain traced the fine scar down her cheek with one fingertip and bared her teeth. 'Perhaps even of raising a treacherous hand against his doting carers.'

Trigg gave a horrified hiss.

'Should some devil send such thoughts your way . . .' The captain leaned down towards the deck. 'Think on the last man to try it.' She came up with the heavy chain and gave it a savage tug, jerking the filthy deck-scrubber from his feet and squawking over in a tangle of limbs, rags, hair. 'Never let this ungrateful creature near a blade!' She stepped onto him where he lay. 'Not an eating knife, not a nail-trimmer, not a fish-hook!' She walked over him, tall heels grinding into his back, losing not the slightest poise in spite of the challenging terrain. 'He is *nothing*, do you hear me?'

'Damn this bitch,' murmured Rulf again as she hopped lightly from the back of the beggar's head.

Yarvi was watching the wretched scrubber as he clambered up, wiped blood from his mouth, retrieved his block, and without a sound crawled stiffly back to his work. Only his eyes showed through his matted hair for an instant as he looked towards the captain's back, bright as stars.

'Now!' shouted Shadikshirram, swarming effortlessly up the ladder onto the roof of the aftcastle and pausing to twirl her ring-crusted fingers. 'South to Thorlby, my little ones! Profits await! And Ankran?'

'My captain,' said Ankran, bowing so low he nearly grazed the deck.

'Bring me some wine, all this blather has given me a thirst.'

'You heard your grandma!' roared Trigg, uncoiling his whip.

There were clatters and calls, the hissing of rope and the creaking of timbers as the few free sailors cast off and prepared the *South Wind* to leave Vulsgard's harbour.

'What now?' muttered Yarvi.

Rulf gave a bitter hiss at such ignorance.

'Now?' Jaud spat into his palms and worked his two strong hands about the polished handles of their oar. 'We row.'

HEAVE

S oon enough, Yarvi wished he had stayed in the flesh-dealer's cellar.

'Heave.'

Trigg's boots ground out a ruthless rhythm as he prowled the gangway, whip coiled in meaty fists, eyes sweeping the benches for slaves in need of its encouragement, blunt voice booming out with pitiless regularity.

'Heave.'

It was no surprise that Yarvi's withered hand was even worse at gripping the handle of a great oar than it had been the handle of a shield. But Trigg made Master Hunnan seem a doting nursemaid in Yarvi's memory. The whip was his first answer to any problem, but when that did not cause more fingers to sprout he lashed Yarvi's crooked left wrist to the oar with chafing thongs.

'Heave.'

With each impossible haul upon the handles of that terrible oar Yarvi's arms and shoulders and back burned worse. Though the hides on the bench were worn to a silky softness, and the handles to a dull polish by his predecessors, with each stroke

84

his arse was worse skinned, his hands worse blistered. With each stroke the whip cuts and the boot bruises and the slow-healing burns about his rough-forged thrall-collar were more stung by salt sea and salt sweat.

'Heave.'

The suffering went far past any point of endurance Yarvi had imagined, but it was astonishing the inhuman efforts a whip in skilful hands could flick from a man. Soon its crack elsewhere, or even the approaching scrape of Trigg's boots on the gangway, would make Yarvi flinch and whimper and pull that fraction harder, spit flecking from his gritted teeth.

'This boy won't last,' growled Rulf.

'One stroke at a time,' murmured Jaud gently, his own strokes endlessly strong, smooth, regular, as though he was a man of wood and iron. 'Breathe slow. Breathe with the oar. One at a time.'

Yarvi could not have said why, but that was some help.

'Heave.'

And the rowlocks clattered and chains rattled, the ropes squealed and the timbers creaked, the oar-slaves groaned or cursed or prayed or kept grim silence, and the *South Wind* inched on.

'One stroke at a time.' Jaud's soft voice was a thread through the haze of misery. 'One at a time.'

Yarvi could hardly tell which was the worse torture – the whip's stinging or his skin's chafing or his muscles' burning or the hunger or the weather or the cold or the squalor. And yet, the endless scraping of the nameless scrubber's stone, up the deck and down the deck and up the deck again, his lank hair swaying and his scar-crossed back showing through his rags and his twitching lips curled from his yellowed teeth, reminded Yarvi that it could be worse.

It could always be worse.

'Heave.'

Sometimes the gods would take pity on his wretched state and send a breath of favourable wind. Then Shadikshirram would smile her golden smile and, with the air of a long-suffering mother who could not help spoiling her thankless offspring, would order the oars unshipped and the clumsy sails of leather-banded wool unfurled, and would airily disclaim on how mercy was her greatest weakness.

With weeping gratitude Yarvi would slump back against the stilled oar of those behind and watch the sailcloth snap and billow overhead and breathe the close stink of more than a hundred sweating, desperate, suffering men.

'When do we wash?' Yarvi muttered, during one of these blissful lulls.

'When Mother Sea takes it upon herself,' growled Rulf.

That was not rarely. The icy waves that slapped the ship's side would spot, spray, and regularly soak them to the skin, Mother Sea washing the deck and surging beneath the footrests until everything was crusted stiff with salt.

'Heave.'

Each gang of three was chained together with one lock to their bench, and Trigg and the captain had the only keys. The oar-slaves ate their meagre rations chained to their bench each evening. They squatted over a battered bucket chained to their bench each morning. They slept chained to their bench, covered by stinking blankets and bald furs, the air heavy with moans and snores and grumbles and the smoke of breath. Once a week they sat chained to their bench while their heads and beards were roughly shaved – a defence against lice which deterred the tiny passengers not at all.

The only time Trigg reluctantly produced his key and opened one of those locks was when the coughing Vansterman was found dead one chill morning, and was dragged from between his blank-faced oarmates and heaved over the side.

The only one who remarked on his passing was Ankran, who plucked at his thin beard and said, 'We'll need a replacement.'

For a moment Yarvi worried the survivors might have to work that fraction harder. Then he hoped there might be a little more food to go around. Then he was sick at himself for the way he had started to think.

But not so sick he wouldn't have taken the Vansterman's share had it been offered.

'Heave.'

He could not have said how many nights he passed limp and utterly spent, how many mornings he woke whimpering at the stiffness of the last day's efforts only to be whipped to more, how many days without a thought but the next stroke. But finally an evening came when he did not sink straight into a dreamless sleep. When his muscles had started to harden, the first raw blisters had burst and the whip had fallen on him less.

The *South Wind* was moored in an inlet, gently rocking. The rain was falling hard, so the sails had been lowered and strung over the deck to make a great tent, noisy with the hissing of drops on cloth. Those men with the skill had been handed rods and Rulf was one, hunched near the rowlock in the darkness, murmuring softly to the fish.

'For a man with but one hand,' said Jaud, chain clinking as he propped one big bare foot up on their oar, 'you rowed well today.'

'Huh.' Rulf spat through the rowlock, and a clipping of Father Moon's light showed the grin on his broad face. 'We may make half an oarsman of you yet.'

And though one of them was born long miles away and the other long years before him, and though Yarvi knew little about them that he could not read in their faces, and though pulling an oar chained in a trading galley was no high deed for the son of King Uthrik of Gettland, Yarvi felt a flush of pride, so sharp it almost brought tears to his eyes, for there is a strange and powerful bond that forms between oarmates.

When you are chained beside a man and share

his food and his misfortune, share the blows of the overseer and the buffets of Mother Sea, match your rhythm to his as you heave at the same great beam, huddle together in the icy night or face the careless cold alone – that is when you come to know a man. A week wedged between Rulf and Jaud and Yarvi was forced to wonder whether he had ever had two better friends.

Though perhaps that said more about his past life than his present companions.

The next day the *South Wind* put in at Thorlby.

Until Sumael, frowning from the forecastle, snapped and steered and bullied the fat galley through the shipping to the bustling wharves, Yarvi had hardly believed he could be living in the same world as the one in which he had been a king. Yet here he was. Home.

The familiar grey houses rose in tiers, crowded upon the steep slopes, older and grander as Yarvi's eye scanned upwards until, squatting on its tunnel-riddled rock, black against the white sky, he gazed upon the citadel where he had been raised. He could see the six-sided tower where Mother Gundring had her chambers, where he had learned her lessons, answered her riddles, planned his happy future as a minister. He could see the copper dome of the Godshall gleaming, beneath which he had been betrothed to his cousin Isriun, their hands bound together, her lips brushing his. He could see the hillside, in view of the howes of his ancestors, where he had sworn his oath in the hearing of gods and men to take vengeance on the killers of his father.

Was King Odem comfortably enthroned in the Black Chair now, loved and lauded by subjects who finally had a king they could admire? Of course.

Would Mother Gundring be standing minister to him, whispering her pithy wisdom in his ear? More than likely.

Had another apprentice taken Yarvi's place as her successor, sitting on his stool, feeding his doves, and bringing the steaming tea every evening? How could it be otherwise?

Would Isriun be weeping bitter tears because her crippled betrothed would never return? As easily as she forgot Yarvi's brother she would forget again.

Perhaps his mother would be the only one to miss him, and that because, in spite of all her cunning, her grip on power would surely crumble without her puppet son perched on his toy chair.

Had they burned a ship and raised an empty howe for him as they had for his drowned Uncle Uthil? Somehow he doubted it.

He realized he had bunched his shrivelled hand into a trembling, knobbled fist.

'What's troubling you?' asked Jaud.

'This was my home.'

Rulf gave a sigh. 'Take it from one who knows, cook's boy. The past is best buried.'

'I swore an oath,' said Yarvi. 'An oath there can be no rowing away from.'

Rulf sighed again. 'Take it from one who knows, cook's boy. Never swear an oath.'

'But once you have sworn,' said Jaud. 'What then?'

Yarvi frowned up towards the citadel, his jaw clenched painfully tight. Perhaps the gods had sent him this ordeal as a punishment. For being too trusting, too vain, too weak. But they had left him alive. They had given him a chance to fulfil his oath. To spill the blood of his treacherous uncle. To reclaim the Black Chair.

But the gods would not wait forever. With every dawn the memory of his father would fade, with every noon his mother's power would wane, with every dusk his uncle's grip on Gettland would grow firmer. With every sunset Yarvi's chances dwindled into darkness.

He would take no vengeance and reclaim no kingdom lashed to an oar and chained to a bench, that much was clear.

He had to get free.

THE MINISTER'S TOOLS

Stroke by backbreaking stroke, Thorlby, and home, and Yarvi's old life slipped into the past. Southwards dragged the *South Wind*, though the wind rarely seemed to blow her oar-slaves much help. Southwards down the ragged coast of Gettland, with its islands and inlets, its walled villages and fishing boats bobbing on the tide, its fenced farmsteads on sheep-dotted hillsides.

And on went Yarvi's pitiless, sinew-shredding, tooth-grinding war against the oar. He could not have said he was winning. No one won. But perhaps his defeats were not quite so one-sided.

Sumael brought them tight to the coast as they passed the mouth of the Helm River, and the ship began to hum with muttered prayers. The oarsmen cast fearful glances out to sea towards a spiral of blackened cloud that tore the sky. They could not see the splintered elf-towers on the broken islands beneath it, but everyone knew they lurked behind the horizon.

'Strokom,' muttered Yarvi, straining to see and fearing to see at once. In ages past men had brought relics from that cursed elf-ruin, but in their triumph they had sickened and died, and the Ministry had forbidden any man to go there.

'Father Peace protect us,' grunted Rulf, making a shambles of holy symbols over his heart, and the slaves needed no whip to double their efforts and leave that shadow far in their wake.

The irony was not lost on Yarvi that this was the very route he would have taken to his Minister's Test. On that voyage Prince Yarvi, swaddled in a rich blanket with his books, would have spared no thought for the suffering of the oar-slaves. Now, chained to the benches, he made the *South Wind* his study. The ship, and the people on it, and how he might use them to get free of it.

For people are the minister's best tools, Mother Gundring always said.

Ebdel Aric Shadikshirram, self-renowned merchant, lover and naval captain, spent most of her time drunk and most of the rest passed out drunk. Sometimes her snoring could be heard through the door of her cabin in the aftcastle, eerily keeping time to the movement of the rowers. Sometimes she would stand upon the forecastle in melancholy mood, one hand on her slouched hip and the other clutching a half-empty bottle, frowning into the wind as though daring it to blow harder. Sometimes she would prowl the gangway slapping backs and telling jokes as though she and her slaves were old friends together. When she passed the nameless deck scrubber she would never miss a chance to kick, throttle or upend the night-bucket over him; then she would swig from her wine, and roar out, 'on to profits!' and the oarsmen would cheer, and a man who cheered especially loudly might get a taste of the captain's wine himself, and a man who stayed silent might get a taste of Trigg's whip instead.

Trigg was the overseer, the chain-master, the grip, second-in-command and with a full share in the enterprise. He ordered the guards, perhaps two dozen of them, and watched over the slaves, and made sure they kept whatever pace the captain asked for. He was a brutal man, but there was a kind of awful justice in him. He had no favourites and made no exceptions. Everyone was whipped alike.

Ankran was the storekeeper and there was no justice in him at all. He slept below decks with the stores, and was the only slave to be regularly let off the ship. It was his task to buy food and clothes and share them out and he worked a thousand tiny swindles every day – buying meat that was halfway spoiled, and trimming every man's rations, and making them mend clothes that were worn to rags – and splitting the profits with Trigg.

Whenever he passed by Rulf would spit with particular disgust. 'What does that crooked bastard want with the money?'

'Some men simply like money,' said Jaud mildly.

'Even slaves?'

'Slaves have the same appetites as other men. It's the chance to indulge them they lack.'

'True enough,' said Rulf, looking wistfully up at Sumael.

The navigator spent most of her time on the roof of one of the castles, checking charts and instruments, or frowning up at sun or stars while she worked quick sums on her fingers, or pointing out some rock or ripple, some cloud or current, and snapping out warnings. While the *South Wind* was at sea she went where she pleased, but when they came into dock the captain's first act was always to lock her by her long, fine chain to an iron ring on the aftcastle. A slave with her skills was probably worth more than their whole cargo.

Sometimes she threaded among the rowers, clambering heedlessly over men, oars and benches to pick at some fixing or other, or to lean over the ship's side to check depths with a knotted plumbline. The only time Yarvi ever saw her smile was when she was perched on one of the mast-heads with the wind tearing at her short hair, as happy there as Yarvi might have been at Mother Gundring's firepit, scanning the coast through a tube of bright brass.

It was Throvenland that ground by now, grey cliffs besieged by the hungry waves, grey beaches where the sea sucked at the shingle, grey towns where grey-mailed spearmen frowned from the wharves at passing ships.

'My home was near here,' said Rulf, as they shipped the oars on one grey morning, a thin drizzle beading everything with dew. 'Two days' hard ride inland. I had a good farm with a good stone chimney, and a good wife who bore me two good sons.'

'How did you end up here?' asked Yarvi, fiddling pointlessly at the strapping on his raw left wrist.

'I was a fighting man. An archer, sailor, swordsman and raider in the summer months.' Rulf scratched at his heavy jaw, already grey stubbled, for his beard seemed to spring out an hour after it was shaved. 'I served a dozen seasons with a captain called Halstam, an easy-going fellow. I became his helmsman and, along with Hopki Strangletoes and Blue Jenner and some other handy men we enjoyed some successes in the raiding business, enough that I could sit with my feet to the fire and drink good ale all winter.'

'Ale never agreed with me, but it sounds a happy life,' said Jaud, gazing into the far distance. Towards a happy past of his own, perhaps.

'The gods love to laugh at a happy man.' Rulf noisily gathered some spit and sent it spinning over the side of the ship. 'One winter, somewhat the worse for drink, Halstam fell from his horse and died, and the ship passed to his oldest son, Young Halstam, who was a different kind of man, all pride and froth and scant wisdom.'

'Sometimes father and son aren't much alike,' muttered Yarvi.

'Against my better judgment I consented to be his helmsman, and not a week from port, ignoring my advice, he tried to take a too-well-guarded merchant ship. Hopki and Jenner and most of the rest went through the Last Door that day. I was one among a handful taken prisoner and sold on. That was two summers ago, and I've been pulling an oar for Trigg ever since.'

'A bitter ending,' said Yarvi.

'Many sweet stories have them,' said Jaud.

Rulf shrugged. 'Hard to complain. In my voyages we must've stolen ten score Inglings and sold 'em for slaves and taken great delight in the profits.' The old raider rubbed his rough palm against the grain of the oar. 'They say the seed you scatter will be the seed you harvest, and so it seems indeed.'

'You wouldn't leave if you could?' muttered Yarvi, with a glance towards Trigg to make sure they were not heard.

Jaud snorted. 'There is a well in the village where I used to live, a well that gives the sweetest water in the world.' He closed his eyes and licked at his lips as if he could taste it. 'I would give anything to drink from that well again.' He spread his palms. 'But I have nothing to give. And look at the last man who tried to leave.' And he nodded towards the scrubber, his block scraping, scraping, scraping endlessly down the deck, his heavy chain rattling as he shuffled stiffly on scabbed knees to nowhere.

'What's his story?' asked Yarvi.

'I don't know his name. Nothing, we all call him. When I was first brought to the *South Wind* he pulled an oar. One night, off the coast of Gettland, he tried to escape. Somehow he got free of his chain and stole a knife. He killed three guards and cut another's knee so he never walked again, and he gave our captain that scar before she and Trigg put a stop to him.'

Yarvi blinked at the shambling scrubber. 'All that with a knife?'

'And not a large one. Trigg wanted to hang him from a mast but Shadikshirram chose to keep him alive as an example to the rest of us.'

'Mercy's ever been her weakness,' said Rulf, and gave a grunt of joyless laughter.

'She stitched her cut,' said Jaud, 'and put that great chain on him, and hired more guards, and told them never to let him get his hands upon a blade, and ever since he has been scrubbing the deck, and never since have I heard him say a word.'

'What about you?' asked Yarvi.

Jaud grinned sideways at him. 'I speak when I have something worth saying.'

'No. I mean, what's your story?'

'I used to be a baker.' Ropes hissed as they brought up the anchor, and Jaud sighed, and worked his hands about the handles his own palms had polished to a gleam. 'Now my story is I pull this oar.'

THE FOOL STRIKES

Jaud pulled their oar, and so did Yarvi, with the calluses thickening even on his crippled hand, his face hardening against the weather and his body turning lean and tough as Trigg's whip. They rounded Bail's Point in a soaking squall, hardly able to see the brooding fortress there for the rain, and turned eastwards into calmer waters, busy with ships of all shapes and nations, Yarvi twisting around at the oar in his eagerness to see Skekenhouse.

It was the elf-ruins he saw first, of course. The giant walls, sheer and perfectly smooth at their bases, were unmarked by Mother Sea's fury but torn off ragged higher up, twisted metal showing in the cracks like splintered bone in a wound, battlements of new masonry perching at their tops, the flags of the High King proudly fluttering.

The Tower of the Ministry loomed over all. Over every building about the Shattered Sea, unless you counted the ruins of Strokom or Lanangad where no man dared tread. For three-quarters of its staggering height it was elf-built: pillars of jointless stone, perfectly square, perfectly true, with giant expanses of black elf-glass still twinkling at some of the great windows.

At perhaps five times the height of the tallest tower in Thorlby's citadel the elf-stone was sheared away, rock melted and congealed in giant tears by the Breaking of God. Above, long generations of ministers had constructed a riotous crown of timber and tile – turrets, platforms, slumping roofs, balconies, sprouting with smoking chimneys and festooned with dangling ropes and chains, all streaked with age and droppings, the rotting work of men ridiculous by comparison with the stark perfection below.

Grey specks circled the highest domes. Doves, perhaps, like the ones Yarvi once tended. Like the one that lured his father to his death. Croaking out messages from the many ministers scattered about the Shattered Sea. Could he even see the odd bronze-feathered eagle carrying the High King's wishes back?

In that ancient tower, Yarvi would have taken the test. There he would have kissed the cheek of Grandmother Wexen when he passed. There his life as a prince would have ended, and his life as a minister begun, and his life as a wretched slave never come to pass.

'Unship the oars!' called Sumael.

'Unship the oars!' bellowed Trigg, to make sure everyone saw he gave the orders.

'Oars out, oars in,' grunted Rulf. 'You'd think they could make up their bloody minds.'

'Skekenhouse.' Yarvi rubbed at the red raw patches on his wrist as the *South Wind* was heaved into its berth while Sumael leant from the aftcastle and screamed at the struggling dockers to take care. 'The centre of the world.'

Jaud snorted. 'Compared to the great cities of Catalia this is a stable.'

'We're not in Catalia.'

'No.' The big man heaved a heavy sigh. 'Sadly.'

The docks stank of old rot and salt decay, and with impressive power to be noticed over the stink of Yarvi and his companions. Many of the berths were vacant. The windows of the decaying buildings behind gaped dark and empty. On the dockside a great heap of mouldering grain sprouted with weeds. Guardsmen in the patched livery of the High King sat idle and threw dice. Beggars slouched in the shadows. Perhaps it was the bigger city, but there was none of the vigour and vitality of Thorlby, none of the bustle or new building.

The elf-ruins might have been stupendous, but the parts of Skekenhouse that men had built seemed quite a disappointment. Yarvi curled his tongue and neatly spat over the side of the ship.

'Nice.' Rulf gave him a nod. 'Your rowing's not up to much, but you're coming on where it really matters.'

'You must struggle by without me, little ones!' Shadikshirram strutted from her cabin in her most garish garments, working an extra ring or two onto her fingers. 'I am expected at the Tower of the Ministry!'

'Our money's expected,' grumbled Trigg. 'How much for a licence this year?'

'My guess would be a little more than last year.' Shadikshirram licked a knuckle so she could twist a particularly gaudy bauble over it. 'There is, in general, an upward trajectory to the High King's fees.'

'Better to toss our money to Mother Sea than to the Ministry's jackals.'

'I'd toss you to Mother Sea if I didn't think she'd toss you straight back.' Shadikshirram held out her jewel-crusted hand at arm's length to admire. 'With a licence we can trade anywhere around the Shattered Sea. Without one . . . pfah.' And she blew all profits away through her fingertips.

'The High King is jealous of his revenues,' muttered Jaud.

'Course he is,' said Rulf as they watched their captain aim a lazy kick at Nothing, then stroll across the bouncing gangplank, Ankran scrambling after her on a short length of chain. 'It's his revenues make him High. Without 'em he'll crash to earth like the rest of us.'

'And great men need great enemies,' said Jaud, 'and wars are a damned expensive hobby.'

'Building temples comes close behind.' Rulf nodded up at the skeleton of a huge building showing itself above the nearest roofs, so covered

in a ramshackle web of scaffolds, hoists and platforms Yarvi could hardly make out its shape.

'That's the High King's temple?'

'To this new god of his.' Rulf spat out of the
rowlock, missed, and spattered the timbers instead.
'A monument to his own vanity. Four years in the
building and still not halfway done.'

'Sometimes I think there can be no such thing
as gods at all,' mused Jaud, stroking thoughtfully
at his pursed lips with a fingertip. 'Then I wonder
who can be making my life such hell.'

'An old god,' said Yarvi. 'Not a new.'

'How d'you mean?' asked Rulf.

'Before the elves made their war upon Her, there
was one God. But in their arrogance they used a
magic so strong it ripped open the Last Door,
destroyed them all and broke the One God into
the many.' Yarvi nodded towards that giant building
site. 'Some in the south believe the One God
cannot ever be truly broken. That the many are
merely aspects of the one. It seems the High King
has seen the merits of their theology. Or at least
Grandmother Wexen has.' He considered that. 'Or
perhaps she sees a profit in currying favour with
the Empress of the South by praying the same
way she does.' He remembered the hungry brightness in her eye as he knelt before her. 'Or she
thinks that folk who kneel to one god will kneel
more easily to one High King.'

Rulf spat again. 'The last High King was bad
enough, but he ranked himself as first among

brothers. The older this one gets the more he's taken with his own power. He and his damn minister won't be happy 'til they're set above their own One God and all the world kneels before their withered arses.'

'A man who worships the One God cannot choose his own path: he is given it from on high,' mused Yarvi. 'He cannot refuse requests, but must bow to commands.' He drew up a length of his chain and frowned down at it. 'The One God makes a chain through the world, from the High King, through the little kings, to the rest of us, each link with its right place. All are made slaves.'

Jaud was frowning sideways. 'You are a deep thinker, Yorv.'

Yarvi shrugged and let his chain drop. 'Less use than a good hand to an oarsman.'

'How can one god make all the world work, anyway?' Rulf held his arms out to encompass the rotting city and all its people. 'How can one god be for the cattle and the fish, and the sea and the sky, and for war and peace both? A lot of damn nonsense.'

'Perhaps the One God is like me.' Sumael sprawled on the aftcastle, propped on one elbow with her head resting on her bony shoulder and one leg dangling.

'Lazy?' grunted Jaud.

She gave a grin. 'She chooses the course, but has lots of little gods chained up to do the rowing.'

'Pardon me, almighty one,' said Yarvi, 'but from where I sit you look to have a chain of your own.'

'For now,' she said, tossing a loop of it over her shoulder like a scarf.

'One God,' snorted Rulf again, still shaking his head towards the quarter-built temple.

'Better one than none at all,' grunted Trigg as he stalked past.

The oar-slaves fell silent at that, all knowing their course would take them past the land of the Shends next, who had no mercy on outsiders, and prayed to no god and knelt to no king, however high he said he was.

Great dangers meant great profits, though, as Shadikshirram informed the crew when she sprang back aboard, holding high her rune-scrawled licence, eyes so bright with triumph one might have thought she had it from the hand of the High King himself.

'That paper won't protect us from the Shends,' someone grunted from the bench behind. 'They skin their captives and eat their own dead.'

Yarvi snorted. He had studied the language and customs of most of the peoples around the Shattered Sea. *The food of fear is ignorance*, Mother Gundring used to say. *The death of fear is knowledge.* When you study a race of men you find they are just men like any others.

'The Shends don't like outsiders since we're always stealing them for slaves. They're no more savage than any other people.'

'As bad as that?' muttered Jaud, eyeing Trigg as he uncoiled his whip.

They rowed east that afternoon with a new licence and new cargo but the same old chains, the Tower of the Ministry dwindling into the haze of distance beyond their wake. At sunset they put in at a sheltered cove, Mother Sun scattering gold on the water as she sank behind the world, painting strange colours among the clouds.

'I don't like the look of that sky!' Sumael had swarmed up one of the masts, legs hooked over the yard, frowning off towards the horizon. 'We should stay here tomorrow!'

Shadikshirram waved her warnings away like flies. 'The storms in this little pond are nothing, and I have always had outstanding weatherluck. We go on.' And she flung an empty bottle into the sea and called to Ankran for another, leaving Sumael to shake her head at the heavens unmarked.

While the *South Wind* rocked gently and the guards and sailors huddled at a brazier on the forecastle to dice for trinkets, one of the slaves began to sing a bawdy song in a voice thin and cracked. At one point he forgot the words and filled them in with nonsense sounds, but at the end there was a scattering of tired laughter, and the hollow thumping of fists on oars in approval.

Another man broke in with a rousing bass, the song of Bail the Builder, who in truth had built nothing but heaps of corpses, and made himself the first High King with fire and sword and a hard word for everyone. Tyrants look far better when looked back on, though, and soon enough other voices joined the first. Eventually Bail passed through the Last Door in battle, as heroes do, and the song came to an end, as songs do, and the singer was rewarded with a round of wood-thumping of his own.

'Who else has a tune?' somebody called.

And to everyone's surprise, not least his own, it turned out Yarvi did. It was one his mother used to sing at night, when he was young and scared in the dark. He did not know why it came to him then, but his voice soared high and free, to places far from the reeking ship and things these men had long forgotten. Jaud blinked at him, and Rulf stared, and it seemed to Yarvi that, chained and helpless in this rotting tub, he had never sung half so well.

There was a silence when he was done, with only the faint creaking of the ship on the shifting water, and the wind in the rigging, and the far, high calls of distant gulls.

'Give us another,' someone said.

So Yarvi gave them another, and another, and another after that. He gave them songs of love lost and love found, of high deeds and low. The Lay of Froki, so cold-blooded he slept through a battle, and the song of Ashenleer, so sharp-eyed she could count every grain of sand on a beach. He sang of Horald the Far-Travelled who beat the black-skinned King of Daiba in a race and in

107

the end sailed so far he fell off the edge of the world. He sang of Angulf Clovenfoot, Hammer of the Vanstermen, and did not mention the man was his great grandfather.

Each time he finished he was asked for another, until Father Moon's crescent showed over the hills and the stars began to peep through heaven's cloth, and the last note of the tale of Bereg, who died to found the Ministry and protect the world from magic, smoked out into the dusk.

'Like a little bird with only one wing.' When Yarvi turned Shadikshirram was looking down at him, adjusting the pins in her tangle of hair. 'Fine singing, eh, Trigg?'

The overseer sniffed, and wiped his eyes on the back of his hand, and in a voice choked with emotion said, 'I never heard the like.'

The wise wait for their moment, Mother Gundring used to say, *but never let it pass*. So Yarvi bowed, and spoke to Shadikshirram in her own language. He did not know it well, but a good minister can make anyone a fine greeting.

'It is my honour,' he said sweetly, while thinking about putting black-tongue root in her wine, 'to sing for one so famous.'

She narrowed her eyes at him. 'Aren't you full of surprises?' And she tossed him her mostly-empty bottle and walked away, humming so tunelessly he could only just tell it was the Lay of Froki.

If he had been served that wine at his father's

108

table he would have spat it in the slave's face, but now it seemed the best he ever tasted, full of sun and fruit and freedom. It was a wrench to share the splash he had, but the sight of Rulf's huge smile after he took his swallow was well worth the price.

As they made ready to sleep, Yarvi found the other slaves were looking at him differently. Or perhaps it was that they were looking at him at all. Even Sumael gave him a thoughtful frown from her place outside the captain's cabin, as though he were a sum she could not quite make add.

'Why are they watching me?' he murmured to Jaud.

'It is rare they get a good thing. You gave them one.'

Yarvi smiled as he pulled the stinking furs to his chin. He would not be cutting the guards down with an eating knife, but perhaps the gods had given him better weapons. Time might be slipping through his fingers. He lacked a full set, after all. But he had to be patient. Patient as the winter.

Once, after his father had hit him in a rage, Yarvi's mother had found him crying. *The fool strikes,* she had said. *The wise man smiles, and watches, and learns.*

Then strikes.

SAVAGES

As a boy, Yarvi had been given a little ship of cork. His brother had taken it from him and thrown it in the sea, and Yarvi had lain on the rocky edge above and watched it tossed and whirled and played with by the waves until it was gone.

Now Mother Sea made the *South Wind* a toy ship.

Yarvi's stomach was in his sick-sour mouth as they crested one surging mountain of water, was sucked into his arse as they plunged into the foam-white valley beyond, pitching and yawing, deeper and deeper until they were surrounded by the towering sea on every side and he was sure they would be snatched into the unknowable depths, drowned to a man.

Rulf had stopped saying he'd been in worse. Not that Yarvi could have heard him. It could hardly be told what was the thunder of the sky and what the roaring of the waves and the groaning of the battered hull, the tortured ropes, the tortured men.

Jaud had stopped saying he thought the sky was brightening. It could hardly be told any longer where lashing sea ended and lashing rain began, the whole a stinging fury through which Yarvi could scarcely see the nearest mast, until the storm gloom was lit by a flash which froze the ship and its cowering crew in an instant of stark black and white.

Jaud's face was grim set, all hard planes and bunched muscle as he wrestled with their oar. Rulf's eyes bulged as he lent his own strength to the struggle. Sumael clung to the ring she was chained to when they were in dock, shrieking something no one could hear over the shrieking wind.

Shadikshirram was less inclined to listen than ever. She stood on the aftcastle's roof, one arm hooked around the mast as though it were a drinking companion, shaking her drawn sword at the sky, laughing and, when the gale dropped enough for Yarvi to hear her, daring the storm to blow harder.

Orders would have been useless now anyway. The oars were maddened animals, Yarvi dragged by the strapping about his wrist as his mother had used to drag him when he was a child. His mouth was salty with the sea, salty with his blood where the oar had struck him.

Never in his life had he been so scared and helpless. Not when he hid from his father in the secret places of the citadel. Not when he looked into Hurik's blood-spotted face and Odem said, *Kill him*. Not when he cowered at the feet of Grom-gil-Gorm. Mighty though they were, such terrors paled against the towering rage of Mother Sea.

The next flash showed the rumour of a coast,

battering waves chewing at a ragged shore, black trees and black rock from which white spray flew.

'Gods help us,' whispered Yarvi, squeezing shut his eyes, and the ship shuddered and flung him back, cracked his head against the oar behind. Men slid and tangled, tumbled from their benches to the furthest extent of their chains, clutching at anything that might spare them from being strangled by their own thrall-collars. Yarvi felt Rulf's strong arm about his shoulder, holding him fast to the bench, and it was some strange comfort to know he would be touching another person as he died.

He prayed as he never had before, to every god that he could think of, tall or small. He prayed not for the Black Chair, or for vengeance on his treacherous uncle, or for the better kiss Isriun had promised him, or even for freedom from his collar.

He prayed only for his life.

There was a grating crash that made the timbers tremble and the ship lurched. Oars shattered like twigs. A great wave washed the deck and dragged at Yarvi's clothes, and he knew that he would surely die the way his Uncle Uthil had, swallowed by the pitiless sea . . .

Dawn came muddy and merciless.

The *South Wind* was beached, listed to one side, helpless as a great whale on the cold shingle. Yarvi hunched soaked through and shivering, bruised but alive at his sharply-angled bench.

The storm had snarled away eastwards in the darkness, but in the pale blue-grey of morning the wind still blew chill and the rain still fell steadily on the miserable oar-slaves, most of them grunting at their grazes, some whimpering at wounds much worse. One bench had been torn from its bolts and vanished out to sea, no doubt bearing its three ill-fated oarsmen through the Last Door.

'We were lucky,' said Sumael.

Shadikshirram clapped her on the back and nearly knocked her over. 'I told you I have outstanding weatherluck!' She at least seemed in the best of moods after her one-sided battle with the storm.

Yarvi watched them circle the ship, Sumael's tongue tip wedged into the notch in her lip as she peered at gouges, stroked at splintered timbers with sure hands. 'The keel and the masts are sound, at least. We lost twelve oars shattered and three benches broken.'

'Not to mention three oar-slaves gone,' grunted Trigg, mightily upset at the expense. 'Two dead in their chains and six more who can't row now and may never again.'

'The hole in the hull is the real worry,' said Ankran. 'There's daylight in the hold. It'll have to be patched and caulked before we can even think of floating her.'

'Wherever will we find some timber?' Shadikshirram swept a long arm at the ancient forest that hemmed in the beach on every side.

'It belongs to the Shends.' Trigg eyed the shadowy

woods with a great deal less enthusiasm. 'They find us here we'll all end up skinned.'

'Then you'd best get started, Trigg. You look bad enough with your skin on. If my luck holds we can handle the repairs and be away before the Shends sharpen their knives. You!' And Shadikshirram stepped over to where Nothing was kneeling on the shingle and rolled him over with a kick in the ribs. 'Why aren't you scrubbing, bastard?'

Nothing crawled after his heavy chain onto the sloping deck and, like a man sweeping his hearth after his house has burned down, painfully set about his usual labour.

Ankran and Sumael exchanged a doubtful glance then set to work themselves, while Shadikshirram went to fetch her tools. Wine, that was, which she started steadily drinking, draped over a nearby rock.

Trigg opened some of the locks – a rarity indeed – and oarsmen who had not left their benches in weeks were put on longer chains and given tools by Ankran. Jaud and Rulf were set to splitting trunks with wedge and mallet, and when the planks were made Yarvi dragged each one to the rent in the ship's side, where Sumael stood, jaw set with concentration as she neatly trimmed them with a hatchet.

'What are you smiling about?' she asked him.

Yarvi's hands were raw with the work and his head hurt from the blow against the oar and he was riddled with splinters from head to toe, but his smile only got wider. On a longer chain everything

114

looked better, and Sumael was by no means an exception.

'I'm free of the bench,' he said.

'Huh.' She raised her brows. 'Don't get used to it.'

'There!' A screech shrill as a cock dropped on a cook slab. One of the guards was pointing inland, face ghostly pale.

A man stood at the treeline. He was stripped to the waist in spite of the weather, body streaked with white paint, hair a black thicket. He had a bow over his shoulder, a short axe at his hip. He made no sudden move, roared no threat, only looked calmly towards the ship and the slaves busy around it, then turned without hurry and disappeared into the shadows. But the panic he sparked could hardly have been greater had he been a charging army.

'Gods help us,' whispered Ankran, plucking at his thrall-collar as if it sat too tight for him to breathe.

'Work faster,' snarled Shadikshirram, so worried she stopped drinking for a moment.

They doubled their efforts, constantly glancing towards the trees for any more unwelcome visitors. At one point a ship passed out at sea and two of the sailors splashed into the surf, waving their arms and screaming for help. A small figure waved back, but the ship made no sign of stopping.

Rulf wiped the sweat from his forehead on one thick wrist. 'I wouldn't have stopped.'

'Nor I,' said Jaud. 'We will have to help ourselves.'

Yarvi could only nod. 'I wouldn't even have waved.'

That was when more Shends slipped noiselessly from the blackness of the forest. Three, then six, then twelve, all armed to the teeth, each arrival greeted with growing horror, by Yarvi as much as anyone. He might have read that the Shends were peaceable enough but these ones did not look as if they had read the same books he had.

'Keep working!' growled Trigg, grabbing one man by the scruff of his neck and forcing him back to the felled trunk he had been stripping. 'We should run them off. Give 'em a shock.'

Shadikshirram tossed her latest bottle across the shingle. 'For every one you see there'll be ten hidden. You'd be the one getting the shock, I suspect. But try it, by all means. I'll watch.'

'What do we do, then?' muttered Ankran.

'I'll be doing my best not to leave them any wine.' The captain pulled the cork from a new bottle. 'If you wanted to save them some trouble I suppose you could skin yourself.' And she chuckled as she took a swig.

Trigg nodded towards Nothing, still on his knees, scrubbing at the deck. 'Or we could give him a blade.'

Shadikshirram stopped laughing abruptly. 'Never.'

The wise wait for their moment, but never let it pass.

'Captain,' said Yarvi, setting down his plank and stepping humbly forward. 'I have a suggestion.'

'You going to sing to them, cripple?' snapped Trigg.

'Talk to them.'

Shadikshirram regarded him through languidly narrowed eyes. 'You know their tongue?'

'Enough to keep us safe. Perhaps even to trade with them.'

The overseer jabbed a thick forefinger at the growing crowd of painted warriors. 'You think those savages will listen to reason?'

'I know they will.' Yarvi only wished he was as certain as he somehow managed to sound.

'This is madness!' said Ankran.

Shadikshirram's gaze wandered to the store-keeper. 'I keenly await your counter-proposal.' He blinked, mouth half open, hands helplessly twitching, and the captain rolled her eyes. 'There are so few heroes left these days. Trigg, you conduct our one-handed ambassador to a parley. Ankran, you toddle along with them.'

'Me?'

'How many cowards called Ankran do I own? You trade for the stores, don't you? Go trade.'

'But nobody trades with the Shends!'

'Then the deals you make should be the stuff of legend.' Shadikshirram stood. 'Everyone needs something. That's the beauty of the merchant's profession. Sumael can tell you what we need.' She leaned close to Yarvi, blasting him with wine-heavy breath, and patted his cheek. 'Sing to 'em, boy. As sweetly as you did the other night. Sing for your life.'

That was how Yarvi found himself walking slowly towards the trees, his empty hands high and his short length of chain held firm in Trigg's meaty fist, desperately trying to convince himself great dangers meant great profits. Ahead, more Shends had gathered, silently watching. Behind, Ankran muttered in Haleen. 'If the cripple manages to make a trade, the usual arrangement?'

'Why not?' answered Trigg, giving a tug on Yarvi's chain. He could hardly believe they were thinking about money even now, but perhaps when the Last Door stands open for them men fall back on what they know. He had fallen back on his minister's wisdom, after all. And a flimsy shield it seemed as the Shends got steadily closer in all their painted savagery.

They did not scream or shake their weapons. They were more than threatening enough without. They simply stepped back to make room as Yarvi came near, herded through the trees by Trigg and into a clearing where more Shends were gathered about a fire. Yarvi swallowed as he realized how many more. They might have outnumbered the whole crew of the *South Wind* three to one.

A woman sat among them, whittling at a stick with a bright knife. Strung around her neck on a leather thong was an elf-tablet, the green card studded with black jewels, scrawled with incomprehensible markings, riddled with intricate golden lines.

The first thing a minister learns is to recognize power. To read the glances, and the stances, the movements and tones of voice that mark the followers from the leader. Why waste time on under-lings, after all? So Yarvi stepped between the men as if they were invisible, looking only into the woman's frowning face, and the warriors shuffled after and hedged him and Trigg and Ankran in with a thicket of naked steel.

For the briefest moment Yarvi hesitated. For a moment, he enjoyed Trigg and Ankran's fear more than he suffered with his own. For a moment he had power over them, and found he liked the feeling.

'Speak!' hissed Trigg.

Yarvi wondered if there was a way to get the overseer killed. To use the Shends to get his freedom, perhaps Rulf's and Jaud's as well . . . But the stakes were too high and the odds too long. The wise minister picks the greater good, the lesser evil, and smooths the way for Father Peace in every tongue. So Yarvi dropped down, one knee squelching into the boggy ground, his withered hand on his chest and the other to his forehead in the way Mother Gundring had taught him, to show he spoke the truth.

Even if he lied through his teeth.

'My name is Yorv,' he said, in the language of the Shends, 'and I come humbly upon bended knee, stranger no longer, to beg the guest-right for me and my companions.'

The woman slowly narrowed her eyes at Yarvi. Then she looked about at her men, carefully sheathed her knife and tossed her stick into the fire. 'Damn it.'

'Guest-right?' muttered one of the warriors, pointing towards the stranded ship in disbelief. 'These savages?'

'Your pronunciation is dismal.' The woman flung up her hands. 'But I am Svidur of the Shends. Stand, Yorv, for you are welcome at our hearth, and safe from harm.'

Another of the warriors angrily flung his axe on the ground and stamped off into the brush.

Svidur watched him go. 'We were very much looking forward to killing you and taking your cargo. We must take what we can, for your High King will make war upon us again when the spring comes. The man is made of greed. I swear I have no idea what we have that he wants.'

Yarvi glanced back at Ankran, who was frowning at the conversation with the deepest suspicion. 'It is my sad observation that some men always want more.'

'They do.' She propped elbow on knee and chin on hand as she watched her crestfallen warriors sit down in disgust, one of them already bunching moss to scrub off his battle-paint. 'This could have been a profitable day.'

'It still can be.' Yarvi clambered to his feet, and clasped his hands the way his mother did when she began a bargain. 'There are things for which my captain would like to trade . . .'

UGLY LITTLE SECRETS

Shadikshirram's cabin was cramped and garish, gloomy from the three slit windows, shadowy from sacks and bags dangling from the low roof-beams. Her bed, heaped with sheets and furs and stained pillows, took up most of the floor. An outsize, iron-bound chest took up most of the rest. Empty bottles had rolled to every corner. The place smelled of tar, salt and incense, stale sweat and stale wine. And yet compared to the life Yarvi had been living – if that even qualified as a life – it seemed the height of indulgent luxury.

'The repair won't last,' Sumael was saying. 'We should head back to Skekenhouse.'

'The wonderful thing about the Shattered Sea is that it forms a circle.' Shadikshirram made a circle in the air with her bottle. 'We will come to Skekenhouse either way.'

Sumael blinked at that. 'But one in days, the other months!'

'You'll keep us going, you always do. The sailor's worst enemy is the sea, but wood floats, no? How difficult can it be? We head on.' Shadikshirram's eyes drifted to Yarvi as he ducked under the low lintel. 'Ah, my ambassador! Since we still have our skins I assume things went well?'

'I need to speak to you, my captain.' He spoke with eyes downcast, the way a minister speaks to their king. 'You alone.'

'Hmmm.' She stuck out her bottom lip and plucked at it like a musician might a harp. 'A man seeking a private audience always intrigues me, even one so young, crippled, and otherwise unattractive as you. Get to your caulk and timber, Sumael, I want us back on the salt by morning.'

The muscles at the sides of Sumael's head bunched as she ground her teeth. 'On it or under it.' And she shouldered past Yarvi and out.

'So?' Shadikshirram took a long swig of wine and set the bottle rattling down.

'I begged the Shends for guest-right, my captain. They have a solemn tradition not to deny a stranger who asks properly.'

'Nimble,' said Shadikshirram, gathering her black-and-silver hair in both hands.

'And I negotiated for the things we need, and made what I consider an excellent trade.'

'Very nimble,' she said, winding her hair into its usual tangle.

But now was when his nimbleness would truly be needed. 'You may not think it quite so excellent a deal as I, my captain.'

Her eyes narrowed slightly. 'How so?'

'Your storekeeper and overseer took their own shares in your profits.'

There was a long pause while, one by one, Shadikshirram slid the pins carefully through her hair to hold it fast. Her face did not change by the slightest detail, yet Yarvi felt suddenly that he was standing at the brink of a precipice.

'Did they?' she said.

He had expected anything but this offhand coolness. Did she know already but not care? Would she send him back to the oar regardless? Would Trigg and Ankran learn he had betrayed them? He licked his lips, knowing he stood on desperately thin ice. But he had no choice but to press on, and hope somehow to reach solid ground.

'Not for the first time,' he croaked.

'No?'

'In Vulsgard you gave money for healthy oar-slaves and they bought the cheapest dregs they could find, myself among them. I've a guess you received little change.'

'Pathetically little.' Shadikshirram picked up her bottle between two fingers and took a long swig. 'But I begin to wonder whether I got a bargain with you.'

Yarvi felt a strange desire to blurt the words out, had to make himself speak calmly, earnestly, just as a minister should. 'They made both arrangements in Haleen, thinking no one would understand. But I speak that language too.'

'And sing in it, no doubt. For an oar-slave you have many talents.'

A minister should endeavour never to be asked

a question they do not already know the answer to, and Yarvi had a lie hanging ready for that. 'My mother was a minister.'

'A minister's belt should remain ever fastened.' Shadikshirram sucked air through her pursed lips. 'Oh, ugly little secret.'

'Life is full of them.'

'So it is, boy, so it is.'

'She taught me tongues, and numbers, and the lore of plants, and many other things. Things that could be of use to you, my captain.'

'A useful child indeed. You may need two hands to fight someone, but only one to stab them in the back, eh? Ankran!' she sang through the open door. 'Ankran, your captain would speak with you!'

The storekeeper's footsteps came fast, but not as fast as Yarvi's heart. 'I've been checking the stores, Captain, and there's a hatchet missing—' He saw Yarvi as he ducked through the doorway, and his face twitched, shock at first, then suspicion, and finally he tried to smile.

'Can I bring you more wine—'

'Never again.' There was an ugly pause, while the captain smiled bright-eyed, and the colour steadily drained from Ankran's face, and the blood in Yarvi's temples surged louder and louder. 'I expect Trigg to rob me: he is a free man and must look to his own interests. But you? To be robbed by one's own possessions?' Shadikshirram drained her bottle, licked the last drops from the neck and weighed it lazily in her hand. 'You must see that is something of an embarrassment.'

The storekeeper's thin lips twisted. 'He's lying, Captain!'

'But his lies match my suspicions so closely.'

'It's all—'

So fast that Yarvi hardly saw it, only heard the hollow thud, Shadikshirram clubbed Ankran with the base of her bottle. He dropped with a grunt and lay blinking, blood streaming down his face. She stepped forward, lifting her boot over his head and, calmly, steadily, frowning with concentration, started stamping on it.

'Swindle me?' she hissed through gritted teeth, heel opening a cut down his cheek.

'Steal from me?' as her boot smashed Ankran's nose sideways.

'Take me for a fool?'

Yarvi looked away into the corner of the room, the breath crawling in his throat as the sick crunching went on.

'After all . . . I've . . . *done* for you!'

Shadikshirram squatted down, forearms resting on her knees and her hands dangling. She thrust her jaw forward and blew a loose strand of hair out of her face. 'I am once again disappointed by the wretchedness of humanity.'

'My wife,' Ankran whispered, bringing Yarvi's eyes crawling back to his ruined face. A bubble of blood formed and broke on his lips. 'My wife . . . and my son.'

'What of them?' snapped Shadikshirram, frowning at a red spatter that had caught the back of her hand and wiping it clean on Ankran's clothes.

'The flesh-dealer . . . you bought me from . . . in Thorlby.' Ankran's voice was squelchy. 'Yoverfell. He has them.' He coughed, and pushed a piece of tooth out of his mouth with his tongue. 'He said he'd keep them safe . . . as long as I brought him their price . . . every time we passed through. If I don't pay . . .'

Yarvi felt weak at the knees. So weak he thought he might fall. Now he understood why Ankran had needed all that money.

But Shadikshirram only shrugged. 'What's that to me?' And she twisted her fingers in Ankran's hair and pulled a knife from her belt.

'Wait!' shouted Yarvi.

The captain looked over at him sharply. 'Really? Are you sure?'

It took everything he had to force his mouth into a watery smile. 'Why kill what you can sell?'

She squatted there a moment, staring at him, and he wondered if she would kill them both. Then she snorted out a laugh, and lowered the knife. 'I do declare. My soft heart will be my undoing. Trigg!'

The overseer paused for just a moment when he stepped into the cabin and saw Ankran on the floor with his face a bloodied pulp.

'It turns out our storekeeper has been robbing me,' said the captain.

126

Trigg frowned at Ankran, then at Shadikshirram, and finally, for a long time, at Yarvi. 'Seems some people think only of themselves.'

'And I thought we were one family.' The captain stood, dusting off her knees. 'We have a new store-keeper. Get him a better collar.' She rolled Ankran towards the door with her foot. 'And put this thing in the space on Jaud's oar.'

'Right y'are, Captain.' And Trigg dragged Ankran out by one arm and kicked the door closed.

'You see that I am merciful,' said Shadikshirram brightly, with merciful gestures of the blood-spotted hand which still loosely held her knife. 'Mercy is my weakness.'

'Mercy is a feature of greatness,' Yarvi managed to croak.

Shadikshirram beamed at that. 'Isn't it? But, great though I am . . . I rather think Ankran has used up all my mercy for this year.' She put her long arm about Yarvi's shoulders, hooking her thumb through his collar, and drew him close, close, close enough to smell the wine on her whisper. 'If another storekeeper betrayed my trust . . .' And she trailed off into silence more eloquent than any words.

'You have nothing to worry about, my captain.' Yarvi looked into her face so close that her black eyes seemed to merge into one. 'I have no wife or children to distract me.' Only an uncle to kill, and his daughter to marry, and the Black Chair of Gettland to reclaim. 'I'm your man.'

'You're scarcely a man, but otherwise, excellent!' And she wiped her knife one way then the other on the front of Yarvi's shirt. 'Then wriggle down to your stores, my little one-handed minister, ferret out where Ankran was hiding my money and bring me up some wine! And smile, boy!' Shadikshirram pulled a golden chain from around her neck and hung it over one of the posts of her bed. A key dangled from it. The key to the oar-slaves' locks. 'I like my friends smiling and my enemies dead!' She spread her arms wide, wriggled the fingers, and toppled back onto her furs. 'Today dawned with such little promise,' she mused at the ceiling. 'But it turns out everyone got what they wanted.'

Yarvi thought it unwise to point out, as he hurried for the door, that Ankran, not to mention his wife and child, would probably not have agreed.

ENEMIES AND ALLIES

To no one's surprise, Yarvi found himself much better suited to the stores than the oars.

At first he could hardly crawl into his shadowy, creaking new domain below decks for the confusion of barrels and boxes, of overspilling chests, of swinging bags hooked to the ceiling. But within a day or two he had everything as organized as Mother Gundring's shelves had been, in spite of the pale new planks of the repair steadily oozing saltwater. It was not a comforting task, bucketing out the brackish puddle that built up every morning.

But a great deal better than being back on the benches.

Yarvi found a length of bent iron to bash at any nail that gave a hint of loosening, and tried not to imagine that just beyond that straining tissue of rough-sawn wood Mother Sea's full crushing weight was bearing in.

The *South Wind* limped eastwards and, wounded and undermanned though she was, within a few days reached the great market at Roystock, a hundred hundred shops pressed onto a boggy

129

island near the mouth of the Divine River. Small, swift ships were caught at the tangle of wharves like flies in a spider's web and their lean and sunburned crews were caught too. Men who had rowed hard weeks upstream, and carried their ships for even harder ones at the tall hauls, were swindled from their strange cargoes for a night or two of simple pleasures. While Sumael cursed and struggled to patch the leaking patches, Yarvi was taken ashore on Trigg's chain, looking for stores and oar-slaves to replace what the storm had taken.

There in narrow lanes aswarm with humanity of every cut and colour, Yarvi bartered. He had watched his mother do it – Laithlin, the Golden Queen, no sharper eye or quicker tongue around the Shattered Sea – and found he had her tricks without thinking. He haggled in six languages, merchants aghast to find their own secret tongues turned against them. He flattered and blustered, snorted derision at prices and contempt at quality, stamped off and was begged back, was first as yielding as oil, then immovable as iron, and left a trail of weeping traders in his wake.

Trigg held the chain with so light a hand that Yarvi almost forgot he was chained at all. Until, when they were done and the saved hacksilver was jingling back into the captain's purse, the overseer's whisper tickled at Yarvi's ear and made his every hair bristle.

'You're quite the cunning little cripple, aren't you?'

Yarvi paused a moment to collect his wits. 'I have . . . some understanding.'

'Doubtless. It's clear you understood me and Ankran, and passed your understandings to the captain. Got quite the vengeful temper, don't she? The tales she tells of herself might all be lies, but I could tell you true ones would amaze you no less. I once saw her kill a man for stepping on her shoe. And this was a big, big man.'

'Perhaps that's why his weight bruised her toes so.'

Trigg yanked at the chain and the collar bit into Yarvi's neck and made him squawk. 'Don't lean too much on my good nature, boy.'

Trigg's good nature did indeed seem too weak a thing to bear much weight. 'I played the hand I was dealt,' croaked Yarvi.

'We all do,' purred Trigg. 'Ankran played his poorly, and paid the price. I don't mean to do the same. So I'll offer you the same arrangement. Half of what you take from Shadikshirram, you give to me.'

'What if I don't take anything?'

Trigg snorted. 'Everyone takes something, boy. Some of what you give to me, I'll pass on to the guards, and everyone's kept friendly. Smiles all round. Give me nothing, you'll make some enemies. Bad ones to have.' He wound Yarvi's chain about his big hand and jerked him closer still. 'Remember cunning children and stupid ones all drown very much the same.'

Yarvi swallowed once more. Mother Gundring

used to say, *A good minister never says no, if they can say perhaps.*

'The captain's watchful. She doesn't trust me yet. Only give me a little time.'

With a shove, Trigg sent him stumbling back towards the *South Wind*. 'Just make sure it's a little.'

That was well enough with Yarvi. Old friends in Thorlby – not to mention old enemies – would not wait for him forever. Charming though the overseer was, Yarvi hoped very much to quit Trigg's company before too long.

From Roystock they turned northwards.

They passed lands that had no name, where fens of mirror pools stretched into unknown distances, thousands of fragments of sky sprinkled across this bastard offspring of earth and sea, lonely birds calling out over the desolation, and Yarvi breathed deep the salt chill and longed for home.

He thought often of Isriun, trying to remember her scent as she leaned close, the brush of her lips, the shape of her smile, sun glowing through her hair in the doorway of the Godshall. Scant memories, turned over and over in his mind until they were worn threadbare as a beggar's clothes.

Was she promised to some better husband, now? Smiling at some other man? Kissing another lover? Yarvi clenched his teeth. He had to get home.

His every idle moment was crowded with plans for escape.

At a trading post where the buildings were so

rough-hewn a man could get splinters just from walking by, Yarvi pointed out a servant-girl to Trigg, then among the salt and herbs acquired some extra supplies while the overseer was distracted. Enough tanglefoot leaf to make every guard on the ship slow and heavy, or even send them off to sleep if the dose was right.

'What about the money, boy?' Trigg hissed as they headed back to the *South Wind*.

'I have a plan for that,' and Yarvi gave a humble smile while he thought of rolling a slumbering Trigg over the side of the ship.

He was a great deal more valued, respected and, being honest, useful as a storekeeper than he had been as a king. The oar-slaves had enough to eat, and warmer clothes to wear, and grunted their approval as he passed. He had the run of the ship while they were on the salt, but like a miser with his profits that much freedom only sharpened his hunger for more.

When Yarvi thought no one could see, he dropped crusts near Nothing's hand, and saw him slip them quickly into his rags. Once their eyes met afterward, and Yarvi wondered if the scrubber could be grateful, for it hardly seemed there was anything human left behind those strange, bright, sunken eyes.

But Mother Gundring always said, *It is for one's own sake that one does good things.* He kept dropping crumbs when he could.

Shadikshirram noted with pleasure the greater

133

weight of her purse, and with even more the improvement in her wine, achieved in part because Yarvi was able to buy in such impressive bulk.

'This is a better vintage than Ankran brought me,' she muttered, squinting at its colour in the bottle.

Yarvi bowed low. 'One worthy of your achievements.' And behind the mask of his smile he considered how, when he sat in the Black Chair once more, he would see her head above the Screaming Gate and her cursed ship made ashes.

Sometimes as darkness fell she would stick one foot at him so he could pull her boots off while she spouted some tale of past glories, the names and details shifting like oil with every telling. Then she would say he was a good and useful boy, and if he was truly lucky would give him scraps from her table and confess, 'my soft heart will be my undoing.'

When he could keep himself from cramming them in his mouth on the spot he would slip them to Jaud, who would pass them to Rulf, while Ankran sat frowning into nowhere between them, his scalp cut from his shaving and his scabbed face a very different shape than it had been before its argument with Shadikshirram's boot.

'Gods,' grunted Rulf. 'Remove this two-handed fool from our oar and give us Yorv again!'

The oar-slaves about them laughed, but Ankran sat still as a man of wood, and Yarvi wondered whether he was turning over his own oath for vengeance. He glanced up and saw Sumael frowning down from her place on the yard. She was always watching, judging, as though at a course she could not approve. Even though they were chained at night to the same ring outside the captain's cabin she said nothing to him beyond the odd grunt.

'Get rowing,' snapped Trigg, shoving past and barging Yarvi into the oar he used to pull.

It seemed he had made enemies as well as friends.

But enemies, as his mother used to say, *are the price of success.*

'Boots, Yorv!'

Yarvi flinched as if at a slap. His thoughts had wandered far away, as they often did. Back to the slopes above his father's burning ship, swearing his oath of vengeance before the gods. Back to the roof of Amwend's holdfast, the smell of burning in his nose. Back to his uncle's calmly smiling face.

You would have been a fine jester.

'Yorv!'

He struggled from his blankets, tugging a length of chain after him, stepping over Sumael, hunched in her own bundle, dark face twitching silently in her sleep. It was growing colder as they headed north, and specks of snow whirled from the night on a keen wind, dotting the furs the oar-slaves huddled under with white. The guards had given up patrolling and the only two awake hunched

135

over a brazier by the forward hatch into the hold, pinched faces lit in orange.

'These boots are worth more than you, damn it!'

Shadikshirram was sitting on her bed, eyes shining wet, straining forward and trying to grab her foot but so drunk she kept missing. When she saw him she sagged back.

'Give me a hand, eh?'

'As long as you don't need two,' said Yarvi.

She gurgled with laughter. 'You're a clever little crippled bastard, aren't you? I swear the gods sent you. Sent you . . . to get my boots off.' Her chuckles became like snores, and by the time he wrestled her second boot off and heaved her leg onto the bed she was sound asleep, head back, hair fluttering over her mouth with each snorting breath.

Yarvi stopped still as stone. Her shirt had come open at the collar and the chain slipped from it. Glinting on the furs beside her neck was the key to every lock on the ship.

He looked towards the door, open a crack, snow flitting outside. He opened the lamp and blew out the flame, and the room sank into darkness. It was an awful risk, but a man with time against him must sometimes throw the dice.

The wise wait for their moment, but never let it pass.

He inched to the bed, skin prickling, and slipped his one-fingered hand under Shadikshirram's head.

Gently, gently he lifted it, shocked at the dead weight, teeth clenched with the effort of moving so slowly. He winced as she twitched and snorted, sure her eyes would flick open, thinking of her heel smashing his face as it had smashed Ankran's.

He took a breath and held it, reached across her for the key, caught by a gleam of Father Moon's light from one of the narrow windows. He strained for it . . . but his itching fingertips came up just short.

There was a choking pressure around his neck. His chain had snagged on something. He turned, thinking to yank it free, and there in the doorway, jaw locked tight and Yarvi's chain gripped firmly in both fists, stood Sumael.

For a moment they were frozen there. Then she began to reel him in.

He let Shadikshirram's head fall as gently as he could, gripped the chain with his good hand and tried to drag it back, breath hissing. Sumael only pulled harder, the collar grinding into Yarvi's neck, the links of the chain cutting into his hand, making him bite his lip to keep from crying out.

It was like the rope contest that the boys used to play on the beach in Thorlby, except only one of them had both hands and one end was around Yarvi's neck.

He twisted and struggled but Sumael was too strong for him, and in silence she dragged him closer, and closer, his boots slipping on the floor, catching a bottle and sending it rolling, until in the end she caught him by the collar and hauled him out into the night, dragging him close.

'You damn fool!' she snarled in his face. 'Are you trying to get yourself killed?'

'What do you care?' he hissed back, her knuckles white around his collar and his knuckles white around her fist.

'I care if they change all the locks because you stole the key, idiot!'

There was a long pause, then, while they stared at each other in the darkness, and it settled on him just how very close they were. Close enough for him to see the angry creases at the bridge of her nose, to see her teeth gleaming through the notch in her lip, to feel her warmth. Close enough for him to smell her quick breath, a little sour, but none the worse for that. Close enough, almost, to kiss. It must have settled on her at the same moment, because she let go his collar as if it was hot, pulled away and twisted her wrist free of his grip.

He turned her words over, and looked at them this way and that, and the realization settled on him.

'Changing the locks would only bother someone who had a key already. Who found a way to copy a key, perhaps?' He sat down in his usual place, rubbing at the chafe marks and the old burns on his neck with his good hand, tucking his bad one into the warmth of his armpit. 'But the only reason a slave would need a key is to escape.'

'Shut your mouth!' She slid down beside him, and there was another pause. The snow drifted, settled upon her hair, across his knees.

It was not until he was giving up hope of her ever speaking again that she finally did, so softly he could scarcely hear it over the wind. 'A slave with a key might free some other slaves. All of them, perhaps. In the confusion, who knows who might slip away?'

'A lot of blood could be spilled,' murmured Yarvi. 'In the confusion, who knows whose? Far safer to put the guards to sleep.' Sumael looked sharply over at him, he could see the gleam of her eyes, the mist of her breath. 'A slave who knew plants, and poured the guards' ale and brought the captain's wine might find a way.' A risk, he knew, but with her help things could be so much easier, and a man with time against him must sometimes throw the dice. 'Perhaps two slaves together could achieve—'

'What one alone couldn't,' she finished for him. 'Best to slip from the ship while in port.'

Yarvi nodded. 'I'd have thought so.' He'd been thinking about little else for days.

'Skekenhouse would be the best chance. The city's busy but the guards are lazy, the captain and Trigg spend a lot of time off the ship—'

'Unless one had friends somewhere around the Shattered Sea.' He let the bait hang there.

She swallowed it whole. 'Friends that might shelter a pair of escaped slaves?'

'Exactly. In, say . . . Thorlby?'

'The *South Wind* will be back through Thorlby within a month or two.' Yarvi could hear the excitement, squeaky in her whisper.

He could not keep it from his own. 'As soon as that a slave with a key . . . and a slave who knew plants . . . could be free.'

They sat in silence, in the cold, in the darkness, as they had so many nights before. But, looking across by Father Moon's pale light, Yarvi thought there was the rare hint of a smile at the corner of Sumael's mouth.

He thought it suited her.

ONE FRIEND

Far north, now, the oar-slaves dragged the *South Wind*, over the black sea with winter on the march. Snow fell often, settling on the roofs of the ship's castles, across the shoulders of the shivering rowers, blowing smoke onto their numbed fingers with each stroke. All night the broken hull groaned. In the morning men leaned over the sides to crack ice from its wounded flanks. At sunset Shadikshirram would wander from her cabin wrapped in furs, eyes and nostrils rimmed with boozy pink, and say she didn't think it overly cold.

'I try to keep love in my heart,' said Jaud, grasping with both hands at the soup Yarvi handed him. 'But gods, I hate the North.'

'There's nowhere more north than this,' answered Rulf, rubbing at the tips of his ears as he frowned out towards the white blanket of the coast.

Ankran, as usual, added nothing.

The sea was an ice-flecked emptiness, groups of lumpen seals watching them sadly from the rocky shoreline. They saw few other ships, and when they did Trigg glowered towards them, hand on his

141

sword, until they were dots in the distance. However powerful the High King thought himself, his licence would not protect them out here.

'Most merchants lack the courage for these waters.' Shadikshirram wedged her boot carelessly on an oarsman's leg, 'but I am not most merchants.' Yarvi silently thanked the gods for that. 'The Banyas who live out in this icy hell worship me as a goddess, for I bring pots and knives and iron tools which they treat like elf-magic, and ask only for pelts and amber which to them are so plentiful as to be next to worthless. They'll do anything for me, poor brutes.' She rubbed her palms together with an eager hissing. 'Here my best profits are made.'

And indeed the Banyas were waiting for the *South Wind* when she finally broke through the shore-ice to a slimy jetty at a grey beach. They made the Shends seem the height of civilization in Yarvi's memory – all swathed in furs so they looked more bears or wolves than men, their shaggy faces pierced with splinters of polished bone and studs of amber, their bows fluttering with feathers and their clubs set with teeth. Yarvi wondered if they were human teeth, and decided people who scratched a living from this miserly land could afford to waste nothing.

'I will be four days away.' Shadikshirram vaulted over the ship's side and clomped down the warped timbers of the jetty, the *South Wind*'s sailors following with her cargo lashed to clumsy sleds. 'Trigg, you're in charge!'

'She'll be better'n when you left her!' the over-seer called back with a grin.

'Four days of idleness,' Yarvi hissed as the last light stained the sky red, fretting at his thrall-collar with his withered thumb. Every night spent on this rotting tub it seemed to chafe him more.

'Patience.' Sumael spoke through closed teeth, scarred lips hardly moving, dark eyes on the guards, and on Trigg in particular. 'A few weeks and we might be with your friends in Thorlby.' She turned her familiar frown on him. 'You'd better have friends in Thorlby.'

'You'd be surprised who I know.' Yarvi wriggled down into his furs. 'Trust me.'

She snorted. 'Trust?'

Yarvi turned his back to her. Sumael might be spiky as a hedgehog but she was tough, and clever, and there was no one on this ship he would rather have had beside him. He needed an accomplice, not a friend, and she knew what to do and when.

He could see it as though it was already done. Every night he lulled himself to sleep with thoughts of it. The *South Wind* rocking gently at a wharf beneath the citadel of Thorlby. The guards snoring a drugged slumber beside their empty ale cups. The key turning smoothly in the lock. He and Sumael stealing together from the ship, chains muffled with rags, through the steep and darkened streets he knew so well, boot-printed slush on the cobbles, snow on the steep roofs.

He smiled as he pictured his mother's face when

143

she saw him. He smiled even more as he pictured Odem's, just before he rammed the knife into his guts . . .

Yarvi stabbed, and cut, and stabbed, his hands slippery hot with traitor's blood and his uncle squealed like a slaughtered pig.

'The rightful King of Gettland!' came the shout and all applauded, none louder than Grom-gil-Gorm who smashed his great hands together with every squelch of the blade and Mother Scaer who shrieked and capered in her joy and turned into a cloud of clattering doves.

The squelching became a sucking and Yarvi looked over at his brother, white and cold on the slab. Isriun leaned over his face, kissing, kissing.

She smiled up at Yarvi through the shroud of her hanging hair. That smile. 'I'll expect a better kiss after your victory.'

Odem propped himself up on his elbows. 'How long is this going to take?'

'Kill him,' said Yarvi's mother. 'One of us at least must be a man.'

'I am a man!' snarled Yarvi, stabbing and stabbing, his arms burning with the effort. 'Or . . . half a man?'

Hurik raised an eyebrow. 'That much?'

The knife was slippery in Yarvi's grip and all the doves were a terrible distraction, staring at him, staring, and the bronze-feathered eagle in their midst with a message from Grandmother Wexen.

'Have you considered the Ministry?' it croaked at him.

'I am a king!' he snarled, cheeks burning, hiding his useless clown's hand behind his back.

'A king sits between gods and men,' said Keimdal, blood leaking from his cut throat.

'A king sits alone,' said Yarvi's father, leaning forward in the Black Chair, the wounds that had been dry all dripping fresh and spilling a slick of blood across the floor of the Godshall.

Odem's screams had turned to giggles. 'You would have been a fine jester.'

'Damn you!' snarled Yarvi, trying to stab harder but the knife was so heavy he could hardly lift it.

'What are you doing?' asked Mother Gundring. She sounded scared.

'Shut up, bitch,' said Odem, and he caught Yarvi around the neck, and squeezed . . .

Yarvi woke with a horrible jolt to find Trigg's hands around his throat.

A crescent of fierce grins swam above him, teeth shining in torchlight. He retched and twisted but he was held fast as a fly in honey.

'You should've taken the deal, boy.'

'What are you doing?' asked Sumael again. He'd never heard her sound scared before. But she sounded nowhere near as scared as Yarvi was.

'I told you to *shut your mouth*!' one of the guards snarled in her face. 'Unless you want to go with him!'

She shrank back into her blankets. She knew what to do, and when. Perhaps a friend would've been better than an accomplice after all, but it was a little late now to find one.

'I told you clever children drown just like stupid ones.' Trigg slid his key into the lock and unfastened Yarvi's chain. Freedom, but not quite how he had pictured it. 'We're going to put you in the water and see if it's true.'

And Trigg dragged Yarvi down the deck like a chicken plucked and ready for the pot. Past the oarsmen sleeping on their benches, the odd one peering from his bald furs. None of them stirred to help him. Why would they? How could they?

Yarvi's heels kicked pointlessly at the deck. Yarvi's hands fumbled at Trigg's, good and bad equally useless. Perhaps he should have bargained, bluffed, flattered his way free, but his bursting chest could only gather the air to make a small wet sound, like a fart.

At that moment the soft arts of the minister were shown to have their limitations.

'We've got a bet going,' said Trigg, 'on how long it takes you to sink.'

Yarvi plucked at Trigg's arm, scratched at his shoulder with his nails, but the overseer scarcely noticed. Out of the corner of his weeping eye he saw Sumael standing, shaking off her blankets. When Trigg unlocked Yarvi's chain he unlocked hers too.

But Yarvi knew he could expect no help from her. He could expect no help at all.

146

'Let this be a lesson to the rest of you!' Trigg stabbed at his chest with his free thumb. 'This is my ship. Cross me and you're done.'

'Let him be!' someone growled. 'He's done no harm.' Jaud, Yarvi saw as he was dragged past. But no one marked the big man. Beside him, from Yarvi's old place, Ankran watched, rubbing at his crooked nose. It did not look like such a bad place now.

'You should've taken the deal,' Trigg bundled Yarvi over the shipped oars like a sack of rags. 'I can forgive a lot in a fine singer, boy, but—'

With a sudden yelp the overseer fell sprawling, hand suddenly loose, and Yarvi jabbed his twisted little finger in Trigg's eye, gave him a wriggling kick in the chest and went tumbling free.

Trigg had tripped on Nothing's heavy chain, pulled suddenly taut. The deck-scrubber hunched in the shadows, eyes gleaming behind his hanging hair. 'Run,' he whispered.

Perhaps Yarvi had made one friend after all.

The first breath he heaved in made his head reel. He scrambled up, sobbing, snorting, careered into the benches, through oar-slaves half asleep, clambering, slithering, under oars and over them.

People were shouting but Yarvi could scarcely hear the words through the throbbing of blood in his ears, like the mindless thunder of a storm.

He saw the forward hatch, wobbling, shuddering. His hand closed around the handle. He hauled it open and pitched face-first into the darkness.

DEATH WAITS

Yarvi fell, knocked his shoulder, cracked his head, tumbled over sacks and sprawled on his face.

Wet on his cheek. In the hold.

He rolled with an effort, dragged himself into the shadows.

Dark down here. Pitch-dark, but a minister must know the ways, and he felt them out now with his fingertips.

Roaring in his ears, burning in his chest, terror tickling at every part of him, but he had to master it, and think. *There is always a way*, his mother used to tell him.

He could hear the guards shouting as they looked down into the hatch, too close, too close behind. He jerked his chain after him, squirming between crates and barrels in the hold, a flicker of light from the torches above catching bands and rivets, guiding him towards the ship's stores.

He slithered through the low doorway, sloshing between shelves and boxes in the freezing puddle that was today's leakage. He crouched against the ship's cold side, breath whooping and wheezing, more light now as the guards brought their torches down after him.

'Where is he?'

There had to be a way. Surely they'd be coming from the other direction soon, from the aft hatch. His eyes flickered to its ladder.

Had to be some way. No time for a plan, all his plans were gone like smoke. Trigg would be waiting. Trigg would be angry.

His eyes darted to every sound, to every glint of light, searching desperately for some means of escape, some place to hide, but there was none. He needed an ally. He pressed himself helplessly back against the wood, felt the icy dampness there, heard the drip of saltwater. And Mother Gundring's voice came to him, soft and careful at the firepit.

When a wise minister has nothing but enemies, she beats one with a worse.

Yarvi dived below the nearest shelf, fumbling in the black, and his fingers closed around the iron bar he kept to knock in nails.

The sailor's worst enemy is the sea, Shadikshirram never tired of saying.

'Where are you, boy?'

He could just see the outlines of Sumael's repair and he rammed the iron bar between hull and fresh timbers and dragged on it with all his strength. He gritted his teeth and worked it deeper and snarled out all his fury and his pain and his helplessness and ripped at that bar as though it was Trigg and Odem and Grom-gil-Gorm combined. He tore at it, strained at it, wedged the wrist of his useless hand around it, the tortured wood creaking, pots and boxes clattering down as he barged the shelves with his shoulder.

He could hear the guards now, near, the glow of their lamps in the hold, their humped shapes in the low doorway, the gleam of their blades.

'Come here, cripple!'

He screamed as he made one last muscle-tearing effort. There was a crack as the timbers suddenly gave, Yarvi lurched flailing backwards, and hissing with the rage of a devil released from hell Mother Sea burst into the stores.

Yarvi brought a shelf crashing down with him, was soaked in an instant in icy water, rolled gasping towards the aft hatch, up and slithering sodden, the din of shouting men and furious sea and splintering wood in his ears.

He floundered to the ladder, the water already to his knees. A guard was at his heels, clutching in the darkness. Yarvi flung the bar at him, sent him stumbling into the jet of water and it tore him across the store like a toy. More leaks had sprung, the sea showering in at a dozen angles, the wails of the guards hardly heard over its deafening roar.

Yarvi dragged himself up the ladder a couple of rungs, heaved the hatch open, slithered through and stood, swaying, wondering if some magic had transported him onto the deck of some other ship in the midst of battle.

The gangway between the benches crawled with

men, struggling in the garish light of burning oil which a broken lamp must have sprayed across the forecastle. Flickering flames danced in the black water, in the black eyes of panicked slaves, on the drawn blades of the guards. Yarvi saw Jaud grab one of them and fling him bodily into the sea.

He was up from his bench. The slaves were freed.

Or some of them. Most were still chained, huddling towards the rowlocks to escape the violence. A few lay bleeding on the gangway. Others were even now leaping over the side, preferring to take their chance with Mother Sea than with Trigg's men, who were flailing about them without mercy.

Yarvi saw Rulf butt a guard in the face, heard the man's nose-bone pop and his sword clatter away across the deck.

He had to help his oarmates. The fingers of his good hand twitched open and closed. Had to help them, but how? The last few months had only reinforced Yarvi's long-held opinion that he was no hero. They were outnumbered and unarmed. He flinched as a guard cut down a helpless slave, axe opening a yawning wound. He could feel the slope in the deck, tilting as the sea rushed in below and dragged the *South Wind* down.

A good minister faces the facts, and saves what he can. A good minister accepts the lesser evil. Yarvi clambered across the nearest bench, towards the ship's side and the black water beyond. He set himself to dive.

He was halfway off the ship when he was snatched

back by his collar. The world tumbled and he crashed down, gasping like a landed fish.

Trigg stood over him, the end of his chain in one fist. 'You're going nowhere, boy.'

He leaned down and planted his other hand around Yarvi's throat, just under his collar so the metal bit into his jaw, but this time the overseer squeezed even harder. He dragged Yarvi up until his kicking boots only just scraped the deck, twisting his face around to look at the carnage that choked the ship. Dead men and wounded men, two guards beating a slave with their sticks in the midst.

'See the trouble you've caused me?' he screeched, one eye red and weepy from Yarvi's finger. The guards were all yammering over each other.

'Where's Jaud and that bastard Rulf?'

'Got onto the jetty. But they'll freeze out there for sure.'

'Gods, my fingers!'

'How'd they get free?'

'Sumael.'

'That little bitch had a key.'

'Where the hell did she get that hatchet?'

'She cut my fingers off! Where are they?'

'What does it matter? They're no use now!'

'He broke the hull!' gasped a soaked guard as he crawled from the aft-hatch. 'There's water flooding in!' And as though to make the point the *South Wind* shuddered again, the deck tilting further so that Trigg had to grab at a bench to stay upright.

'Gods help us!' screeched one of the chained oar-slaves, clawing at his collar.

'Are we sinking?' asked another, wide eyes rolling down.

'How are we going to explain this to Shadikshirram?'

'Gods damn it!' roared Trigg, and he smashed Yarvi's head against the blunt end of the nearest oar, filling his skull with light and his mouth with scalding sick, then drove him down against the deck and started choking him in earnest.

Yarvi struggled mindlessly but the overseer's full weight was on him and he couldn't breathe, couldn't see anything but Trigg's snarling mouth, and that growing blurrier, as though it was at the end of a tunnel down which Yarvi was being steadily dragged.

He'd cheated Death half a dozen times in the last few weeks, but no matter how strong or clever, no matter how good your weaponluck or your weatherluck, none can cheat her forever. Heroes and High Kings and Grandmothers of the Ministry all pass through her door in the end: she makes no exceptions for one-handed boys with big mouths and bitter tempers. The Black Chair would be Odem's, his father unavenged, his oath forever unfulfilled . . .

Then, through the surging of trapped blood in his ears, Yarvi heard a voice.

It was a broken, whispering voice, rough as a scrubbing block. Had it been Death's voice he would not have been surprised. Except by what it said.

'Did you not hear Shadikshirram?'

With an effort Yarvi forced his weeping eyes towards it.

Nothing stood in the middle of the deck. His grease-matted hair was pushed back and for the first time Yarvi could see his face, bent and lop-sided, scarred and broken, twisted and hollowed, his eyes wide and gleaming wet.

His heavy chain was wound around and around one arm, and from his fist the hasp dangled free, a chunk of splintered wood and nails still attached. In his other hand he held the sword Rulf had knocked from a guard's hand.

Nothing smiled. A broken smile full of broken teeth and speaking of a broken mind. 'She told you never to give me a blade.'

'Put the sword *down*!' Trigg barked the last word, but his voice creaked with something Yarvi had never heard there before.

Fear.

As if it was Death indeed that stood before him on the deck.

'Oh, no, Trigg, no.' Nothing's smile grew broader, and madder, and the tears brimmed in his eyes and left shining streaks on his pitted cheeks. 'I think it will put you down.'

A guard charged at him.

Scrubbing the deck Nothing had seemed old, and painfully slow. A brittle remnant. A man of twigs and string. With sword in hand he flowed like water, danced like flickering fire. It was as if the blade had its own mind, quick and merciless as lightning, and Nothing was pulled after.

The sword darted out, its point glinted between the charging guard's shoulder-blades and was gone, left him tottering, wheezing, hand clasped to his chest. Another guard swung an axe and Nothing slipped out of its way and let it chop splinters from the corner of a bench. It went up again and with a click of metal the arm that held it spun off into the darkness. The guard sank to his knees, eyes goggling, and Nothing's bare foot knocked him flat.

A third came at him from behind, sword raised. Without looking, Nothing thrust his blade out, took the guard through the throat and left him spluttering blood, then knocked a club away with his chain-wrapped arm and smashed the pommel of his sword into the mouth of its owner, teeth flying, dropped soundlessly to scythe the legs from under another and send him spinning onto the deck face-down.

All this in the space of time that Yarvi might have taken one breath. If he could have taken a breath.

The first guard still stood, fumbling at his pierced chest, trying to speak but saying only red froth. Nothing pushed him gently out of his way with the back of his arm as he passed, the balls of his bare feet making no sound. He looked down at the blood-soaked boards and clicked his tongue.

'The deck is very dirty.' He looked up, wasted

face all black-dashed and red-speckled. 'Shall I scrub it, Trigg?'

The overseer backed away while Yarvi fumbled helplessly with his hand. 'Come closer and I kill him!'

'Kill him.' Nothing shrugged. 'Death waits for us all.' The guard with the ruined legs was whimpering as he tried to drag himself up the tilted deck. Nothing stabbed him through the back in passing. 'Today she waits for you. She reaches for her key, Trigg. She unlocks the Last Door.'

'Let's talk about it!' Trigg backed off with one palm up. The deck was tipping further now, black water welling from the aft-hatch. 'Let's just talk!'

'Talk only makes problems.' Nothing lifted the sword. 'Steel is always the answer.' And he spun it in his hand so the blade caught the light and danced red and white and yellow and all the colours of fire. 'Steel does not flatter or compromise. Steel tells no lies.'

'Just give me a chance!' whined Trigg, water pouring over the sides of the ship now, flooding among the benches.

'Why?'

'I've got dreams! I've got plans! I've got—'

With a hollow click the sword split Trigg's skull down to his nose. His mouth kept making words for a moment, but no breath came to give them sound. He flopped back, kicking a little, and Yarvi tore free of his limp hand, gasping in air, and coughing, and trying to drag his collar free so he could breathe.

'Perhaps I shouldn't,' said Nothing, twisting the sword from Trigg's head, 'but I feel much better.'

All around them men were screaming. If any guards survived they'd preferred the sea to Nothing's sword. Some slaves were trying to clamber over their sinking benches to drier ones behind, others straining at their chains as the water surged higher and higher, others with faces only just showing, mouths sucking at the air and their eyes bulging with horror. Still others, Yarvi knew, must already be below the black surface, holding their breath for a few more moments while they struggled hopelessly at their locks.

He dropped to his hands and knees, retching, head spinning, digging at Trigg's bloody clothes for his key, struggling not to look at his split face but catching a glimpse anyway of features distorted and fleshy pulp gleaming inside the great wound and he swallowed vomit, rooting again for the key, the wails of the trapped slaves loud in his ears.

'Leave it.' Nothing stood over him, standing far taller than Yarvi had ever imagined he might, blood-spotted sword hanging from one hand.

Yarvi blinked up at him, and then down the tipping deck towards the drowning slaves. 'But they'll die.' His voice was a tiny croak.

'Death waits for us all.'

Nothing caught Yarvi by his thrall-collar, hefted him into the air and over the rail, and once again Mother Sea took him in her icy embrace.

III

THE LONG ROAD

BENDING WITH CIRCUMSTANCE

Someone slapped Yarvi's face. He saw the hand, heard the noise, but hardly felt it.

'Run,' hissed Jaud's voice.

The closest Yarvi could manage was a shivering shamble, his flapping chain and his soaked clothes dragging him down with every step, the shingle clutching at his waterlogged boots. He tripped often, but whenever he fell strong arms would be there to haul him up, to haul him on into the darkness.

'Go,' grunted Rulf.

Near the snow-covered top of the beach Yarvi snatched one look back, and forced out, 'Gods,' through his rattling teeth.

Mother Sea was hungrily swallowing the *South Wind*. The forecastle was wreathed in fire, rigging made lines of flame, the top of the mast, where Sumael used to perch, ablaze. The benches where Yarvi had struggled were flooded, tangled oars sticking up helplessly like the legs of a turned-over woodlouse. Only one corner of the aftcastle still showed above waters alive with the reflections of fire. The hold, the stores and the captain's cabin were drowned in the silence beneath.

There were black figures on the shore, on the jetty, staring. Guards who had escaped Nothing's sword? Slaves who had somehow got free of their chains? Yarvi wondered if he could hear faint cries above the keening of the wind. Faint screams above the crackling of the flames. There was no way to know who luck had saved from that ordeal of fire and water, who was living and who dead, and Yarvi was too cold to be glad he had survived one more disaster, let alone to be sad that anyone else had not. No doubt the regrets would come soon enough.

If he lived out the night.

'Move,' said Sumael.

They bundled him over the crest and he tumbled down the far side, came to rest on his back in a drift, skin on fire with the cold, each icy gasp like a knife in his throat. He saw Rulf's broad face with a glimmer of orange down one cheek, Sumael's gaunt and twitching in the light of Father Moon.

'Leave me,' he tried to say, but his mouth was too numb to make the words, his teeth chilled to the roots, and all that came was a weak puff of smoke.

'We go together,' said Sumael. 'Wasn't that the deal?'

'I thought it was finished when Trigg started throttling me.'

'Oh, you won't wriggle out of it that easily.' She caught him by his crooked wrist. 'Get up.'

He had been betrayed by his own family, his own people, and found loyalty among a set of slaves who owed him nothing. He was so pathetically glad of it he wanted to weep. But he had a feeling he would need his tears later.

With Sumael's help he managed to get up. With Rulf's and Jaud's to flounder on, hardly thinking about the course except to keep the sinking *South Wind* somewhere at his back. The icy wetness squelched in his boots, the wind cut through his soaked and chafing clothes as though he wore nothing.

'Did you have to pick the coldest place the gods have made for your escape?' growled Rulf. 'And the coldest time of year?'

'I had a better plan.' Sumael sounded less than delighted with the total ruin of it, too. 'But it sunk with the *South Wind*.'

'Plans must sometimes bend with circumstance,' said Jaud.

'Bend?' growled Rulf. 'This one's snapped in pieces.'

'Over there.' Yarvi pointed with the frozen stub of his finger. Up ahead a stunted tree clawed at the night, each branch picked out on top in white, underneath in the faintest flickering of orange. He hardly dared believe his own eyes but he started towards it as fast as he could even so, half walking, half crawling, all desperate. At that moment, even a dream of fire seemed better than nothing.

'Wait!' hissed Sumael, 'we don't know who—'

'We don't care,' said Rulf, floundering past.

The fire had been built in a hollow beneath that twisted tree where there was some shelter from the wind, the fragments of a broken crate carefully arranged, the smallest flame flickering in their midst. Hunched over it, coaxing it into life with his smoking breath, was Ankran.

Had Yarvi made the choice of who to save Ankran's name would have been far from the first on his lips. But freeing Rulf and Jaud meant freeing their oarmate, and Yarvi would have thrown himself at Odem's feet right then had he offered warmth. He flopped onto his knees, holding his shaking hands towards the flames.

Jaud planted his fists on his hips. 'You made it, then.'

'Some turds float,' said Rulf.

Ankran only rubbed at his crooked nose. 'If my stench bothers you, you could find your own fire.'

A hatchet slid silently from Sumael's sleeve, the dangling blade gleaming. 'I like this one.'

The ex-storekeeper shrugged. 'Then far be it from me to turn the desperate away. Welcome one and all to my mansion!'

Sumael had already shinned up the frozen rocks to the tree and neatly lopped off a branch. Now she wedged it in the ground so its twigs were towards the fire. She snapped her fingers at Yarvi. 'Get your clothes off.'

'Romance yet survives!' said Rulf, fluttering his lashes at the sky.

Sumael ignored him. 'Wet clothes will kill you in the night sure as any enemy.'

Now the cold was loosening its grip Yarvi was

feeling his bruises – every muscle aching and his head sore and his neck throbbing from Trigg's hands. Even had he wanted to, he lacked the strength to object. He peeled off his soaked clothes, some of the hems already stiff with ice, and huddled as close to the fire as he dared, near naked but for collar and chain.

Rulf dumped an old fleece around his shuddering shoulders. 'I'm lending that,' he said, 'not giving it.'

'Much appreciated . . . either way,' Yarvi forced through his chattering teeth as he watched Sumael hang his clothes facing the flames, where they began to gently steam.

'What if someone sees the light?' Jaud was asking, frowning back the way they had come.

'If you'd rather freeze, sit in the darkness. You'll find plenty of it.' Ankran tried to prod more warmth from the fire with a twig. 'For my part I suspect the fight, then the ship aflame, then the ship sinking, will have dampened their appetite for a search.'

'As long as we're well gone before dawn,' said Rulf.

'Gone where?' asked Sumael, squatting beside Yarvi.

East was the obvious choice. East along the coast the way the *South Wind* had brought them. But west was where Yarvi needed to go. West to Vansterland. West to Gettland. West to Odem, and vengeance, and the sooner the better. He glanced around this motley fellowship, all huddled over the life-giving flames, faces pinched and strange in its light, wondering how he could possibly convince them to go the wrong way.

'East of course,' said Rulf. 'How long ago did we pass that trading post?'

Sumael spent a moment reckoning on her fingers. 'On foot we might make it in three days.'

'It'll be hard going.' Rulf scrubbed with his nails at his stubbly chin. 'Damn hard going, and—'

'I'll be going west,' said Ankran, bent jaw clenched and his eyes fixed on the flames.

There was silence as they all looked at him. 'West to where?' asked Jaud.

'Thorlby.'

Yarvi could only raise his brows at help from such an unexpected quarter. Rulf burst out laughing. 'Thank you for giving me one good chuckle before I die, Master Ankran! Our ex-storekeeper's walking to Gettland.'

'To Vansterland. I'll try to find a ship to take me from there.'

Rulf chuckled again. 'So you're only going to walk to Vulsgard? And how long a stroll do you reckon that to be, oh navigator?'

'At least a month on foot.' Sumael said it so quickly she already must have worked it out.

'A month of this!' Rulf waved his broad hand towards the snow-covered emptiness they had struggled through already, and Yarvi had to admit the thought was by no means a heartening one. 'With what gear?'

'I have a shield.' Jaud swung it off his back and knocked at it with one fist. A large, round shield of rough wood with an iron boss. 'I thought to use it as a float.'

'And a generous guard lent me his bow.' Rulf plucked at the string as if it was a harp. 'But with no arrows it plays no music. Does anyone have a tent? Extra clothes? Blankets? Sleds?' Silence, aside from the moaning of the chill wind just outside their firelit hollow. 'Then the very best of luck, Master Ankran! It's been my pleasure to row beside you but I fear our ways must part. The rest of us will be going east.'

'What fool put you in charge?'

They all spun about as the voice croaked from the darkness, and Nothing was there. He was streaked with soot as well as his usual dirt, rags and hair and beard all blackened. He had Trigg's boots on, and Trigg's jacket, blood crusting one shoulder. Over the other he carried a great roll of singed sailcloth, and cradled in one arm, like a babe against the freezing night, the sword with which Yarvi had seen him kill six men.

He dropped cross-legged beside the fire as though it was a meeting long arranged and gave a satisfied sigh as he held his palms to the flames. 'West to Gettland sounds well. We will be followed.'

'Trigg?' asked Sumael.

'You need give no more thought to our overseer. My debt to him is paid. But between me and Shadikshirram the account is still open.' Nothing licked a finger and polished a blemish from the blade of his sword. 'We must put her far behind us.'

'Us?' snapped Sumael, and Yarvi noticed that, just behind her back, the hatchet was ready. 'You're inviting yourself along?'

The firelight shifted in Nothing's mad eyes. 'Unless someone else wants to invite me?'

Yarvi held his hands up between them and smoothed the way for Father Peace. 'We need all the help we can get. What's your name, even?'

Nothing stared off into the night sky as though the answer might be written in the stars. 'I have had three names . . . perhaps four . . . but all of them brought me bad luck. I would hate them to bring you bad luck too. If you must talk to me, Nothing will do, but I am no great talker. Shadikshirram will be coming, and she will expect us to go east.'

'Because going west is madness!' Rulf rounded on Sumael. 'Tell them!'

She pressed her scarred lips together and narrowed her eyes at the fire. 'East is quicker. East is easier.'

'There!' barked Rulf, slapping his thigh.

'I'm going west,' said Sumael.

'Eh?'

'East there will be people. Anyone who got off the ship. Then that trading post was crawling with slavers.'

'And Vansterland isn't?' asked Rulf. 'Because we always did good business in Inglings there.'

'East is dangerous,' said Sumael.

'West is nothing but weeks of wilderness!'

'There is forest. Forest might mean fuel. Might mean food. East has the trading post, but then? Only the fens and the wild, hundreds of miles of it. West is Vansterland. West is civilization. West is . . . maybe . . . ships that go further west. That go home.'

'Home.' Jaud stared into the flames as though he glimpsed his village there, and that well with the sweetest water in the world.

'We head inland,' said Sumael, 'out of sight of any ships. Then west.'

Rulf flung up his hands. 'How will you find your way out in the snows? You'll end up walking in circles!'

Sumael slid a leather package from inside her coat, unrolled it to show her eye-glass and instruments. 'I'll find my way, old man, don't worry on that score. I can't say I much look forward to either route. Especially in this company. But west might be the better chance.'

'Might be?'

Sumael shrugged. 'Sometimes, might be is the best you can hope for.'

'Three for west.' Ankran had the first smile Yarvi had seen him give since Shadikshirram knocked his two front teeth out. 'What about you, big man?'

'Hmm.' Jaud propped his chin thoughtfully on one fist and looked about the circle. 'Huh.' He carefully eyed each one of them, and ended on

Sumael's instruments. 'Heh.' He shrugged his heavy shoulders, and took a long breath. 'There is no man I would rather have beside me in a fight, Rulf. But when it comes to getting from a place to a place . . . I trust Sumael. I go west. If you will have me.'

'You can hold your shield over me when it snows,' said Sumael.

'You're all bloody mad!' Rulf slapped down a heavy hand on Yarvi's shoulder. 'Looks like it's just you and me, Yorv.'

'I'm very flattered by the offer . . .' Yarvi slipped from under Rulf's hand and his fleece together and back into his shirt, not altogether dry but close enough. 'But the first thing we have to do is stick together. Stick together or die apart.' That and his chair, and his oath, and his vengeance all waited for him in Gettland, and the longer they waited, the less his chance of ever claiming them. 'We'll all be going west.' And Yarvi gave Rulf a grin, and slapped him on the shoulder with his good hand. 'I prayed for younger help but I'll take what I can get.'

'Gods!' Rulf pressed at his temples with the heels of his hands. 'We'll all regret this.'

'It can keep the rest of my regrets company.' Nothing stared off into the darkness as though he saw a ghostly host beyond the firelight. 'There are enough of them.'

FREEDOM

Sumael led the way at a furious pace and they all walked her course with as little question as they had rowed it. Through a broken land of black rock and white snow they floundered, where stunted trees had all been swept into tortured shapes by the wind, bowing mournfully toward the sea.

'How many steps to Vansterland?' called Rulf.

Sumael checked her instruments, lips moving with silent sums, peered up at the smudge of Mother Sun in the iron sky, and headed on without answering.

Few in the citadel of Thorlby would have reckoned it a treasure, but Nothing's roll of mildewed sailcloth became their most valued possession. With the care of pirates dividing a stolen hoard they tore it up between them and wound it under their clothes, around their frozen heads and hands, stuffed their boots with it. Half, Jaud carried with him so they could huddle beneath it when night came. No doubt it would scarcely be warmer than the utter darkness outside, but they knew they would be grateful for that little.

That little would be the difference between life and death.

They took turns breaking new ground, Jaud forging ahead without complaint, Rulf venting curses on the snow as though it was an old enemy, Ankran struggling on with arms hugged around himself, Nothing with head up and sword clutched tight, as though he fancied he was made from steel himself and no weather could chill or warm him, even when in spite of Yarvi's prayers snow began to settle across the shoulders of his stolen jacket.

'Bloody wonderful,' muttered Rulf at the sky.

'It works for us,' said Ankran. 'Covers our tracks, keeps us hidden. With luck our old mistress will think we froze out here.'

'Without luck we will,' muttered Yarvi.

'No one cares either way,' said Rulf. 'No one's mad enough to follow us here.'

'Ha!' barked Nothing. 'Shadikshirram is too mad to do anything else.' And he tossed the end of his heavy chain over his shoulder like a scarf and cut that conversation down as dead as he had the *South Wind*'s guards.

Yarvi frowned back the way they had come, their tracks snaking off into the grey distance. He wondered when Shadikshirram would find the wreck of her ship. Then he wondered what she would do when she did. Then he swallowed, and floundered after the others just as fast as he could.

At midday, Mother Sun no higher than Jaud's shoulder at her feeble zenith, their long shadows struggling after them across the white, they paused to huddle in a hollow.

'Food,' said Sumael, giving voice to every thought among them.

No one was keen to volunteer. They all knew food was worth more than gold out here. It was Ankran who surprised them all by first reaching into his furs and bringing out a packet of salted fish.

He shrugged. 'I hate fish.'

'The man who used to starve us now feeds us,' said Rulf. 'Who says there's no justice?' He came up with a few biscuits well past their best, if they had ever had one. Sumael followed that with two dried loaves.

Yarvi could only spread his empty palms and try to smile. 'I'm humbled . . . by your generosity . . .?'

Ankran rubbed gently at his crooked nose. 'It warms me just a little to see you humbled. How about you two?'

Jaud shrugged. 'I had little time to prepare.'

Nothing held up his sword. 'I brought the knife.'

They all considered their meagre larder, scarcely enough for one decent meal for the six of them.

'I suppose I'd better be mother,' said Sumael.

Yarvi sat, slavering like his father's dogs waiting for scraps, while she rationed out six fearsomely equal and awfully tiny shares of bread. Rulf swallowed his in two bites, then watched as Ankran chewed every crumb a hundred times with eyes closed in ecstasy.

'Is that all we eat?'

Sumael wrapped up the precious bundle again, jaw tight, and pushed it into her shirt without speaking.

'I miss Trigg,' said Rulf, mournfully.

Sumael would have made a fine minister. She had been thinking clearly enough on her way off the ship to grab two of Shadikshirram's abandoned wine bottles, and now they packed them with snow and took turns to carry them inside their clothes. Yarvi soon learned only to sip the results, since unwrapping to piss in that cold was an act of heroism that earned grunted congratulations from the others, all the more heartfelt since everyone knew sooner or later they would have to present their own nethers to the searing wind.

For all it felt like a month of torture the day was short, and as evening came the heavens blazed with stars, glittering swirls and burning trails, bright as the eyes of the gods. Sumael pointed out strange constellations, for every one of which she had a name – the Bald Weaver, the Crooked Way, Stranger-Come-Knocking, the Eater of Dreams – and as she spoke them steaming into the dark she smiled, a happiness in her voice that he had never heard from her before, and made him smile too.

'How many steps to Vansterland, now?' he asked.

'Some.' She looked back to the horizon, happiness swiftly snuffed out, and upped the pace.

He toiled on after her. 'I haven't thanked you.'

'You can do it when we don't end up a pair of frozen corpses.'

'Since I might not get that chance . . . thank you. You could've let Trigg kill me.'

'If I'd taken a moment to think about it, I would have.'

He could hardly complain at that. He wondered what he would have done if she had been the one Trigg throttled, and did not like the answer. 'I'm glad you didn't think, then.'

There was a long pause, with just the crunching of their boots in the snow. Then he saw her frown over her shoulder at him, and away. 'So am I.'

The second day they joked to keep their spirits up.

'You're being stingy with the stores again, Ankran! Pass back the roast pig!' And they laughed.

'I'll race you to Vulsgard! Last one through the gate gets sold to pay for ale!' And they chuckled.

'I hope Shadikshirram brings some wine when she comes for us.' Not so much as a smile.

When they slithered from their wretched tent at dawn on the third day, if you could call that watery gloom a dawn, they were all grumbling.

'I do not care for this old blunderer in front,' croaked Nothing, after tripping over Rulf's heels for a third time.

'I'm not sure I like this madman's sword at my back,' snapped Rulf over his shoulder.

'You could have it through your back instead.'

'How many years between you and still you act

175

like children?' Yarvi pushed his way into step between them. 'We need to help each other or the winter will kill us all.'

Faintly, just ahead, he heard Sumael say, 'More than likely it will kill us all anyway.'

He did not disagree.

By the fourth day, the freezing fog lying over the white land like a shroud, they were silent. Just a grunt now as one or another stumbled, just a grunt as one or another helped them up and on to nowhere. Six silent figures in the great emptiness, in the great, cold void, each struggling under their own burden of chill misery, under their own chafing thrall-collar and ever heavier chain, each with their own pain, and hunger, and fear.

At first Yarvi thought about the men drowned on the ship. How many dead? The planks cracking and the sea pouring in. So that he could save himself? The slaves straining at their chains for one more gasp before Mother Sea dragged them down, down, down.

But his mother had always said, *never worry about what has been done. Only about what will be.*

There was no changing it, and guilt over the past and worry about the future began both to fade, leaving only taunting memories of food. The four dozen pigs roasted for the visit of the High King, so much for such a little, grey-haired man and his hard-eyed minister. The feast when Yarvi's brother passed his warrior's test that Yarvi had done no more than pick at, knowing he could never pass himself. The beach before his ill-fated raid, men cooking the meal that might be their last, meat turning above a hundred fires, heat like a hand on your face, a ring of hungry grins lit by flame, fat sizzling and the crackling blackened—

'Freedom!' roared Rulf, opening his arms wide to hold the vast expanse of empty white. 'Freedom to freeze where you please! Freedom to starve where you like! Freedom to walk 'til you drop!'

His voice died quickly in that thin sharp air.

'Finished?' asked Nothing.

Rulf let his arms flop down. 'Yes.' And they slogged on.

It was not the thought of his mother that kept Yarvi going, step after floundering step, stride after aching stride, fall after chilling fall, dogged in the tracks of the others. It was not the thought of his betrothed, or his dead father, or even his stool beside Mother Gundring's fire. It was the thought of Odem, smiling with his hand on Yarvi's shoulder. Of Odem, promising to be his shoulder-man. Of Odem, asking gently as the spring rain if a cripple should be King of Gettland.

'I think *not*,' Yarvi snarled in smoke through his cracked lips. 'I think *not* . . . I think *not*.'

And step after torturous step, Gettland edged ever closer.

The fifth day was clear and icy crisp, the sky blinding blue, so that it seemed Yarvi could see almost all the way to the sea, a strip of black and white on the far horizon of a land of black and white.

'We've done well,' he said. 'You have to admit.'

Sumael, shading her eyes from the brightness as she frowned westward, had to do no such thing. 'We've had good weatherluck.'

'I don't feel lucky,' muttered Rulf, hugging himself. 'Do you feel lucky, Jaud?'

'I feel cold,' said Jaud, rubbing at the pinked tips of his ears.

Sumael shook her head at the sky, which aside from a distant bruise far off to the north looked unusually clear. 'Maybe tonight, maybe tomorrow, you'll learn what bad weatherluck looks like. There's a storm coming.'

Rulf squinted up. 'You're sure?'

'I don't tell you how to snore, do I? Don't tell me how to navigate.'

Rulf looked at Yarvi, and shrugged. But before dark, as usual, she was proved right. That bruise on the sky grew, and swelled, and darkened, and turned odd colours.

'The gods are angry,' muttered Nothing, frowning up.

'When aren't they?' said Yarvi.

The snow began to fall in giant flakes, in curtains and eddies. The wind blew up in shrieking gusts, bludgeoning from every way at once, barging them left and right. Yarvi took a fall and, when he clambered up, couldn't see any of the others. He blundered on in a panic and ran straight into Jaud's back.

'We have to get out of this!' he screeched, hardly able even to hear his own voice over the wind.

'I will not argue!' Jaud bellowed back.

'We need deep snow!'

'Snow we have!' roared Ankran.

They floundered to the bottom of a narrow gully, the most promising slope Yarvi could hope to find with the snow coming in such flurries that the others were little more than ghosts. He dug like a rabbit, scooping snow between his legs, burrowing desperately inwards then, when he'd tunnelled a body's length, up. His hands burned with the cold inside their wrappings of wet sail-cloth, his muscles burned with the effort but he forced himself on. He dug as if his life depended on it.

It did.

Sumael wormed her way after him, growling through her gritted teeth and using her hatchet like a trowel. They dug out first a shelf, then a hollow, then a tiny chamber. Ankran wriggled in behind, tongue wedged into the gap in his front teeth as he scooped the snow back. Rulf came next into the cold dimness, then Jaud worked his great shoulders up into the growing cave, and finally Nothing poked his head in.

'Neat,' he said.

'Keep the entrance clear,' Yarvi muttered, 'or we'll be buried in the night,' and he hunched against the packed snow, unwound the soaked wrappings and blew into his cupped hands. He had few enough fingers already: he could afford to lose no more.

'Where did you learn this?' asked Sumael, sitting back beside him.

'My father taught me.'

'I think he has saved our lives.'

'You must thank him, when you see him.' Ankran wriggled his shoulders into place. They were tightly squeezed, but they had been for days. There was no room for pride, or distaste, or enmity out here in the wastes.

Yarvi closed his eyes, then, and thought of his father, laid out pale and cold on the slab. 'My father's dead.'

'I am sorry,' came Jaud's deep voice.

'It's good that one of us is.'

Yarvi let his hand drop, and realized a moment later it had fallen against Sumael's, her upturned fingers pressed into his palm. It felt good there, warm where her skin touched his. He did not move it. Nor did she.

Slowly he closed his fingers around hers.

There was a long silence then, the wind whining soft outside their shelter and the breath coming heavy inside, and Yarvi began to feel about as close to comfortable, packed under strides of frozen snow, as he had since they left Ankran's fire.

'Here.' He felt the breath of the word on his face, felt Sumael gently take him by the wrist. His eyes flicked open but he could not guess at her expression in the darkness.

She turned his hand over and pressed something

into his palm. Stale, and sour, and halfway between soggy and frozen, but it was bread, and by the gods he was glad to get it.

They sat pressed together, all eking out their shares, all chewing with something like contentment, or at least relief, and one by one swallowing, and falling silent, and leaving Yarvi wondering whether he dared take Sumael's hand again.

Then she said, 'That's the last food.'

Another silence, but this one far less comfortable.

Rulf's voice came muffled in the darkness. 'How far to Vansterland?'

No one answered.

THE BETTER MEN

'Gettlanders are the better men,' came Nothing's breathy croak. 'They fight as one. Each guarded by the shield of his shoulder-man.'

'Gettlanders? Hah!' Rulf snorted smoke as he struggled on up the snowy slope after Sumael. 'A herd of bloody sheep driven bleating to the butcher! When the shoulder-man falls, what then? Throvenmen have fire in them!'

They'd been arguing all day. Whether sword or bow was superior. Whether Hemenholm was south of Grenmer Island. Whether painted wood or oiled were more loved by Mother Sea and hence made for a more favoured vessel. Yarvi could not imagine where they found the breath. He hardly had enough for breathing with.

'Throvenmen?' croaked Nothing. 'Hah! When the fires burn out what then?' First they would argue their case, then settle to stating their position with ever more certainty, and finally to a contest of scornful grunting. In Yarvi's hearing neither had conceded a hair's breadth since they left the *South Wind* sinking.

It was three days since the food ran out, and Yarvi's hunger was an aching void inside him that swallowed every hope. When he had unwrapped the sailcloth from his hands that morning he had hardly recognized them: they were shrivelled and bloated at once. The skin on his fingertips had a waxy look, prickly-numb to the touch. Even Jaud was hollow about the cheeks. Ankran had a limp he was trying and failing to hide. Rulf's breath came with a wheeze that made Yarvi wince. Nothing had frost in his straggling eyebrows. Sumael's scarred lips were thinner and greyer and tighter pressed with every mile they trudged.

All Yarvi could think about, as this debate of the damned droned on, was which of them would die first.

'Gettlanders know discipline,' droned Nothing. 'Gettlanders are—'

'What kind of fool even gives a damn?' snarled Yarvi, rounding on the two old men and stabbing his stub of a finger in their faces, suddenly furious. 'Men are just men, good or bad depending on their luck! Now save your breath for walking!' And he wedged his hands back under his armpits and forced himself on up the slope.

'He's a cook's boy and a philosopher,' he heard Rulf wheeze.

'I can hardly decide which is the more useless out here,' muttered Nothing. 'I should have let Trigg kill him. Gettlanders are clearly . . .'

He fell silent as he crested the ridge. They all

did. A forest lay before them, stretching away in every direction until it was lost in the grey veil of the falling snow.

'Trees?' whispered Sumael, as though she hardly dared believe her own senses.

'Trees could mean food,' said Yarvi.

'Trees could mean fire,' said Ankran.

Suddenly they were all plunging down the hillside, whooping like children freed from their chores. Yarvi fell, tumbled in a shower of snow and was up again. They floundered eagerly between the stunted outliers, then in amongst towering firs with trunks so thick Yarvi could scarcely have linked his hands around them. Mighty pillars as in some sacred place and they unwelcome trespassers.

They slowed from run to jog, from jog to cautious shuffle. No fruit fell from the sparse branches. No deer flung themselves onto Nothing's sword. Such fallen wood as they found was soaked and rotted. Beneath the snow the ground was treacherous with tangled roots and countless years of rotted needles.

Their laughter guttered out and the wood was perfectly quiet, not so much as a bird's chirrup to scratch the heavy silence.

'Gods,' whispered Ankran. 'We're no better here than out there.'

Yarvi scrambled to a tree trunk, breaking off a piece of half-frozen fungus with a trembling hand.

'Have you found something?' asked Jaud, squeaky with hope.

'No.' Yarvi tossed it aside. 'This kind can't be eaten.' And despair began to float down with the snow and settle on Yarvi even more heavily than before.

'Fire is what we need,' he said, trying to keep the flickering of hope alive. Fire would warm them, and raise their spirits, and bring them together, and keep them going a little longer. Where that might take them he could not afford to think about. One stroke at a time, as Jaud had always told him.

'For a fire we need dry wood,' said Ankran. 'Might the cook's boy know where to find some?'

'I'd know where to buy it in Thorlby,' Yarvi snapped back. In truth, he probably wouldn't have. There had been slaves for that.

'Higher ground should be drier ground.' Sumael set off at a jog and Yarvi struggled after, sliding down a slope and into a treeless dip, covered in clean white snow. 'Maybe up here . . .'

She hurried out into that scar in the forest and Yarvi followed the trail of her quick footprints. Gods he was tired. He could scarcely feel his feet. There was something strange about the ground here, flat and hard under a thin blanket of snow, black patches scattered. At Sumael's next step there came a strange creaking.

She froze, frowning down.

'Wait!' Nothing stood on the slope behind them, clutching a tree with one hand and his sword with the other. 'It's a river!'

Yarvi stared at his feet, every hair on him prickling with horror. The ice pinged, clicked, shifted under his boots. It gave a long groan as Sumael turned towards him, her wide eyes flicking up to his. There was no more than a stride or two between them.

Yarvi swallowed, hardly daring even to breathe, and held out his hand to her.

'Tread softly,' he whispered.

She took a step and, without so much as a gasp, vanished through the ice.

First he stood frozen.

Then his whole body twitched as if to dash forward.

He stopped himself with a moan, floundered down onto all fours and wriggled to where she had disappeared. Black water, and splinters of ice floating, and not the slightest sign of her. He stared over his shoulder to see Jaud bounding down the bank in a shower of snow.

'Stay!' shrieked Yarvi. 'You're too heavy!'

He thought he saw movement under the ice, dragged himself to it sprawled out on his face, scrubbed away snow, could see nothing down there but blackness, lonely bubbles shifting.

Ankran teetered out onto the river, arms spread wide, skittered to a halt as the frozen surface groaned. Nothing was floundering through the snow downstream, towards a patch of bare ice where jagged rocks poked through.

Awful silence stretched out.

'Where is she?' screamed Yarvi. Rulf only stared from the bank, mouth hanging helplessly.

How long could someone hold their breath? Not this long, surely.

He saw Nothing hop a few steps from the bank and raise his sword high, point downwards.

'Are you mad?' Yarvi screeched, before he realized.

Of course he was.

The sword darted down, spray fountained up, and Nothing dropped on the ice and thrust his other arm into the water.

'I have her!' He hauled Sumael from the river, limp as rags and streaming freezing water, dragged her towards the bank where Jaud and Rulf were waiting.

'Is she breathing?' screamed Yarvi, crawling on hands and knees for fear of going through himself.

'How do I tell?' asked Jaud, kneeling beside her.

'Put your cheek to her mouth!'

'I don't think so!'

'Lift her feet!' Yarvi scrambled from the frozen river and forced his leaden legs along the snow-covered bank.

'What?'

'Get her upside-down!'

Jaud dumbly lifted her by her ankles, her loose head dragging in the snow, and Yarvi struggled up and forced two fingers into her mouth, hooked them round and down her throat.

'Come on!' he growled, spitting, and straining.

187

'Come on!' He had seen Mother Gundring do it once, to a boy who fell in a mill-pond.

The boy had died.

Sumael didn't move. She was clammy-cold, like a dead thing already, and Yarvi snarled a mess of prayers through his clenched teeth, he hardly even knew who to.

He felt Nothing's hand on his shoulder. 'Death waits for us all.'

Yarvi shrugged him off and pushed harder. 'Come on!'

And as suddenly as a child pinched awake Sumael jerked and coughed out water, rasped in half a breath and coughed out more.

'Gods!' said Rulf, taking a dumbstruck step back.

Yarvi was almost as surprised as he was, and certainly had never been so glad to have a handful of cold puke.

'You going to put me down?' croaked Sumael, eyes swivelling to the corners. Jaud let her drop and she hunched on the snow, plucking at her thrall-collar, and coughing and spitting, and starting to shiver hard.

Rulf was staring as if he had witnessed a miracle. 'You're a sorcerer!'

'Or a minister,' murmured Ankran.

Yarvi had no wish to let anyone pick at that scab. 'We need to get her warm.'

They struggled to coax a fire with Ankran's little flint, tearing sheets of moss from the trees for kindling, but everything was wet and the few sparks would not take. One after another they tried while Sumael stared, eyes fever-bright, shivering harder and harder until they could hear her clothes flapping against her.

Jaud who had once lit the ovens in a bakery every morning could do nothing, and Rulf who had set fires on beaches windswept and rain-lashed all about the Shattered Sea could do nothing, and even Yarvi made a futile effort, fumbling the flint in his useless stub of a hand until his fingers were cut while all the while Ankran muttered a prayer to He Who Makes the Flame.

But the gods were working no more miracles that day.

'Can we dig a shelter?' Jaud rocked back on his heels. 'Like we did in the blizzard?'

'Not enough snow,' said Yarvi.

'With branches, then?'

'Too much snow.'

'Got keep going.' Sumael suddenly wobbled to her feet, Rulf's outsize coat dropping in the snow behind her. 'Too hot,' she said, unwinding the sailcloth from her hands so it flapped free, tugging her shirt open and pulling at the chain inside. 'Scarf's too tight.' She took a couple more shambling steps and pitched straight on her face. 'Got keep going,' she mumbled into the snow.

Jaud gently rolled her, sat her up, hugging her with one arm.

'Father won't wait forever,' she whispered, faintest breath of smoke spilling from her blued lips.

'The cold's in her head.' Yarvi put his palm against her clammy skin and found his hand shook. He might have saved her from drowning but without fire or food the winter would take her through the Last Door still, and he could not stand the thought of it. What would they do without her?

What would he do without her?

'Do something!' hissed Rulf, gripping hard at Yarvi's arm.

But what? Yarvi chewed at his cracked lip, staring off into the forest as though some answer might present itself among those barren trunks.

There is always a way.

He frowned for a moment, then shook Rulf off and hurried to the nearest tree, tearing the wrappings from his good hand. He plucked a red-brown tuft of something from the bark, and the embers of hope sparked to life once again.

'Wool,' muttered Ankran, holding up another tuft. 'Sheep passed this way.'

Rulf tore it from his fingers. 'Were driven?'

'Southwards,' said Yarvi.

'How can you tell?'

'The moss grows out of the wind on the west side of the trunks.'

'Sheep mean warmth,' said Rulf.

'Sheep mean food,' said Jaud.

Yarvi did not say what he was thinking. That sheep meant people, and people might not be friendly. But to weigh your choices you need more than one.

'I'll stay with her,' said Ankran. 'You bring help, if you can.'

'No,' said Jaud. 'We go together. We are all oarmates now.'

'Who'll carry her?'

Jaud shrugged. 'When you have a load to lift, you're better lifting than weeping.' And he slipped his arms underneath Sumael and grimaced as he lifted her, stumbled just a little, then settled her twitching face against his shoulder and without another word started southwards, head held high. She must not have weighed much now but, cold and hungry and tired as Yarvi was, it seemed a feat almost impossible.

'I've lived a while,' muttered Rulf, blinking at Jaud's back. 'But I can't say I ever saw a finer thing.'

'Nor I,' said Yarvi, clambering up and hurrying after. How could he complain, or doubt, or falter, with that lesson in strength before him?

How could any of them?

KINDNESS

They huddled in the damp brush, and looked down towards the steading.

One building was stone-built, so old it had settled into the land, a thin plume of smoke drifting from the snow-humped roof which made Yarvi's mouth water and his skin prickle at misty memories of food and warmth. Another building, which from the occasional muffled bleating was the barn where the sheep were kept, looked to be made from the hull of an upended ship, though how it might have come this far inland he had no notion. Others were rough-hewn sheds almost lost under the drifted snow, the gaps between them blocked by a fence of sharpened logs.

Just outside the entrance, by a hole in the ice and with his fishing rod propped on a pair of sticks, a small boy sat swaddled in furs, and from time to time noisily blew his nose.

'This worries me,' whispered Jaud. 'How many will be in there? We know nothing about them.'

'Except that they are people and people are never to be trusted,' said Nothing.

'We know they have food, and clothes, and

192

shelter.' Yarvi looked at Sumael, hunched in every thread they could spare, which was few enough. She was shivering so hard her teeth rattled, lips grey-blue like slate, eyelids drooping, closing, opening and drooping again. 'Things we need to survive.'

'Then it is simple.' Nothing unwrapped the cloth from the hilt of his sword. 'Steel is the answer.'

Yarvi stared at him. 'You're going to kill that boy?'

Rulf wriggled his shoulders uncomfortably, but Nothing only shrugged his. 'If it is a choice between his death or ours then, yes, I will kill him, and anyone else down there. They can join my regrets.' He started to rise but Yarvi grabbed his ragged shirt and dragged him back down, found himself staring into his hard, flat, grey eyes. Close up, they looked no more sane. Quite the reverse.

'The same goes for you, cook's boy,' whispered Nothing.

Yarvi swallowed, but he did not look away, and he did not let go. Sumael had risked her life for his on the *South Wind*. It was time to repay the debt. And besides, he was tired of being a coward.

'First we'll try talking.' He stood, tried to think up some gesture that might make him look less like a ragged beggar at the utter extremes of desperation, and failed.

'Once they have killed you,' said Nothing. 'Will steel be the answer?'

Yarvi breathed a smoky sigh. 'I expect so.' And he shuffled down the slope towards the buildings.

All was still. No sign of life but for the boy. Yarvi stopped perhaps a dozen steps from him.

'Hey.'

The lad jerked up, upsetting his fishing rod, stumbled back and nearly fell, then ran towards the house. Yarvi could only wait, and shiver. Shiver with the cold, and with the fear of what was coming. You could not expect too much kindness from folk who lived in land as harsh as this.

They spilled from the stone building like bees from a broken hive. He counted six, each well-wrapped in furs, each with a spear. Three of them had stone points rather than metal, but all were gripped with grim purpose. Silently they rushed to make half a circle around him, spears pointing in.

All Yarvi could do was lift his hands, empty apart from their swaddlings of filthy sailcloth, send up a silent prayer to Father Peace and croak out, 'I need your help.'

The figure in the centre planted their spear butt-down in the snow, and walked slowly up to Yarvi. She pushed her hood back to show a shag of yellow-grey hair and a face deep-lined, worn by work and weather. For a moment, she studied him.

Then she stepped forward and, before Yarvi could cringe away, threw her arms about him and hugged him tight.

'I am Shidwala,' she said in the Tongue. 'Are you alone?'

'No,' he whispered, fighting to hold back his tears of relief. 'My oarmates are with me.'

The inside of the house was low, and narrow, and stank of sweat and woodsmoke, and it seemed a palace. An oily stew of roots and mutton was doled out from a blackened pot into a wooden bowl polished with years of use. Yarvi dug into it with his fingers and had never tasted anything finer. Benches followed the curving walls, and Yarvi and his friends sat on one side of the sizzling firepit and their hosts on the other – Shidwala, and four men he took to be her sons, and the boy from the ice pool, who stared at Sumael and Jaud as if they were elves stepped out of legend.

Back in Thorlby, these people would have seemed beyond poor. Now the room was crammed with riches. Tools of wood and bone were bracketed on the walls, cunning instruments for hunting, and fishing, and digging shelter, and teasing a living from the ice, skins of wolf and goat and bear and seal on every surface. One of the hosts, a man with a thick brown beard, scraped out the pot to hand Jaud a second bowl, and the big man nodded his thanks and started to stuff it in, eyes closed in ecstasy.

Ankran leaned close to him. 'I think we have eaten all their dinner.'

Jaud froze with his fingers in his mouth and the bearded man laughed and leaned across the fire to clap him on the shoulder.

195

'I'm sorry,' said Yarvi, putting his own bowl aside.

'You are hungrier than us, I think,' said Shidwala. They spoke the Tongue with a strange accent. 'And also remarkably far from your way.'

'We are heading to Vulsgard from the land of the Banyas,' said Ankran.

The woman considered that a moment. 'Then you are remarkably close to your way, but I find your way a very strange one.'

Yarvi could only agree with that. 'If we had known the hardship of it, we might have chosen another.'

'So it is with many choices.'

'All we can do now is see it through.'

'So it is with many choices.'

Nothing leaned close to Yarvi and whispered in his ground-down stub of a voice. 'I do not trust them.'

'He wants to thank you for your hospitality,' said Yarvi, quickly.

'We all do,' said Ankran. 'You, and the gods of your house.'

Yarvi brushed ashes from the prayer stone that was set into the hearth and read the runes there. 'And She Who Breathes Out the Snows.'

'Well said and well reckoned.' Shidwala narrowed her eyes. 'Where you come from she is a small god, eh?'

Yarvi nodded. 'But here a tall one, I think.'

'Like many things, gods seem bigger when you are closer to them. Here, She Who Breathes Out the Snows is ever at our elbows.'

'She shall have our first prayers waking,' said Ankran.

'Wise,' said Shidwala.

'And you'll have our second,' said Yarvi. 'You've saved our lives.'

'Here all the living must be friends.' She smiled, and the deep creases in her face reminded Yarvi of Mother Gundring, and for a moment he was sick for home. 'The winter is enemy enough for all of us.'

'We know it.' Yarvi looked over at Sumael, hunched close to the fire with her eyes shut, rocking gently with a blanket about her shoulders. Most of the colour had come back to her face.

'You could wait with us, until winter passes.'

'I cannot,' said Ankran, voice cracking as he set his jaw hard. 'I must get to my family.'

'And I to mine,' said Yarvi, though his pressing need was to kill one of his rather than save them. 'We must go on, but there are many things we need . . .'

Shidwala took in their wretched state and raised her brows. 'Indeed there are. We would happily trade.'

At the word 'trade' Shidwala's sons smiled, and nodded their approval.

Yarvi glanced at Ankran, and Ankran spread his empty palms. 'We have nothing to trade.'

'There is the sword.'

Nothing frowned even harder, cradled the blade a little closer, and Yarvi was painfully aware he

197

had been happy to kill these people a few moments before.

'He will not part with it,' said Yarvi.

'There is one thing I could make good use of.' The man with the brown beard was staring across the fire at Sumael.

Jaud stiffened, and Rulf gave an unhappy grunt, and Ankran's voice had a harsh edge when he spoke. 'We will not sell one of our own. Not at any price.'

Shidwala laughed. 'You misunderstand. Metal here is scarce.' She came around the fire on her haunches, reached into Sumael's collar where steel glinted and drew out a length of her fine chain. 'This is what we want.'

Yarvi felt the smile spread across his face. It had been a while, and it felt fine there. 'In that case . . .' He unwound his scarf of frayed sailcloth and drew out his own heavier chain. 'You might want this one too.'

The bearded man's eyes lit up as he weighed it in his hand, then his jaw dropped as Nothing jerked open his own collar. 'And there is this,' he said, dragging out the heavy links.

Now everyone was smiling. Yarvi leaned in close to the fire, and clasped his hands the way his mother used to. 'Let us trade.'

Nothing leaned to whisper in his ear. 'I told you steel would be the answer.'

With a final crash the rusted bolt sheared away and Nothing's collar sprang open.

'That was a stubborn one,' said the bearded man, frowning at his ruined chisel.

Somewhat unsteadily Nothing stood from the block, reached with one trembling hand to touch his neck, the skin leathery with the chafing of years.

'For twenty years I wore that collar,' he whispered, tears glimmering in his eyes.

Rulf slapped him on the shoulder. 'I wore mine only three, and still I feel light as air without it. You must feel like you could float away.'

'I have,' whispered Nothing. 'I will.'

Yarvi stroked absently at the old burns where his own collar used to sit, watching Ankran carefully pack the things their chains had bought them. A fishing rod and bait. A shovel made from the shoulder-blade of a moose. A bronze knife that looked like a relic from a time soon after the Breaking of God. Nine arrows for Rulf's bow. A wooden bowl for drinking. Dried moss to start a fire. Rope woven from wool. Ewe's cheese and mutton and dried fish. Furs too, and rough over-clothes stitched from fleeces, and raw wool to stuff inside them. Leather sacks to carry it all. Even a sled to pull it on.

What silly things these would have seemed once, what beggar's junk. Now it was a treasure hoard.

Sumael was wrapped up to her chin in a thick white fur, eyes closed and a rare grin on her face, white tooth showing through the notch in her lip.

'Feels good?' Jaud asked her.

'I am warm,' she whispered, without opening her eyes. 'If I'm dreaming, don't wake me.'

Shidwala tossed Nothing's open collar clattering into a barrel alongside their chains. 'If you want advice—'

'Always,' said Ankran.

'Head north and west. In two days you will come upon a country that fires under the earth make hot. At its edges the streams run with warm water and the fish teem.'

'I've heard tales of such a country,' said Yarvi, remembering Mother Gundring's voice droning over the firepit.

'We will go north and west,' said Ankran.

Shidwala nodded. 'And may the gods walk with you.' She turned to go but Nothing dropped suddenly to his knees, took her hand and pressed his cracked lips to it.

'I will never forget this kindness,' he said, wiping tears on the back of his hand.

'None of us will,' said Yarvi.

With a smile she pulled Nothing to his feet, and patted his grizzled cheek. 'That is its own reward.'

THE TRUTH

Rulf slipped from the trees with a huge grin on his face, bow over one shoulder and a stringy deer over the other. To leave no one in any doubt as to the quality of his archery he had left the arrow sticking from its heart.

Sumael raised one brow at him. 'So you're not just a beauty.'

He winked back. 'To an archer, arrows make all the difference.'

'Do you want to skin, cook's boy, or shall I?' Ankran held out the knife with the hint of a twisted grin. As though he knew Yarvi would refuse. He was no fool. The few times Yarvi had been dragged out to hunt his hand had stopped him drawing bow or holding spear and he had felt sick when it came to the butchery. His father had scalded him and his brother had mocked him and their men had barely bothered to conceal their contempt.

Much like the rest of his childhood, then.

'You can skin this time,' said Yarvi. 'I'll give you some pointers if you go wrong.'

After they ate Jaud sat with his bare feet to the fire, rubbing fat into the cracks between his thick toes. Rulf tossed the last bone aside and wiped his greasy hands on his fleece jacket.

'Some salt would've made all the difference.'

Sumael shook her head. 'Have you ever had a thing you didn't complain about?'

'If you can't find anything to complain about you aren't looking hard enough.' Rulf settled back on one elbow, smiling into the darkness and scratching at his thick growth of beard. 'Though I never was disappointed in my wife. I thought I'd die at that bloody oar. But since I still seem to be casting a shadow I've a mind to see her again. Just to say a hello. Just to know that she's well.'

'If she has any sense she'll have moved on,' said Sumael.

'She had more'n her share. Too much to waste life waiting.' Rulf sniffed, and spat into the fire. 'And better men than me aren't hard to find.'

'There we can agree.' Nothing sat a little way from the fire with his stiff back to the rest of them and his naked sword on his knees, polishing the blade with a rag.

Rulf only grinned over at him. 'And what about you, Nothing? You spent years scrubbing a deck, will you spend the rest of them scrubbing that sword? What will you do once we get to Vulsgard?'

Yarvi realized it was the first time since the *South Wind* went beneath the waves that any one of them had talked about what might come next. It was the first time it had looked as if they might make it.

'I have scores to settle. But they have kept fresh twenty years.' Nothing bent back to his frantic polishing. 'It can rain blood later.'

'Anything but snow would be an improvement in the weather,' said Jaud. 'I will be finding passage south, back to Catalia. Najit is the name of my village, and from its well comes the sweetest water in the world.' He clasped his hands over his stomach, and smiled the way he always did when he mentioned the place. 'I mean to drink from that well again.'

'Perhaps I'll join you,' said Sumael. 'It won't be far out of my way.'

'Your way where?' Yarvi asked. Though they had slept within reach of each other for months he hardly knew a thing about her, and found he wanted to. She frowned at him, as if wondering whether to open a door so long kept bolted, then shrugged.

'The First of Cities, I expect. I grew up there. My father was a famous man, in his way. A shipwright to the empress. His brother still is . . . perhaps. I hope. If he's alive. A lot can change in the time I've been away.'

And she fell silent, and frowned into the flames, and so did Yarvi, worrying over what might have changed in Thorlby while he was gone.

'Well, I will not be turning down your company,' said Jaud. 'Someone who actually knows where they are going can be a considerable help on a long journey. What about you, Ankran?'

'In Angulf's Square in Thorlby there is a flesh-dealer's shop.' Ankran growled the words at the

203

fire, his bony face full of shadows. 'The one where Shadikshirram bought me. From a man called Yoverfell.' He flinched when he said the name. The way Yarvi might have when he thought of Odem's. 'He has my wife. He has my son. I have to get them back.'

'How do you plan to do that?' asked Rulf.

'I will find a way.' Ankran made a fist, and thumped it harder and harder against his knee until it had to be painful. 'I *must.*'

Yarvi blinked across the fire. When he first laid eyes on Ankran he had hated him. He had tricked him, watched him beaten and stolen his place. Then he had accepted him, walked beside him, taken his charity. Come to trust him. Now he found what he had never thought to. That he admired him.

All Yarvi had done was for himself. His freedom, his vengeance, his chair. What Ankran had done was for his family.

'I could help,' he said.

Ankran looked up sharply. 'You?'

'I have . . . friends in Thorlby. Powerful friends.'

'This cook you were apprenticed to?' snorted Rulf.

'No.'

Yarvi was not sure why he chose that moment. Perhaps the closer he was bound to this band of misfits the heavier the lie sat on him. Perhaps some spot of pride had somehow survived and chose that moment to chafe. Perhaps he thought Ankran

204

was putting the truth together anyway. Or perhaps he was just a fool.

'Laithlin,' he said. 'Wife of the dead king, Uthrik.'

Jaud gave a smoking sigh, and settled down into his fur. Rulf did not bother even to chuckle. 'And what are you to the Golden Queen of Gettland?'

Yarvi kept his voice level even though his heart was suddenly thumping. 'Her youngest son.'

And that gave them all some pause.

Yarvi the most, for it came to him then he could have stayed a cook's boy, and gone anywhere. Traipsed after Rulf to say hello to his wife or followed Nothing to whatever madness his cracked mind settled on. Gone with Jaud to drink from that well in far Catalia, or on with Sumael to the wonders of the First of Cities. The two of them, together . . .

But now there was nowhere to go but into the Black Chair. Except through the Last Door.

'My name isn't Yorv, it's Yarvi. And I am the rightful King of Gettland.'

There was a long silence. Even Nothing had forgotten his polishing and twisted about on his stone to stare with eyes fever-bright.

Ankran softly cleared his throat. 'That would explain your shitty cooking.'

'You're not joking, are you?' asked Sumael.

Yarvi returned her gaze, long and level. 'Do you hear me laughing?'

'Then if I may ask, what was the King of Gettland doing lashed to an oar on a rotting trading galley?'

Yarvi pulled his fleece tight about his shoulders and looked into the fire, the flames taking on the shapes of things done and faces past. 'Because of my hand . . . or the lack of it, I was to give up my birthright and join the Ministry. But my father, Uthrik, was killed. Betrayed by Grom-gil-Gorm and his minister, Mother Scaer . . . or so I was told. I led twenty-seven ships on a raid against them. My Uncle Odem laid the plans.' He found his voice was quivering. 'Which included killing me and stealing my chair.'

'Prince Yarvi,' murmured Ankran. 'Uthrik's younger son. He had a crippled hand.' Yarvi held it up to the light and Ankran considered it, thoughtfully stroking the side of his crooked nose. 'When we last passed through Thorlby there was talk of his death.'

'The announcement was made a little early. I fell from a tower, and Mother Sea washed me into the arms of Grom-gil-Gorm. I pretended to be a cook's boy, and he put a collar on me and sold me to slavers in Vulsgard.'

'And there Trigg and I bought you,' mused Ankran, turning the story over for truth as a merchant might turn over a ring, trying to fathom how much gold was in the alloy. 'Because you told me you could row.'

Yarvi could only shrug as he pushed his crippled hand back inside the warmth of his fleece. 'As you can see, not the biggest lie I've ever told.'

Jaud puffed out his cheeks. 'No doubt every man has his secrets, but that is larger than the average.'

'And a good deal more dangerous,' said Sumael, eyes narrowed. 'Why break the silence?'

Yarvi thought about that for a moment. 'You deserve to know the truth. And I deserve to tell it. And it deserves to be told.'

More silence. Jaud rubbed more fat into his feet. Ankran and Sumael exchanged a lingering frown. Then Rulf pushed his tongue between his lips and made a loud farting sound. 'Does anyone believe this rubbish?'

'I believe.' Nothing stood, eyes black and huge, lifting his sword high. 'And I now swear an oath!' He rammed the blade into the fire, sparks whirling and everyone shuffling back in surprise. 'A sun-oath and a moon-oath. Let it be a chain about me and a goad within me. I will not rest until the rightful King of Gettland sits in the Black Chair once again!'

This silence was even longer, and no one was more stunned than Yarvi.

'Did you ever feel you were living in a dream?' muttered Rulf.

Jaud gave another of his sighs. 'Often.'

'A nightmare,' said Sumael.

Early the next day they crested a ridge and were greeted by a sight straight out of a dream. Or perhaps a nightmare. Instead of white hills ahead they saw black, distant mountains ghostly in a haze of steam.

'The hot country,' said Ankran.

'A place where the gods of fire and ice make war upon each other,' whispered Nothing.

'Looks pleasant enough,' said Yarvi, 'for a battlefield.'

There was a stretch of verdant green between the white land and the black, vegetation shifting with the breeze, clouds of coloured birds wheeling above, water glimmering in the thin sun.

'A strip of spring cut out from the winter,' said Sumael.

'I do not trust it,' said Nothing.

'What do you trust?' asked Yarvi.

Nothing held up his sword, and did not so much smile as show his broken teeth. 'Only this.'

No one mentioned yesterday's revelation as they trudged on. As though they did not know whether to believe him, or what to do if they decided they did, and so had settled on pretending it had never happened and treating him just as they had before.

That was well enough with Yarvi, in the end. He always had felt more like a cook's boy than a king.

The snow grew thin under his ragged boots, then melted and worked its way into them, then left him slipping in mud, then was gone altogether. The ground was patched with moss, then covered with tall green grass, then speckled with wildflowers that even Yarvi did not know the names of. Finally they stepped onto a shingle bank beside a wide pool, steam rising from the milky water, a twisted tree spreading rustling orange leaves over their heads.

'I have spent the last few years, and the last few

days in particular, wondering what I did to earn such a punishment,' said Jaud. 'Now I wonder how I deserved such a reward.'

'Life ain't about deservings,' said Rulf, 'so much as snatching what can be got. Where's that fishing rod?'

And the old raider began to pluck pale fish from that cloudy water as quickly as he could bait his hook. It had started to snow again but it would not settle on the warm ground, and dry wood was everywhere, so they set a fire and Ankran cooked a banquet of fish on a flat stone above it.

Afterwards Yarvi lay back with his hands on his full belly and his battered feet soaking in warm water and wondered when he was last this happy. Not taking yet another shameful beating in the training square, that was sure. Not hiding from his father's slaps or wilting under his mother's glare, for certain. Not even beside Mother Gundring's fire. He lifted his head to look at the faces of his mismatched oarmates. Who would be worse off if he never went back? Surely an oath unfulfilled was not the same as an oath broken . . .

'Perhaps we should just stay here,' he murmured.

Sumael had a mocking twist at the corner of her mouth. 'Who'd lead the people of Gettland to a brighter tomorrow then?'

'I've a feeling they'd get by. I could be king of this pond, and you my minister.'

'Mother Sumael?'

'You always know the right path. You could find me the lesser evil and the greater good.'

She snorted. 'Those aren't on any map. I need to piss.' And Yarvi watched her stride off into the long grass.

'I've a feeling you like her,' murmured Ankran.

Yarvi's head jerked towards him. 'Well . . . we all like her.'

'Of course,' said Jaud, grinning broadly. 'We'd be lost without her. Literally.'

'But you,' Rulf grunted, eyes closed and hands clasped behind his head, '*like* her.'

Yarvi worked his mouth sourly, but found he could not deny it. 'I have a crippled hand,' he muttered. 'The rest of me still works.'

Ankran gave something close to a chuckle. 'I've a feeling she likes you.'

'Me? She's harder on me than anyone!'

'Exactly.' Rulf was smiling too as he wriggled his shoulders contentedly into the ground. 'Ah, I remember what it was, to be young . . .'

'Yarvi?' Nothing was standing tall and stiff on a rock beside that spreading tree, showing no interest in who liked who and staring off the way they had come. 'My eyes are old and yours are young. Is that smoke?'

Yarvi was almost glad of the distraction as he clambered up beside Nothing, squinting southwards. But the gladness did not last long. It rarely did. 'I can't tell,' he said. 'Maybe.' Almost certainly. He could see faint smudges against the pale sky.

Sumael joined them, shading her eyes with one hand and giving no sign of liking anyone. Her jaw muscles tightened. 'It's coming from Shidwala's steading.'

'Maybe they've made a bonfire,' said Rulf, but his smile was gone.

'Or Shadikshirram has,' said Nothing.

A good minister hopes always for the best, but prepares always for the worst. 'We need to get up high,' said Yarvi. 'See if anyone's following.'

Nothing pursed his lips to gently blow a speck of dust from the bright blade of his sword. 'You know she is.'

And she was.

Squinting through the strange round window of Sumael's eye-glass from the rocky slope above the pool, Yarvi could see specks on the snow. Black specks moving, and the hope drained out of him like wine from a punctured skin. Where hope was concerned, he had long been a leaky vessel.

'I count two dozen,' said Sumael. 'Banyas I think, and some of the sailors from the *South Wind*. They have dogs and they have sleds and more than likely are well armed.'

'And intent on our destruction,' muttered Yarvi.

'That or they're very, very keen to wish us well on our journey,' said Rulf.

Yarvi lowered the eye-glass. It was hard to imagine they had been laughing just an hour before. His friends' faces were back in the drawn and worried shapes which had become so wearyingly familiar.

Apart from Nothing, of course, who looked precisely as mad as he always did.

'How far back are they?'

'My guess is sixteen miles,' said Sumael.

Yarvi was used to counting her guesses as facts. 'How long will it take them to cover that?'

Her lips moved silently as she worked through the sums. 'Pushing hard with sleds, they might be here at first light tomorrow.'

'Then we'd better not be,' said Ankran.

'No.' Yarvi looked away from his placid little kingdom, up the hill of bare scree and shattered rock above. 'In the hot land their sleds will be no help.'

Nothing frowned into the white sky, scratching at his neck with the backs of his filthy fingernails. 'Sooner or later, steel must be the answer. It always is.'

'Later, then,' said Yarvi, hefting his pack. 'Now, we run.'

RUNNING

They ran.

Or they jogged. Or they waddled, and stumbled, and shuffled over a hellish landscape of blasted stone where not a plant grew or a bird flew, Father Earth tortured into a hot waste as empty of life as the cold had been.

'The winds of fate have blown me to some glamorous places of late,' mused Ankran as they crested a ridge and stared out at another vista of smoking rock.

'Are they still following?' asked Jaud.

'Hard to see men in this broken country.' Sumael peered through her eye-glass to scan the desolation behind them, which was misted with stinking steam. 'Especially ones who'd rather not be seen.'

'Perhaps they've turned back.' Yarvi sent up a prayer to He Who Turns the Dice for a little rare luck. 'Perhaps Shadikshirram couldn't convince the Banyas to follow us.'

Sumael wiped grimy sweat across her face. 'Who wouldn't want to come here?'

'You do not know Shadikshirram,' said Nothing. 'She can be most persuasive. A great leader.'

'I saw scant sign of it,' said Rulf.

'You were not at Fulku, when she led the fleet of the empress to victory.'

'But you were, I suppose?'

'I fought on the other side,' said Nothing. 'I was champion to the King of the Alyuks.'

Jaud's forehead wrinkled with disbelief. 'You were a king's champion?' Looking at him it was hard to imagine, but Yarvi had watched great warriors in the training square, and never seen the like of Nothing's blade-work.

'Our flagship was aflame.' The old man's knuckles were white about his sword's grip as he remembered. 'Roped by a dozen galleys, slick with the blood of the fallen, crawling with the soldiers of the empress when Shadikshirram and I first fought. I was tired from battle and sore with wounds and unused to the shifting deck. She played the helpless woman, and in my pride I believed her and she made me bleed. So I came to be her slave. The second time we fought I was weak from hunger, and she had steel in her hand and strong men at her back and I stood alone with only an eating knife. She made me bleed a second time, but in her pride she let me live.' His mouth twisted into that mad smile and made flecks of spit as he barked the words. 'Now we shall meet a third time, and I have no pride to weigh me down, and the ground shall be of my choosing, and she shall bleed for me. Yes, Shadikshirram!'

He raised his sword high, cracked voice echoing

from the bare rocks, bouncing about the valley. 'The day is here! The time is now! The reckoning comes!'

'Could it come after I'm safely back in Thorlby?' asked Yarvi.

Sumael grimly tightened her belt a notch. 'We have to move.'

'What have we been doing?'

'Dawdling.'

'What's your plan?' asked Rulf.

'Kill you and leave your corpse as a peace offering?'

'Don't think she's come all this way for peace, do you?'

Sumael's jaw muscles worked. 'Sadly, no. My plan is to reach Vansterland ahead of them.' And she started down the slope, gravel trickling from every footstep.

The ordeal by steam was almost worse than the ordeal by ice had been. Though the snow was falling it grew hotter and hotter, and layer by layer they stripped off their jealously-hoarded clothes until they were slogging along half-naked, sweat-soaked, dust-smeared as labourers emerging from a mine. Thirst took the place of hunger, Ankran rationing out the cloudy, foul-tasting water in their two bottles more stingily than ever he had the stores on the *South Wind*.

There had been fear before. Yarvi could not remember the last time he had been without it. But it had been the slow fear of cold and hunger and exhaustion. Now it was a crueller spur. The fear of sharpened steel, the sharp teeth of the Banyas' dogs, the even sharper vengeance of their owner.

They struggled on until it was so dark Yarvi could scarcely see his withered hand before his face, Father Moon and all his stars lost in the gloom, and they crawled in silence into a hollow in the rocks. He fell into an ugly mockery of sleep and was shaken awake what felt like moments later, bruised and aching at the first grey glimmer of dawn, to struggle on again with the splinters of his nightmares still niggling at him.

To keep ahead was all they thought of. The world became no bigger than the stretch of bare rock between their heels and their pursuers, a space ever shrinking. For a while Rulf dragged a pair of sheepskins after them on ropes: an old poacher's trick to put off the dogs. The dogs were not fooled. Soon enough they were all bruised, grazed, bloodied from a hundred slips and falls, but with only one good hand Yarvi did worse than the others. Yet each time he went down Ankran was there with a steadying hand, to help him up, to help him on.

'Thanks,' said Yarvi, once he had lost count of his falls.

'You'll get your chance to repay me,' said Ankran. 'In Thorlby, if not before.'

For a moment they scrambled on in awkward silence, then Yarvi said, 'I'm sorry.'

'For falling?'

'For what I did on the *South Wind*. For telling Shadikshirram . . .' He winced at the memory of the wine bottle cracking into Ankran's head. The heel of the captain's boot crunching into his face.

Ankran grimaced, tongue wedged into the hole in his front teeth. 'What I hated most about that ship wasn't what was done to me, but what I was made to do. No. What I chose to do.' He stopped for a moment, bringing Yarvi to a halt and looking him in the eye. 'I used to think I was a good man.'

Yarvi put a hand on his shoulder. 'I used to think you were a bastard. Now I'm starting to have some doubts.'

'You can weep over each other's hidden nobility when we're safe!' called Sumael, a black outline on a boulder above them, pointing off into the misty grey. 'For now, we have to turn south. If we reach the river ahead of them we'll need some way to cross. We won't make a raft from stones and steam.'

'Will we make it to the river before we die of thirst?' asked Rulf, licking the last drops from one of the bottles and peering hopefully into it as though some might be stuck in there.

'Thirst.' Nothing barked out a chuckle. 'It's a Banya spear in your back you need to worry about.'

They slid down endless slopes of scree, hopped between boulders as big as houses, clambered down spills of black rock like waterfalls frozen. They crossed valleys where the ground was painful to touch it was so hot, choking steam hissing from cracks like devil's mouths, skirting pools of bubbling water slick with many-coloured oil. They toiled upward, sending stones clattering down dizzy drops, clinging with cut fingertips, Yarvi pawing at cracks with his useless hand, finally looking back from the heights . . .

To see those black dots through Sumael's eye-glass still following, and always slightly closer than before.

'Do they never tire?' asked Jaud, wiping the sweat from his face. 'Will they never stop?'

Nothing smiled. 'They will stop when they are dead.'

'Or we are,' said Yarvi.

DOWNRIVER

They heard the river before they saw it, a whisper through the woods that put a little lost spring in Yarvi's ruined legs and a little lost hope in his aching heart. The whisper became a growl, then a surging roar as they finally burst from the trees, all filthy with sweat, dust, ash. Rulf flung himself down the shingle onto his face and started lapping up water like a dog. The rest of them were not far behind him.

When the burning thirst of a day's hard scrambling was quenched, Yarvi sat back and stared across the river to the trees on the far side, so like the ones about them, yet so different.

'Vansterland,' muttered Yarvi. 'Thank the gods!'

'Thank 'em once we're across,' said Rulf, clean mouth and patch of beard pale in his ash-streaked face. 'That doesn't look like friendly water to this sailor.'

Nor did it to Yarvi. His relief was already turning to dread as he took in the width of the Rangheld, the steep far bank perhaps twice bowshot away, the river high with meltwater from the burning land at their backs. On the black surface patterns

219

of frothing white showed swift currents and ripping eddies and hinted at hidden rocks, deadly as traitor's knives.

'Can you build a raft to cross this?' he muttered.

'My father was the foremost shipwright in the First of Cities,' said Sumael, peering into the woods. 'He could pick the best keel from a forest with one look.'

'Doubt we'll have time for a carved figurehead,' said Yarvi.

'Maybe we could mount you on the front,' said Ankran.

'Six small trunks for the raft, then a larger one cut in half for crossbeams.' Sumael hurried to a nearby fir, running her hand up the bark. 'This will do for one. Jaud, you hold it, I'll chop.'

'I'll keep watch for our old mistress and her friends.' Rulf shrugged the bow from his shoulder and turned back the way they came. 'How far back do we reckon 'em now?'

'Two hours if we're lucky, and we generally aren't.' Sumael slid out her hatchet. 'Yarvi, find the rope, then look for some wood that might make a paddle. Nothing, when we've felled the trunks, you trim the branches.'

Nothing hugged his sword tight. 'This is no saw. I will need the blade keen when Shadikshirram comes.'

'We hope to be long gone by then,' said Yarvi, too much water sloshing in his aching belly as he rooted through the packs.

Ankran held out his hand. 'If you won't use it give me the sword—'

Faster than seemed possible the immaculate point was grazing Ankran's stubbled throat. 'Try to take it and I will give it to you point first, store-keeper,' murmured Nothing.

'Time presses,' hissed Sumael through her gritted teeth, sending splinters flying from the base of her chosen tree with short, quick blows. 'Use your sword or snap them off in your arse, but trim the bloody branches. And leave some long so we have something to hold on to.'

Soon Yarvi's right hand was cut and dirty from dragging lengths of timber, his left wrist, which he hooked underneath them, riddled with splinters. Nothing's sword was slathered in sap, Jaud's fuzzy growth of hair was full of wood dust, Sumael's right palm was bloody from wielding the hatchet and still she chopped, chopped, chopped.

They sweated and strained, snapping at each other through bared teeth, not knowing when the Banyas' dogs would be snapping at them instead, but knowing it could not be long.

Jaud heaved up the trunks with a grunting effort, veins bulging from his thick neck, and nimble as a dressmaker sewing a hem Sumael weaved the rope in and out while Nothing hauled out the slack. Yarvi stood and watched, startling at every sound and, not for the first or the last time, wishing he had two good hands.

Considering the tools they had and the time they

221

didn't, their raft was a noble effort. Considering the surging torrent they would have to navigate, it was a terrifying one – hacked and splintered timbers bound with a hairy tangle of wool rope, their moose-shoulder shovel as one paddle, Jaud's shield as another, and a vaguely spoon-shaped branch Yarvi had found as a third.

With arms folded about his sword, Nothing gave voice to Yarvi's thoughts. 'I do not care for the look of this raft and this river together.'

The fibres in Sumael's neck stood out starkly as she dragged at the knots one more time. 'All it has to do is float.'

'No doubt it will, but will we still be on it?'

'That depends how well you hold on.'

'And what will you say when it breaks up and floats out to sea in pieces?'

'I imagine I'll be forever silent by then, but with the satisfaction of knowing as I drown that you were killed first by Shadikshirram, here, on this forsaken bank.' Sumael raised one brow at him. 'Or are you coming with us?'

Nothing frowned at them, then off into the trees, weighing his sword in one hand, then he cursed and threw his weight in between Jaud and Yarvi. The raft began to grind slowly towards the water, their boots sliding in the shingle. Yarvi slipped into the mud in panic as someone came springing from the bushes.

Ankran, his eyes wild. 'They're coming!'

'Where's Rulf?' asked Yarvi.

'Just behind me! This is it?'

'No, this is a joke,' hissed Sumael. 'I have a war galley of ninety oars hidden behind that tree.'

'Only asking.'

'Stop asking and help us launch the bastard!'

Ankran flung his weight to the raft and with all of them pushing it slithered down the bank into the river. Sumael dragged herself on, her kicking foot catching Yarvi in the jaw and making him bite his tongue. He was up to his waist in water, thought he heard shouting behind him in the trees. Nothing was on now: he seized the wrist of Yarvi's useless hand and hauled him up, one of the torn branches gouging his chest. Ankran snatched their packs from the beach and started to fling them onto the raft.

'Gods!' Rulf burst from the trees, cheeks puffing with every huge breath. Yarvi could see shadows in the woods beyond him, could hear wild calls in a language he did not know. Then the barking of dogs.

'Run, you old fool!' he screeched. Rulf charged down the shingle and sloshed out into the water and between them Yarvi and Ankran hauled him aboard while Jaud and Nothing began to paddle like madmen.

The only effect was that they began to slowly spin.

'Keep us straight!' snapped Sumael as the raft picked up speed.

'I'm trying!' growled Jaud, digging away with his shield and showering them all with water.

'Try harder! Do you know any decent oarsmen?'

'Do you have any decent oars?'

'Shut your mouth and paddle!' snarled Yarvi, water washing across the raft and soaking his knees. Dogs spilled from the forest – huge dogs, the size of sheep they seemed, all snarling teeth and drool, bounding up and down the shingle, barking.

Then men came. Yarvi could not have said how many in that snatched glance over his shoulder. Ragged shapes among the trees, kneeling on the bank, the curve of a bow.

'Get down!' roared Jaud, clambering to the back of the raft and huddling behind his shield.

Yarvi heard the bowstrings, saw the black splinters drifting up. He crouched, fascinated, his eyes fixed on them. They seemed to take an age to fall, each with a gentle whisper. One plopped in the water a couple of strides away. Then there were two quiet clicks as arrows stuck into Jaud's shield. A fourth lodged shuddering in the raft beside Yarvi's knee. A hand's width to one side and it would have been through his thigh. He blinked at it, mouth open.

There the difference between one side of the Last Door and the other.

He felt Nothing's hand at the scruff of his neck, forcing him to the edge of the raft. 'Paddle!'

More men were spilling from the trees. There might have been a score of them. There might have been more.

'Thanks for the arrows!' Rulf bellowed at the bank.

One of the archers let fly another but they were moving out into swifter water now and his arrow fell well short. A figure stood with hands on hips, looking after them. A tall figure, with a curved sword, and Yarvi caught a glimpse of gleaming crystal on a dangling belt.

'Shadikshirram,' murmured Nothing. He had been right. She had been tracking them all along. And though Yarvi did not hear her make a sound, could not even see her face over that distance, he knew then she would not stop.

Not ever.

ONLY A DEVIL

They might have escaped a fight with Shadikshirram, but soon enough the river was giving them more fight than even Nothing could have hoped for.

It showered them with cold water, soaked them and all their gear right through, made the raft buck and twist like an unbroken horse. Rocks battered at them, overhanging trees clutched at them, caught Ankran's hood and might have plucked him from the raft had Yarvi not been clinging to his shoulder.

The banks grew steeper, higher, narrowed, until they were hurtling down a rocky gorge between broken cliffs, water spurting up through the gaps between the logs, their raft spinning like a leaf in spite of Jaud's effort to use his arrow-stuck shield as a rudder. The river soaked the ropes and tore at the knots and began to work them loose, the raft flexing with the current, threatening to rip apart all together.

Yarvi could not hear Sumael's screamed orders over the thunder of the river, and he gave up all pretence of influencing the outcome, closed his eyes and clung on for his life, good hand and bad hand burning with the clenched effort, one moment cursing the gods for putting him on this raft, the next begging them to get him off it with his life. There was a wrench, a drop, the raft tipped under Yarvi's knees, and he squeezed his eyes shut, waiting for the end.

But suddenly the waters were calm.

He prised one eye open. They all were huddled in the middle of the flopping, foundering raft, clinging to the branches, clinging to each other, shivering and bedraggled, water lapping at their knees as they ever so gently spun.

Sumael stared at Yarvi, hair plastered to her face, gulping for air.

'Shit.'

Yarvi could only nod. Unclenching the fingers of his good hand from their branch was an aching effort.

'We're alive,' croaked Rulf. 'Are we alive?'

'If I'd known,' muttered Ankran, 'what this river would be like . . . I would've taken my chances . . . with the dogs.'

Daring to look past the ring of haggard faces, Yarvi saw the river had widened and slowed. It grew much broader still ahead, smooth water with barely a ripple, trees on wooded slopes reflected in the mirror surface.

And off on their right, flat and inviting, lay a wide beach scattered with rotting driftwood.

'Get paddling,' said Sumael.

One by one they slid from their disintegrating raft, hauled it between them as far onto the beach as they could, dragged off their sodden gear, tottered a few steps and without a word flopped on the shingle among the rest of the flotsam, no strength left even to celebrate their escape, unless lying still and breathing counted.

'Death waits for us all,' said Nothing. 'But she takes the lazy first.' By some magic he was standing, frowning upriver for any sign of pursuit. 'They will be following.'

Rulf worked himself up onto his elbows. 'Why the hell would they?'

'Because this is just a river. That some men call this side Vansterland will mean nothing to the Banyas. It will certainly mean nothing to Shadikshirram. They are as bound together now in their pursuit as we are in our escape. They will build their own rafts and follow, and the river will be too swift for them to land just as it was for us. Until they come here.' Nothing smiled. Yarvi was starting to get nervous when Nothing smiled. 'And they will come ashore, tired and wet and foolish, just as we have, and we will fall upon them.'

'Fall upon them?' said Yarvi.

'We six?' asked Ankran.

'Against their twenty?' muttered Jaud.

'With a one-handed boy, a woman and a store-keeper among us?' said Rulf.

'Exactly!' Nothing smiled wider. 'You think just as I do!'

228

Rulf propped himself on his elbows. 'There is no one, ever, who's thought as you do.'

'You are afraid.'

The old raider's ribs shook with chuckles. 'With you on my side? You're damn right I am.'

'You told me Throvenlanders had fire.'

'You told me Gettlanders had discipline.'

'For pity's sake, anything but that!' snarled Yarvi as he stood. It was not a hot and mindless anger that came upon him, as his father's rages had been, or his brother's. It was his mother's anger, calculating and patient, cold as winter, and for the time being it left no room for fear.

'If we have to fight,' he said, 'we'll need better ground than this.'

'And where will we find this field of glory, my king?' asked Sumael, with her notched lip curled.

Yarvi blinked into the trees. Where indeed?

'There?' Ankran was pointing up towards a rocky bluff above the river. It was hard to say with the sky bright behind but, squinting towards it, Yarvi thought there might be ruins at the summit.

'What was this place?' asked Jaud, easing through the archway, and at the sound of his voice birds clattered from perches high in the broken walls and away.

'It's an elf-ruin,' said Yarvi.

'Gods,' muttered Rulf, making a sign against evil, and badly.

'Don't worry.' Sumael kicked heedlessly through

a heap of rotten leaves. 'I doubt there'll be any elves here now.'

'Not for thousands upon thousands of years.' Yarvi ran his hand over one of the walls. Not made from mortared stone but smooth, and hard, without joint or edge as though it had been moulded more than built. From its crumbling top rods of rusted metal sprouted, unruly as an idiot's hair. 'Not since the Breaking of God.'

There had been a great hall here, with pillars proudly marching down both sides and archways to rooms on the right and left. But the pillars had toppled long ago, and the walls were thickly webbed with dead creeper. Part of the far wall had vanished entirely, claimed by the hungry river far below. The roof had fallen centuries since and above them was only the white sky and a shattered tower wreathed in ivy.

'I like it,' said Nothing, striding across the rubble-strewn ground, thick with dead leaves, rot and bird-droppings.

'You were all for staying on the beach,' said Rulf.

'I was, but this is a stronger place.'

'I'd like it better with a good gate.'

'A gate only postpones the inevitable.' Nothing made a ring with filthy thumb and forefinger and peered with one bright eye through it towards the empty archway. 'That invitation will be their undoing. They will be funnelled through, without room to make their numbers count. Here we have a chance of winning!'

'So your last plan was certain death?' said Yarvi.

Nothing grinned. 'Death is life's only certainty.'

'You surely know how to build morale,' muttered Sumael.

'We are outnumbered four to one and most of us are no fighters!' Ankran's bulging eyes had a desperate look. 'I can't afford to die here! My family are—'

'Have more faith, storekeeper!' Nothing hooked one arm about Ankran's neck and one about Yarvi's and dragged them close with shocking strength. 'If not in yourself, then in the rest of us. We are your family now!'

It was even less reassuring, if anything, than it had been when Shadikshirram told them as much aboard the *South Wind*. Ankran stared at Yarvi and all Yarvi could do was stare back.

'And anyway, there is no way out now, and that is good. People fight hardest when they have no way out.' Nothing gave them a parting squeeze then hopped up onto the base of a broken pillar, pointing towards the entrance with his naked sword. 'Here I shall stand, and take the brunt of their attack. Their dogs at least cannot have made the river journey. Rulf, you will climb that tower with your bow.'

Rulf peered up at the crumbling tower, then around the others, and finally blew his grey-bearded cheeks out with a heavy sigh. 'I daresay it's sad to think of a poet's death, but I'm a fighting man, and in that trade you're bound to go sooner or later.'

Nothing laughed, a strange and jagged sound. 'I

dare say we've both lasted longer than we deserve! Together we braved the snow and the hunger, the steam and the thirst, together we will stand. Here! Now!'

It was hard to believe this man, standing straight and tall with steel in hand, wild hair pushed back and eyes burning bright, could be the pitiful beggar Yarvi had stepped over on his way onto the *South Wind*. He seemed a king's champion indeed now, with an air of command none questioned, an air of mad confidence that gave even Yarvi some courage.

'Jaud, take your shield,' said Nothing, 'Sumael your hatchet, and guard our left. That is our weaker side. Let none get around me. Keep them where I and my sword may look them in the eyes. Ankran, you and Yarvi will guard our right. That shovel will do as a club: anything can kill if you swing it hard enough. Give Yarvi the knife since he has just one hand to hold it. One hand, perhaps, but the blood of kings in his veins!'

'It's keeping it there that worries me,' said Yarvi under his breath.

'You and I, then.' Ankran offered out the knife. A makeshift thing without so much as a crosspiece, wooden handle wrapped with leather cord and the blade greened down the back but the edge keen enough.

'You and I,' said Yarvi, taking it from him and gripping it tight. He would never have believed when he first looked on the storekeeper in the stinking slave-pits of Vulsgard that he might one day stand as his shoulder-man, but he found in spite of his fear he was proud to do it.

'With a good bloody ending this journey will make a fine song, I think.' Nothing held his free arm out, fingers spread, towards the archway through which Shadikshirram and her Banyas would no doubt soon be spilling, fixed on murder. 'A band of brave companions escorting the rightful King of Gettland to his stolen chair! A last stand amidst the elf-ruins of yore! You cannot expect all the heroes to survive a good song, you know.'

'He's a damn devil,' murmured Sumael, jaw muscles clenching and unclenching as she weighed her hatchet in her hand.

'When you're in hell,' murmured Yarvi, 'only a devil can point the way out.'

THE LAST STAND

Rulf's voice split the quiet. 'They're coming!' And it felt as if Yarvi's guts would drop out of his arse.

'How many?' called Nothing eagerly.

A pause. 'Might be twenty!'

'Gods,' whispered Ankran, chewing at his lip.

Until that moment there had been the hope that some might have turned back or drowned in the river but, as with so many of Yarvi's hopes, it had withered before bearing fruit.

'The greater their numbers, the greater our glory!' shouted Nothing. The blacker their plight the happier he grew. At that moment there seemed a lot to be said for inglorious survival, but the choice was made now, if there had ever been a choice.

No more running, no more tricks.

Yarvi might have mouthed a dozen prayers over the last few moments, to every god, tall or small, that might be the slightest help. But now he closed his eyes and sent up one more. Perhaps he had been touched by Father Peace, but this one he sent to Mother War alone. To guard his friends, his oarmates, his family. For each in their own way had proved themselves worth saving.

That, and to bring his enemies a red day. For Mother War likes a prayer with blood in it, that's no secret.

'Fight or die,' murmured Ankran, and he offered out his hand and Yarvi gave his own, useless though it was. They looked into each other's faces, he and this man that he had hated, plotted against, seen beaten, then struggled through the wastes beside and come to understand.

'If I don't get glory but . . . the other thing,' said Ankran, 'would you find a way to help my family?'

Yarvi nodded. 'I swear it.' What difference if he failed to keep a second oath, after all? He could only be damned once. 'If I get the other thing . . .' Asking Ankran to kill his uncle seemed too high an expectation. He shrugged. 'Weep me a river?'

Ankran grinned. A shaky grin with the front teeth missing, but he managed it still, and it seemed at that moment high heroism to marvel at. 'Mother Sea will rise with my tears.'

The long silence stretched out, split into aching moments by the pounding of Yarvi's heart.

'What if we both die?' he whispered.

Nothing's grating voice came before the answer. 'Ebdel Aric Shadikshirram! Welcome to my parlour!'

'Like you, it's a little past its best.' Her voice.

Yarvi pressed himself to a crack in the wall, eye straining towards the archway.

'We all are less than we used to be,' called Nothing.

'You were an admiral once. Then a captain. And now—'

'Now I am nothing, just like you.' Yarvi saw her, in the shadows of the archway, eyes gleaming as she peered in. Trying to make out what was inside, and who. 'An empty jug. A broken vessel with all the hopes leaked out.' He knew she couldn't see him, but even so he shrank away behind the crumbling elf-stone.

'I sympathize,' called Nothing. 'It hurts, to lose everything. Who knows better than I?'

'And what do you think the sympathy of nothing for nothing is worth?'

Nothing laughed. 'Nothing.'

'Who's with you in there? That lying little bitch who used to cap my mastheads? That sneaking maggot with the turnip for a hand?'

'I have a higher opinion of them than you, but, no. They went on ahead. I am alone.'

Shadikshirram barked a laugh at that, and as she leaned forward into the archway Yarvi saw the glimmer of drawn steel. 'No, you're not. But you soon will be.' He peered up towards the tower, saw the curve of Rulf's bow, the string full drawn. But Shadikshirram was too canny to offer him a shot. 'I am too merciful! That has always been my fault. I should have killed you years ago.'

'You can try today. Twice we have met before in battle, but this time I—'

'Tell it to my dogs.' And Shadikshirram gave a shrill whistle.

Men spilled through the archway. Or things that looked like men. The Banyas. Wild and ragged shadows, glimpses of white faces gaping, studs of amber and bone and bared teeth shining, weapons of polished rock and walrus tooth and whale jaw. They screeched and gibbered, whooped and wailed, mad sounds, like beasts, like devils, as if that archway was a gate to hell and what lay beyond was vomiting into the world.

The foremost dropped gurgling with one of Rulf's arrows in his chest but the others plunged into the ruin and Yarvi stumbled from the crack as though slapped. The urge to run was almost more than he could stand, but he felt Ankran's hand on his shoulder then, and stood, shaking like a leaf, every breath a wheezing whimper.

But he stood.

The screaming started. Crashes, the sounds of steel, of rage, of pain, almost worse for not being able to see who made them, or why. He heard the shrieking of the Banyas, but more horrible still was Nothing's voice. A bubbling moan, a whispering sigh, a jagged growl. The rattle of final breath.

Or could it be laughter?

'Do we help?' whispered Yarvi, though he doubted he could move his rooted feet.

'He said wait.' Ankran's crooked face was chalk-white. 'Should we wait?'

Yarvi turned to look at him, and over his shoulder saw a figure drop from the wall.

He was more boy than man, hardly older than Yarvi. One of the sailors from the *South Wind*. Yarvi had seen him laughing on the rigging, but had never known his name. It seemed a little late for introductions now.

'There,' he croaked, and Ankran turned just as another man dropped down. Another of the sailors, bigger, bearded, and he held a mace in his hand, its heavy head spiked with steel. Yarvi felt his eyes drawn to the awful weight of that weapon, wondering what it might do to his skull, swung in anger. The man smiled as though guessing his thoughts, then leaped at Ankran, the two of them going down and rolling in a snarling tangle.

Yarvi knew he had a debt to pay, knew he should plunge to help his friend, his shoulder-man, but instead he turned to face the lad, as if they were couples pairing off at a harvest dance, somehow sensing who was their proper partner.

Like dancers they circled, knives held out before them, prodding at the air as if testing for the right bit of it. They circled, circled, the snarling and snapping of Ankran and the bearded man ignored, their struggle for life and death dismissed in the pressing need to survive the next few moments. Beyond the dirt and the bared teeth, he looked scared, this lad. Almost as scared as Yarvi felt. They circled, circled, eyes flickering between the glinting knife and—

The lad darted forward, stabbing, and Yarvi stumbled back, caught his heel on a root and only just kept his balance. The boy came at him again but Yarvi slipped away, cut at nothing and made the lad totter against the wall.

Could it really be one of them had to kill the other? To end everything he was, everything he might ever be?

So it seemed. But it was hard to see the glory in it.

The boy lunged again and Yarvi saw the knife flash through a shaft of daylight. By some dim instinct of the training square he caught it on his own, gasping, blades scraping. The lad crashed into him with a shoulder and Yarvi fell against the wall.

They spat and snarled in each other's faces, close enough that Yarvi could see the black pores on the lad's nose, the red veins in the whites of his bulging eyes, close enough that Yarvi could have stuck his tongue out and licked him.

They strained, grunting, trembling, and Yarvi knew he was the weaker. He tried to push his finger into the lad's face but his crooked wrist was caught, twisted away. The blades scraped again and Yarvi felt a burning cut on the back of his hand, felt the point of the knife brush his stomach, cold through his clothes.

'No,' he whispered. 'Please.'

Then something scratched Yarvi's cheek and the pressure was gone. The lad tottered back, lifting a trembling hand to his throat, and Yarvi saw an arrow there, its dripping head toward him, a line of blood running down the lad's neck into his collar. His face was going pink, cheeks quivering as he dropped to his knees.

Through a notch in the crumbling elf-wall behind him Yarvi saw Rulf squatting on top of the tower, nocking another arrow to his bow. The lad's face was turning purple and he gulped and clucked – cursing Yarvi, or begging him for help, or asking the gods for mercy, but all he could say was blood.

'I'm sorry,' whispered Yarvi.

'You will be.'

Shadikshirram stood a few strides away in a fallen archway.

'I thought you were a clever boy,' she said. 'But you turn out something of a disappointment.'

Her finery was crusted with mud, and her hair fell across her face in a filthy tangle, the pins lost, one fever-bright eye showing in its sunken socket. But the long, curved, blade of her sword was deadly clean.

'Only the latest in a lengthy string of them.' She kicked the dying lad onto his back and stepped over his jerking legs. Strutted, strolled, without fuss or hurry. Just as she had used to walk on the deck of the *South Wind*. 'But I suppose I have brought it on myself.'

Yarvi edged back, crouching, breathing hard, eyes darting between the ruined walls for some way out, but there was none.

He would have to fight her.

'I have too soft a heart for this hard world of

ours.' She glanced sideways, towards the notch Rulf's arrow had come through, then ducked smoothly under it. 'That has always been my one weakness.'

Yarvi scrambled back through the rubble, the grip of the knife sweaty in his palm. He could hear screams, the sounds of fighting. The others, more than busy with their own final bloody steps through the Last Door. He snatched a glance over his shoulder, saw the place where the broken elf-walls ended at the brink, sapling trees spreading their branches into empty air above the river.

'I cannot tell you how it pleases me to have the chance to say goodbye.' Shadikshirram smiled. 'Goodbye.'

No doubt she was far better armed than him. And taller, stronger, more skilful, more experienced. Not to mention her considerable advantage in number of hands. And in spite of her protestations he did not think she would be too weighed down by softness of heart.

There is always a way, his mother used to say, but where would he find a way to beat Shadikshirram? He, who in a hundred shameful showings in the training square had never won a match?

She raised her brows, as though she had been working at the same sum and happened upon the same answer. 'Perhaps you should just jump.'

She took another step, slowly herding him backwards, the point of her sword glinting as it passed through a chink of sunlight. He was running out of ground, could sense the space opening behind him, could feel the high breeze on the back of his neck, could hear the angry river chewing at the rocks far below.

'Jump, cripple.'

He edged back again and heard stones clattering into the void, the verge dissolving at his heels.

'Jump!' screamed Shadikshirram, spit flecking from her teeth.

And Yarvi caught movement at the corner of his eye. Ankran's pale face sliding around the crumbling wall, creeping up with his tongue pressed into the gap in his bared teeth and his club raised. Yarvi couldn't stop his eyes flickering across.

Shadikshirram's forehead creased.

She spun quick as a cat, twisted away from the moose-bone shovel so that it whistled past her shoulder and without much effort, without much sound, slid her sword straight through Ankran's chest.

He gave a shuddering breath, eyes bulging.

Shadikshirram cursed, pulling back her sword-arm.

Mercy is weakness. Yarvi's father used to say. *Mercy is failure.*

In an instant he was on her. He drove his claw of a hand under her armpit, pinned her sword, his knobbly palm pushing up into her throat, and with his right fist he hit her, punched her, dug at her.

They drooled and spat and snorted, whimpering,

squealing, lurching, her hair in his mouth. She twisted and growled and he clung to her, punching, punching. She tore free and her elbow caught him in the nose with a sick crunch, snapped his head up and the ground hit him in the back.

Calls far away. The echo of steel.

A distant battle. Something important.

Had to stand. Could not let his mother down.

Had to be a man. His uncle would be waiting.

He tried to shake the dizziness away, the sky flashed as he rolled over.

His arm flopped out into space, black river far below, white water on rocks.

Like the sea beneath the tower of Amwend. The sea he had plunged into.

Breath whooped in as he came back to himself. He scrabbled from the crumbling brink, head spinning, face throbbing, heels clumsy, mouth salty with blood.

He saw Ankran, twisted on his back, arms wide. Yarvi gave a whimper, scrambling towards him, reaching out. But his trembling fingertips stopped short of Ankran's blood-soaked shirt. The Last Door had opened for him. He was past help.

Shadikshirram lay on the rubble beside his body, trying to sit up and looking greatly surprised that she could not. The fingers of her left hand were tangled with the grip of her sword. Her right was clasped against her side. She peeled it away and her palm was full of blood. Yarvi blinked down at his own right hand. The knife was still in it, the blade slick, his fingers, his wrist, his arm red to the elbow.

'No,' she snarled. She tried to lift the sword but the weight of it was too much.

'Not like this. Not here.' Her bloody lips twisted as she looked up at him. 'Not you.'

'Here,' said Yarvi. 'Me. What was it you said? You may need two hands to fight someone. But only one to stab them in the back.'

And he realized then that he had not lost all those times in the training square because he lacked the skill, or the strength, or even a hand. He had lacked the will. And somewhere on the *South Wind*, somewhere in the trackless ice, somewhere in this ancient ruin, he had found it.

'But I commanded the ships of the empress,' Shadikshirram croaked, her whole right side dark with blood. 'I was a favoured lover . . . of Duke Mikedas. The world was at my feet.'

'That was long ago.'

'You're right. You're a clever boy. I am too soft.' Her head dropped back and she stared at the sky. 'That's . . . my one . . .'

The hall of the elf-ruin was scattered with bodies.

The Banyas had been devils from a distance. Close up they were wretched. Small and scrawny as children, bundles of rags, decked with whale-bone holy signs that had been no shield against Nothing's pitiless steel.

One that still breathed reached towards Yarvi, his other hand clutching at an arrow lodged in his ribs. His eyes held no hate, only doubt, and fear, and pain. Just as Ankran's had done when Shadikshirram killed him.

Only people, then, who Death ushered through the Last Door like any others.

He tried to make a word as Nothing walked up to him. The same word, over and over, shaking his head.

Nothing put a finger to his lips. 'Shhhh.' And he stabbed the Banya through the heart.

'Victory!' roared Rulf as he leapt the last distance to the ground. 'I never saw sword-work like it!'

'Nor I such archery!' said Nothing, folding Rulf in a crushing embrace. The closest of friends now, united in slaughter.

Sumael stood in an archway, gripping one shoulder, blood streaking her arm to the fingertips. 'Where's Ankran?' she asked.

Yarvi shook his head. He didn't dare speak in case he was sick. Or started crying. Or maybe both at once. With the pain and the fading fury. With relief that he was alive. With sorrow that his friend was not. Sorrow that weighed heavier with every moment.

Jaud sunk down onto a fallen lump of elf-stone, and let the scarred shield drop from his arm, and Sumael put one bloody hand on his shaking shoulder.

'I freely acknowledge now that Gettlanders are the best!' frothed Rulf.

'Just as I begin to doubt it!' Nothing frowned over. 'I was expecting Shadikshirram.'

Yarvi looked down at her curved sword in his hand, as if for evidence. 'I killed her.'

Perhaps he should have fallen to his knees and given thanks to the gods for their unlikely victory, but the red harvest sword-hacked and arrow-stuck about that ruin did not look like a thing to give thanks for.

So he sat down beside the others, and picked the crusted blood from under his broken nose.

He was the King of Gettland, after all, was he not?

He had knelt enough.

BURNING THE DEAD

The dead burned.

The flames that wreathed them made strange shadows flow across the walls of the elf-ruin. They sent a roiling of smoke into the pinking sky, the proper thing to thank Mother War for their victory. So Nothing said, and few were on such friendly terms with her as he. If Yarvi squinted hard enough he fancied he could still see the bones in the fire, of the nine dead Banyas and the three dead sailors, of Ankran and Shadikshirram.

'I will miss him,' said Yarvi, struggling to hold back his tears.

'We all will,' said Jaud, wiping his on the heel of his hand.

Nothing let his spill freely down his scarred cheeks as he nodded at the flames. 'I will miss her.'

Rulf snorted. 'I bloody won't.'

'Then you are more a fool than I first took you for. The gods give no finer gift than a good enemy. Like a good whetstone on the blade,' and Nothing frowned down at his sword, clean of blood though his fingernails were still crusted with it, and gave the steel another shrieking lick with his stone. 'A good enemy keeps you ever sharp.'

'I'm happier blunt,' grunted Jaud.

'Pick your enemies more carefully than your friends,' Nothing was muttering at the flames. 'They will be with you longer.'

'Don't worry.' Rulf clapped Nothing on the shoulder. 'If life has taught me one thing it's that your next enemy is never far away.'

'You can always make enemies of your friends,' said Sumael, pulling Shadikshirram's coat tight about her shoulders. 'Making friends of your enemies is harder labour.'

Yarvi knew that to be true enough. 'Do you think this is what Ankran would have wanted?' he muttered.

'To be dead?' said Jaud. 'I doubt it.'

'To be burned,' said Yarvi.

Jaud glanced over at Nothing, and shrugged. 'Once the men of violence get a notion it is hard to put them off. Especially when they still have the smell of blood in their noses.'

'And why make the attempt?' Sumael scratched again at the dirty bandages Yarvi had bound around her cut arm. 'These are the dead. Their complaints are easily brushed aside.'

'You fought well, Yarvi,' called Nothing. 'Like a king indeed.'

'Does a king let his friends die for him?' Yarvi glanced guiltily across at Shadikshirram's sword, and remembered the feeling, punching, punching, the red knife in his red hand, and shivered under his stolen cloak. 'Does a king stab women in the back?'

The tears were still wet on Nothing's wasted face. 'A good one sacrifices everything to win, and stabs who he must however he can. The great warrior is the one who still breathes when the crows feast. The great king is the one who watches the carcasses of his enemies burn. Let Father Peace spill tears over the methods. Mother War smiles upon results.'

'That's what my uncle would have said.'

'A wise man, then, and a worthy enemy. Perhaps you will stab him in the back and we can watch him burn together.'

Yarvi rubbed gently at the swollen bridge of his nose. The thought of more corpses on fire gave him scant comfort, no matter who they belonged to. Over and over the moment went through his mind, his eyes flicking to Ankran, giving him away, Shadikshirram spinning, the blade darting out. Over and over he sorted through the things he might have done differently, the things that might have left his friend alive, but he knew it was all wasted effort.

There was no going back.

Sumael turned, frowning into the night. 'Did anyone hear—'

'Hold!' echoed a voice from the darkness, harsh as a whip crack. Yarvi twisted about, heart leaping, and saw a tall warrior step through the archway. Huge, he seemed, in the light of the corpse-fire, bright helm and mail, strong sword and shield all gleaming.

'Give up your weapons!' came another call and a second man slipped from the shadows, a drawn bow levelled, long braids hanging about his face. A Vansterman, then. Others came after, and more, and within a breath or two a dozen warriors had formed a crescent about them.

Yarvi had not thought his spirits could drop further. Now he discovered the scale of his error.

Rulf's eyes drifted to his bow, well out of reach, and he slumped back on one elbow. 'Where do Vanstermen come on your list of the most worthy?'

Nothing nodded at them appraisingly. 'In these numbers, high enough.'

What strength the gods had given Yarvi he had more than used up that day. He poked Shadikshirram's sword away with his toe. Jaud raised his empty hands. Sumael held up her hatchet between finger and thumb and tossed it into the shadows.

'What about you, old man?' asked the first of the Vanstermen.

'I am considering my position.' Nothing gave his sword another grating stroke with the stone. It might as well have been applied directly to Yarvi's nerves.

'If steel is the answer they have a great deal of it,' he muttered.

'Put it down.' The second Vansterman full drew his bow. 'Or we'll burn your corpse with the rest.'

Nothing stabbed his sword point down into the earth, and sighed. 'He makes a persuasive case.'

Three of the Vanstermen started forward to gather the weapons and search them for more while their captain watched. 'What brings you five to Vansterland?'

'We are travellers . . .' said Yarvi, as he watched one of the warriors shake out the sorry contents of his pack. 'On our way to Vulsgard.'

The archer raised his brows at the pyre. 'Travellers burning corpses?'

'What is the world coming to when an honest man cannot burn corpses without suspicion?' asked Nothing.

'We were waylaid by bandits,' ventured Yarvi, thinking as fast as he was able.

'You should keep your country safe to travel,' said Rulf.

'Oh, we thank you for making us safer.' The captain peered at Yarvi's neck, then twitched Jaud's collar back to show the scars. 'Slaves.'

'Freed men,' said Sumael. 'I was their mistress. I am a merchant.' And she reached into her coat to carefully produce a crumpled piece of parchment. 'My name is Ebdel Aric Shadikshirram.'

The man frowned at the High King's licence, but recently removed from its rightful owner's corpse. 'You are ragged for a merchant.'

'I didn't say I was a good one.'

'And young,' said the captain.

'I didn't say I was an old one.'

'Where is your ship?'

'At sea.'

'Why are you not aboard?'

'I thought it wise to leave before it touched the bottom.'

'A poor merchant indeed,' muttered one of the men.

'With a cargo of lies,' said another.

The captain shrugged. 'The king can decide what to believe. Bind them.'

'King?' asked Yarvi, as he offered his wrists.

The man gave the thinnest of smiles. 'Grom-gil-Gorm has come north to hunt.'

So it seemed that Rulf was right. The next enemy was closer than any of them had thought.

FLOATING TWIGS

Yarvi was no stranger to hard men. His father had been one. His brother another. Dozens more had taken their turn in the training square each day in Thorlby. There had been hundreds gathered on the sand to see King Uthrik howed. To sail with young King Yarvi on his ill-fated raid to Amwend. Faces that smiled only in battle and hands worn to the shape of their weapons.

But he had never seen such a gathering as Grom-gil-Gorm had brought with him to hunt.

'I never saw so many Vanstermen in one place,' muttered Rulf. 'And I spent a year in Vulsgard.'

'An army,' grunted Nothing.

'And an ugly one,' said Jaud.

They bristled with weapons and puffed with menace, glared daggers and spoke swords. They wore their scars as proudly as a princess might her jewels while, by way of music, a woman's voice shrill as a whetstone keened out a love song to Mother War, of spilled blood and notched steel and lives lost too soon.

Into the midst of this bear pit, roped and hobbled helpless, between fires over which fresh carcasses dripped red gravy, Yarvi and his friends were herded stumbling at spearpoint.

'If you have a plan,' hissed Sumael from the corner of her mouth, 'now would be the time.'

'I have a plan,' said Nothing.

'Does it involve a sword?' asked Jaud.

A pause. 'All my plans do.'

'Do you have a sword?'

Another. 'No.'

'How will your plan work without one?' muttered Sumael.

A third. 'Death waits for us all.'

Where this company of killers was tightest knotted Yarvi saw the outline of a great chair, and upon it a great figure with a great cup in his great fist, but instead of the fear that might once have gripped him Yarvi felt the ticklings of opportunity. Not a plan, scarcely even an idea but, as Mother Gundring used to tell him, *drowning men must clutch at whatever twigs they find floating.*

'There are better things one can do with enemies than kill them,' he whispered.

Nothing snorted. 'And what would that be?'

'Make allies of them.' And Yarvi took a deep breath and roared out, 'Grom-gil-Gorm!' His voice smoked shrill and cracked and as far from kingly as could be imagined, but loud enough to be heard all about the camp, and that was what mattered. A hundred firelit faces turned towards him. 'King of Vansterland! Bloodiest son of Mother War! Breaker of Swords and maker of orphans, we meet again! I—'

A well-judged blow in the stomach drove his breath out in a mournful sigh. 'Stop your tongue before I rip it out, boy!' snarled the captain, shoving Yarvi coughing onto his knees.

But his words had their effect.

First a heavy silence settled, then an even heavier tread approached, and finally the sing-song voice of Grom-gil-Gorm himself. 'You bring guests!'

'Though they look like beggars.' And though he had not heard it since they put the collar on him, Yarvi knew the icy tone of Mother Scaer from his dreams.

'We found them in the elf-ruin above the river, my king,' said the captain.

'They do not have the look of elves,' said Gorm's minister.

'They were burning corpses.'

'A noble enterprise if they are the right ones,' said Gorm. 'You speak as though I know you, boy. Would you have me play a guessing game?'

Struggling for breath to speak, Yarvi raised his head, once again taking in the boots, the belt, the thrice-looped chain, and finally far above the craggy head of the King of Vansterland, most bitter enemy to his father, his country, his people.

'Last time we met . . . you offered me your knife.' And Yarvi fixed Gorm with his eye. On his knees, ragged and bloodied, beaten and bound, but fixed him still. 'You told me to seek you out if I changed my mind. Would you give it to me now?'

The King of Vansterland frowned, fingering that

chain of dead men's pommels about his trunk of a neck, and with the other hand pushed his many blades carefully into his belt. 'That might not be prudent.'

'I thought Mother War breathed on you in your crib, and it had been foreseen no man could kill you?'

'The gods help those who help themselves.' Mother Scaer grabbed Yarvi's jaw with bruising fingers and twisted his face into the light. 'It is the cook's boy caught at Amwend.'

'That it is,' murmured Gorm. 'But he is changed. He has a stern eye upon him now.'

Mother Scaer narrowed her own eyes. 'And you have lost the collar I gave you.'

'It chafed. I wasn't born to be a slave.'

'And yet you kneel again before me,' said Gorm. 'What were you born to be?'

His men spilled lickspittle laughs, but Yarvi had been laughed at all his life and it had lost its sting.

'The King of Gettland,' he said, and this time his voice was cold and hard as the Black Chair itself.

'Oh, gods,' he heard Sumael breathe. 'We're dead.'

Gorm gave a huge smile. 'Odem! You are younger than I remember.'

'I am Odem's nephew. Uthrik's son.'

The captain cuffed Yarvi across the back of the head and knocked him on his broken nose. Which was particularly galling, since with hands bound he could do nothing to break his fall. 'Uthrik's son died with him!'

'He had another son, fool!' Yarvi wriggled back onto his knees, mouth salty with blood. A taste he was tiring of.

Fingers were twisted in Yarvi's hair and he was dragged up. 'Shall I hire him for a jester or hang him for a spy?'

'That is not your place to decide.' Mother Scaer merely raised one finger, elf-bangles on her long arm rattling, but the captain let go as if he had been slapped. 'Uthrik did have a second son. Prince Yarvi. He was training for the Ministry.'

'But never took the test,' said Yarvi. 'I took the Black Chair instead.'

'So that the Golden Queen might keep her grip on power.'

'Laithlin. My mother.'

Mother Scaer considered him for a long moment, and Yarvi raised his chin and stared back in as close to a kingly manner as his bleeding nose, bound hands and stinking rags would allow. Perhaps it was enough, at least to plant the seed of doubt.

'Free his hands.'

Yarvi felt his ropes cut and, with a suitable sense of theatre, slowly held his left hand to the light. The muttering about the campfires at the sight of the twisted thing seemed for once most gratifying.

'Was this what you were looking for?' he asked.

Mother Scaer took it in hers, and turned it over, and kneaded at it with strong fingers. 'If you were student to Mother Gundring, whose student was she?'

Yarvi did not hesitate. 'She was taught by Mother Wexen, then minister to King Fynn of Throvenland, now Grandmother of the Ministry and first servant of the High King himself.'

'How many doves does she keep?'

'Three dozen, and one more with a black patch upon its brow that will carry news to Skekenhouse when Death opens the Last Door for her.'

'Of what wood is the door to the King of Gettland's bedchamber?'

Yarvi smiled. 'There is no door, for the king is one with the land and its people, and can have no secrets from them.'

The look of disbelief on Mother Scaer's gaunt face was the source of much rare satisfaction for Yarvi.

Grom-gil-Gorm raised one crag of brow. 'He spoke pure answers?'

'He did,' murmured his minister.

'Then . . . this crippled pup is truly Yarvi, son of Uthrik and Laithlin, the rightful King of Gettland?'

'So it would appear.'

'It's true?' croaked Rulf.

'It's true,' breathed Sumael.

Gorm was busy laughing. 'Then this has been my best hunting trip in many long years! Send a bird, Mother Scaer, and find out what King Odem will pay us for the return of his wayward nephew.' The King of Vansterland began to turn away.

Yarvi stopped him with a snort. 'The great and terrible Grom-gil-Gorm! In Gettland they call you a madman, drunk on blood. In Throvenland they call you a savage king of a savage land. In Skekenhouse, in the elf-built halls of the High King . . . why, there you hardly warrant mention.'

Yarvi heard Rulf give a worried grunt, the captain growling with suppressed fury, but Gorm only stroked thoughtfully at his beard. 'If you aim to flatter me you miss the mark. Your point?'

'Would you prove them right, and make so small a profit from the golden chance the gods have sent you?'

The King of Vansterland raised a brow at his minister. 'My ears are open to greater gains.'

Sell them what they want, Yarvi's mother always said, *not what you have*. 'Every spring you gather your warriors and raid across the border into Gettland.'

'It has been known.'

'And this spring?'

Gorm pursed his lips. 'A small jaunt perhaps. Mother War demands vengeance for your uncle's outrages at Amwend.'

Yarvi thought it best not to point out that he had been king at the start of those outrages if not their end. 'All I ask is that you push a little further this year. All the way to the walls of Thorlby itself.'

Mother Scaer hissed her disgust. 'Only that?'

But Gorm's curiosity was tickled. 'What would I gain for granting such a favour?'

Proud men like Yarvi's dead father, and his

259

murdered brother, and his drowned Uncle Uthil, would no doubt have spat their last breath in Grom-gil-Gorm's face rather than sought his help. But Yarvi had no pride. It had been shamed out of him by his father. Tricked out of him by Odem. Beaten out of him on the *South Wind*. Frozen out of him in the wasteland.

He had been kneeling all his life, to kneel a little longer was no hardship.

'Help me take back my throne, Grom-gil-Gorm, and I shall kneel in Odem's blood before you as King of Gettland, your vassal and subject.'

Nothing leaned close, hissing angrily through clenched teeth, 'Too high a price!'

Yarvi ignored him. 'Uthil, Uthrik and Odem. The brothers that have been your great enemies shall all three be gone through the Last Door and around the Shattered Sea you shall stand second in power only to the High King himself. Perhaps . . . in time . . . higher yet.'

The more powerful a man is, Mother Gundring always used to say, *the more he craves power.*

Gorm's voice was slightly hoarse. 'That would be a fine thing.'

'A fine thing indeed,' agreed Mother Scaer, her eyes narrower than ever as she glared at Yarvi. 'If it could be managed.'

'Only give me and my companions passage to Thorlby and I will make the attempt.'

'They are strange retainers you have gathered,' said Mother Scaer, eyeing them without enthusiasm.

'Strange circumstances demand them.'

'Who is this crooked creature?' asked Gorm. The others were wisely looking to the ground, but Nothing stared back unbowed, bright eyes burning.

'I am a proud Gettlander.'

'Ah, one of those.' Gorm smiled. 'Up here we prefer our Gettlanders shamed and bloody.'

'Pay him no mind, my king. He is Nothing.' And Yarvi brought Gorm's eyes back to his with the honeyed tone his mother used to use, for men of violence thrive on rage but know not what to do with reason and good sense. 'If I fail, you'll still have the plunder taken on your march south.'

Nothing growled his disgust, and small wonder. The towns of Gettland burning, the land ravaged, the people driven off or made slaves. Yarvi's land and Yarvi's people, but he was too deep in the mire now to return. The only way out was through, and to drown in the attempt or rise filthy but breathing on the other side. To take back the Black Chair he needed an army, and Mother War now placed their swords in his withered hand. Or their boots on his scarred neck, at least.

'You have all to gain,' he coaxed, softly, softly, 'nothing to lose.'

'There is the High King's favour,' said Mother Scaer. 'He has commanded that there be no war until his temple is finished—'

'There was a time Grandmother Wexen's eagles brought requests.' Gorm's sing-song voice held a note of anger now. 'Then they brought demands.

Now she sends commands. Where does it end, Mother Scaer?'

His minister spoke softly. 'The High King has the Lowlanders and most of the Inglings praying to his One God now, ready to fight and die at his order—'

'And does the High King rule Vansterland too?' scoffed Yarvi. 'Or does Grom-gil-Gorm?'

Mother Scaer's lip wrinkled. 'Don't play too close to the fire, boy. We all answer to someone.'

But Gorm was far away, already spreading flame and murder across the steadings of Gettland, no doubt. 'Thorlby has strong walls,' he murmured, 'and many strong warriors to man them. Too many. If I could take that city my skalds would already be singing of my victory.'

'Never,' whispered Nothing, but no one listened. The deal was done.

'That is the best thing of all,' crooned Yarvi. 'You need only wait outside. I will give you Thorlby.'

PART IV

THE RIGHTFUL KING

CROWS

Yarvi pulled the fur collar of his borrowed cloak up against the wind and wrinkled his nose at the salt tang of the sea. That and the stink of the slaves pulling the oars. He had grown used to it when he was one of them, slept with his face in Rulf's armpit and scarcely noticed. He had stunk just as bad as the rest, he knew. But that made their smell no better now.

All the worse, in fact.

'Poor dogs.' Jaud frowned over the rail of the aftcastle at them struggling below. For such a strong man he had a weak heart.

Rulf scrubbed at the grey-brown hair that had sprouted above his ears, though his pate was bald as ever. 'Be nice to set 'em free.'

'Then how would we get to Thorlby?' said Yarvi. 'Someone has to row. Will you pull an oar?'

His old oarmates both looked sharply across at him. 'You have changed,' said Jaud.

'I've had to.' And he turned away from them and the benches where he had once struggled. Sumael stood at the rail, a huge smile on her face as the salt wind tore at her hair, grown longer now than it had been, black as raven's feathers.

'You look pleased,' said Yarvi, happy to see her happy. He had not seen it often enough.

'Glad to be on the sea again.' She spread her arms wide, wriggling her fingers. 'And with no chains!'

He felt his smile fade, for he still had a chain he could not break. The one he had forged himself with his own oath. The one that drew him back to Thorlby, and bound him to the Black Chair. And he knew then that sooner or later Sumael would stand at the rail of another ship. One that would carry her back to the First of Cities, and away from him forever.

Her smile faltered too, as though she had the same thought at the same moment, and they looked away from each other to watch Father Earth grinding by in awkward silence.

For two lands so bitterly opposed, Vansterland and Gettland looked very much the same. Barren beaches, forest and fen. He had seen few people, and those hurrying inland, fearful at the sight of a ship. Narrowing his eyes to the south, he saw a little tooth upon a headland, the smoke of houses smudging the white sky.

'What's that town?' he asked Sumael.

'Amwend,' she said. 'Near the border.'

Amwend, where he had led the raid. Or flopped from a ship without a shield and straight into a trap, at least. That was the tower, then, where Keimdal had died. Where Hurik had betrayed him. From which Odem had thrown him down, down into the bitter sea, and even more bitter slavery.

Yarvi realized he had ground his shrivelled hand into the rail until it hurt. He turned his eyes away from land, towards the white-churned water in their wake, the marks of the oars quickly fading to leave no sign of their passing. Would it be so with him? Faded and forgotten?

Sister Owd, the apprentice Mother Scaer had sent with them, was looking straight at him. A furtive sort of look, then quickly down at something she was writing on a tiny slip of paper, tugged and twitched under her charcoal by the wind.

Yarvi walked slowly to her. 'Keeping an eye on me?'

'You know I am,' she said, without looking up. 'That's what I'm here for.'

'Do you doubt me?'

'I just tell Mother Scaer what I see. She chooses what to doubt.'

She was small and round-faced, one of those people whose age is hard to guess, but even so Yarvi did not think she could be older than him. 'When did you take the Minister's Test?'

'Two years ago,' she said, shielding the little slip of paper with her shoulder.

He gave up trying to see it. Ministers have their own signs anyway: he doubted he could read them. 'What was it like?'

'Not hard, if you're prepared.'

'I was prepared,' said Yarvi, thinking back to that

night Odem came in out of the rain. The flames reflected in the jars, the creases in Mother Gundring's smile, the purity of question and answer. He felt a surge of longing, then, for that simple life with no uncles to kill or oaths to keep or hard choices to be made. For the books and the plants and the soft word spoken. He had to force it away to the back of his mind with an effort. He could not afford it now. 'But I never got the chance to take it.'

'You didn't miss much. A lot of fussing outside the door. A lot of being stared at by old women.' She finished the message and began to roll it up into a tiny pellet. 'Then the honour of being kissed by Grandmother Wexen.'

'How was that?'

Sister Owd puffed out her cheeks and gave a long sigh. 'Wisest of all women she may be, but I was hoping my last kiss would be from someone younger. I saw the High King, from a distance.'

'So did I, once. He seemed small, and old, and greedy, and complained about everything, and was scared of his food. But he had many strong warriors with him.'

'Time hasn't changed him much, then. Except he worships the One God now, he's more gripped with his own power than ever, and by all accounts can't stay awake longer than an hour at a time. And those warriors have multiplied.' She rolled up the canvas cover on the cage. The birds inside did not move, did not startle at the light, only stared levelly at Yarvi with half a dozen pairs of unblinking eyes. Black birds.

Yarvi frowned at them. 'Crows?'

'Yes.' Sister Owd pulled up her sleeve, unhooked the tiny door and skilfully wormed a white arm inside the cage, took a crow about the body and drew it out, still and calm as a bird made from coal. 'Mother Scaer hasn't used doves for years.'

'Not at all?'

'Not since I've been her apprentice.' She made the message fast about the bird's ankle and spoke softly. 'The rumour is a dove sent from Mother Gundring tried to claw her face. She doesn't trust them.' She leaned close to the black bird and cooed, 'We are a day from Thorlby.'

'Thorlby,' spoke the crow in its croaking voice, then Sister Owd flicked it into the skies where it clattered away to the north.

'Crows,' murmured Yarvi, watching it skim the white-flecked waves.

'Promises of obedience to your master, Grom-gil-Gorm?' Nothing stood beside Yarvi, still hugging his sword like a lover even though he had a perfectly good sheath for it now.

'He's my ally, not my master,' answered Yarvi.

'Of course. You are a slave no longer.' Nothing rubbed gently at the scars all about his stubbled neck. 'I remember our collars coming off, in that friendly farmstead. Before Shadikshirram burned it. No slave, you. And yet you made the deal with the Vanstermen kneeling.'

269

'We were all on our knees at the time,' growled Yarvi.

'My question is, are we still? You will win few friends when you take back the Black Chair with the help of Gettland's worst enemy.'

'I can win friends once I'm in the chair. It's getting enemies out of it that concerns me now. What should I have done? Let the Vanstermen burn us?'

'Perhaps there was middle ground between letting Gorm kill us and selling him the land of our birth.'

'Middle ground has been hard to find of late,' Yarvi forced through gritted teeth.

'It always is, but a king's place is upon it. There will be a price for this, I think.'

'You are quick with the questions but tardy on the answers, Nothing. Did you not swear an oath to help me?'

Nothing narrowed his eyes at Yarvi, the wind blowing up and lashing the grey hair about his battle-beaten face. 'I swore an oath, and mean to see it through or die.'

'Good,' said Yarvi, turning away. 'I will hold you to it.'

Below them the oar-slaves were working up a sweat, teeth clenched at their benches, grunting in time as the overseer stalked between them, whip coiled behind his back. Just as Trigg had done on the deck of the *South Wind*. Yarvi remembered well enough the burning in his muscles, the burning of the lash across his back.

But the closer he came to the Black Chair the heavier weighed his oath, and the shorter grew his patience.

Someone has to row.

'More speed!' he growled at the overseer.

YOUR ENEMY'S HOUSE

Sumael sprang from ship to jetty and shoved through the press to the table where Thorlby's dockmistress sat flanked by guards. Yarvi followed with a little less agility and a lot less authority across the gangplank, onto the ground that should have been his kingdom, eyes down and hood up, the others at his back.

'My name is Shadikshirram,' Sumael said, flicking the paper carelessly open and dropping it onto the table, 'and I carry a licence to trade from the High King, stamped with the rune of Grandmother Wexen herself.'

They had waited until the most junior dockmistress took her turn at the table in the hope she would wave them through. Instead she frowned at the licence long enough for everyone to get twitchy, fingering the two keys about her neck, one of her household and one of her office. Yarvi noticed with a wave of sick nerves that one corner of the licence was brown with old blood. The blood of its rightful owner, indeed, and spilled by Yarvi's own hand. The dockmistress peered up at Sumael, and spoke the words he had been dreading.

'You're not Shadikshirram.' One of the guards shifted his gloved hand slightly on the haft of his spear, and Nothing shifted his thumb in his belt towards his sword, and Yarvi's sickness swelled to dread. Would it all end here, in an ugly little brawl on the docks? 'I saw her come ashore here often, usually drunk—'

Sumael dealt the tabletop a fearsome blow, snarling into the dockmistress's face and making her shrink back, astonished. 'You speak of my mother, Ebdel Aric Shadikshirram, and you'll speak with more respect! She is gone through the Last Door. Drowned in the icy waters of the North.' Her voice cracked, and she dabbed at her dry eyes with the back of her hand. 'Her business she entrusted to me, her loving daughter Sumael Shadikshirram.' She snatched the licence back from the table and shouted again, flecking dockmistress, guards, and Yarvi too with spit. 'And I have business with Queen Laithlin!'

'She is queen no—'

'You know who I speak of! Where is Laithlin?'

'Usually at her counting house—'

'I will have words with her!' And Sumael turned on her heel and stalked off up the jetty.

'She may not take visitors . . .' the dockmistress muttered weakly after her.

Sister Owd gave the table a friendly pat as Yarvi and the rest filed past. 'If it's any consolation, she's like this with everyone.'

'A winning performance,' said Yarvi as he caught

up to Sumael, hurrying past the fish hanging and the nets heaped and the fishers shouting prices for the morning's catch. 'What would we do without you?'

'I nearly wet myself,' she hissed back. 'Is anyone following?'

'Not even looking.' The dockmistress was busy venting her frustrations on the next arrival and they soon left her behind.

Home at last, but Yarvi felt like a stranger. It all seemed smaller than he remembered, less busy, berths and stalls standing empty, buildings abandoned. His heart leapt whenever he saw a familiar face and, like a thief passing the place of his crime, he shrank further into his hood, back prickling with sweat despite the cold.

If he was recognized King Odem would soon hear of it, and lose no time in finishing what began on the roof of Amwend's tower.

'Those are the howes of your ancestors, then?'

Nothing was staring through his tangle of hair towards the North, down the long and lonely sweep of beach and the file of grassy humps above it, the nearest with just a few months of patchy green on its fallow flanks.

'Of my murdered father Uthrik.' Yarvi worked his jaw. 'And my drowned uncle Uthil, and kings of Gettland back into the darkness of history.'

Nothing scratched at his grizzled cheek. 'Before them you swore your oath.'

'As before me you swore yours.'

'Never fear.' Nothing grinned as they threaded through a crowded gate in the outermost wall of the city. That mad, bright-eyed grin that gave Yarvi more fears rather than less. 'Flesh may forget, but steel never does.'

Sister Owd seemed to know the ways of Thorlby better even than Yarvi, its native son. Its king. She led them up narrow streets zigzagging the steep hillside, houses crammed tall and narrow between outcroppings of rock, the grey bones of Gettland showing through the city's skin. She led them across bridges over surging streams where slaves leaned out to fill the jugs of the wealthy. She led them finally to a long, slim yard in the shadow of the lowering citadel where Yarvi had been born, and raised, and daily humiliated, and studied to be a minister, and found out he was a king.

'The house is here,' said Sister Owd. It was in plain sight. One Yarvi had often walked past.

'Why does Gorm's minister keep a house in Thorlby?'

'Mother Scaer says the wise minister knows her enemy's house better than her own.'

'Mother Scaer is as prone to pithy phrases as Mother Gundring,' grunted Yarvi.

Owd turned the key. 'It's what the Ministry is all about.'

'Take Jaud with you,' Yarvi drew Sumael to one side and spoke softly to her. 'Go to the counting house and speak to my mother.' If his luck held, Hurik would be at the training square now.

'And say what?' asked Sumael. 'That her dead son has come calling?'

'And that he's finally learned to fasten his cloak-buckle. Bring her here.'

'What if she doesn't believe me?'

Yarvi pictured his mother's face, then, as she used to frown down at him, and thought it very likely she would doubt. 'Then we must think of something else.'

'And if she doesn't believe me, and orders me dead for the insult?'

Yarvi paused. 'Then *I* must think of something else.'

'Who among you has been sent bad weatherluck or bad weaponluck?' came a ringing voice from across the square. A crowd had gathered before a grand building, new-raised, pillars of white marble at its front, and before them a priest in robes of humble sack cloth stood with arms spread and wailed his message. 'Who among you finds their prayers to the many gods ignored?'

'My prayers were ignored so much I stopped making 'em,' muttered Rulf.

'It would be small wonder!' called out the priest. 'For there are not many gods but one! All the arts of the elves could not break her! The arms of the One God, and the gates of her temple, are flung wide for all!'

'Temple?' Yarvi frowned. 'My mother built that place to be a mint. They were going to stamp coins there, every one the same weight.' Now the seven-rayed sun of the One God – the High King's god – was raised above the doorway.

'Her comfort, her mercy, her shelter, is freely given!' roared the priest. 'Her only demand is that you love her as she loves you!'

Nothing spat on the stones. 'What have gods to do with love?'

'Things have changed here,' said Yarvi, glancing about the square and pulling his hood a little lower.

'New king,' said Sumael, licking at her scarred lip, 'new ways.'

GREAT STAKES

They heard the door open, and Yarvi stiffened. They heard footsteps in the hallway, and Yarvi swallowed with an effort. The door swung open and Yarvi took a halting step towards it, hardly able to breathe—

Two slaves ducked through, hands on their swords. Two huge-shouldered Inglings with silver collars. Nothing bristled, steel glinting as he drew.

'No!' said Yarvi. He knew these two. Slaves of his mother's.

And now their owner swept into the room with Sumael just behind.

She was not changed.

Tall and stern, golden hair oiled and piled in shining coils. She wore few jewels but those of humbling size. The great Queen's Key, key to the treasury of Gettland, was gone from her chain, and in its place was a smaller, set with dark rubies like drops of spilled blood.

Yarvi might have had trouble convincing his companions he was a king, but his mother filled that small room to its corners with an effortless majesty.

'Gods,' croaked Rulf, and with a wince lowered himself to his knees, and Sister Owd, and Jaud and Sumael, and the two slaves hurried to follow him. Nothing knelt last, eyes and sword's point on the floor, so that only Yarvi and his mother were left standing.

She did not so much as acknowledge them. She stared at Yarvi, and he at her, as though they were alone. She walked to him, neither smiling nor frowning, until she stood but a stride away, and she seemed to him so beautiful it hurt his eyes to look at her, and he felt in them the burning of tears.

'My son,' she whispered, and folded him in her arms. 'My son.' And she held him so tight that it was almost painful, and her tears wetted his head while his wetted her shoulder.

Yarvi had come home.

It was some time before his mother let him go, and held him at arm's length, and carefully wiped her cheeks. He realized he looked up into her face no longer. He had grown, then. Grown in many ways.

'It seems your friend spoke the truth,' she said.

Yarvi slowly nodded. 'I am alive.'

'And have learned to fasten your cloak-buckle,' she said, giving it a searching tug and finding it secure.

In silence she listened to his story.

In silence she heard of the raid and the burning of Amwend. Of Odem's betrayal and Yarvi's long fall into the bitter sea.

Shall Gettland have half a king?

In silence she heard him made a slave, and sold a slave, only her eyes moving to the faint scars on his neck.

These are some wretched leavings.

In silence he made his escape, endured the long ordeal in the ice, fought for his life in the elf-ruin, and all the while Yarvi thought what a song it would make if he lived to have it set to music.

You cannot expect all the heroes to survive a good song.

And when it came to Ankran's death and then to Shadikshirram's, Yarvi thought of the red knife in his hand, and his grunting and hers, and his throat closed, and he shut his eyes and could not speak.

You may need two hands to fight someone, but only one to stab them in the back.

Then he felt his mother's hand on his. 'I am proud. Your father would have been proud. All that matters is that you have come back to me.'

'Thanks to these four,' said Yarvi, swallowing sour spit.

Yarvi's mother swept his companions with her searching gaze. 'You all have my thanks.'

'It was nothing,' grunted Nothing, eyes locked to the floor, face hidden behind his tangle of hair.

'My honour,' said Jaud, bowing his head.

'We couldn't have made it without him,' muttered Rulf.

'He was a sore pain in my arse every mile,' said

Sumael. 'If I had it to do again I'd leave him in the sea.'

'And then where would you find a ship to take you home?' asked Yarvi, grinning at her.

'Oh, I would think of something else,' she said, grinning back.

Yarvi's mother did not join them. She took in every detail of the look they gave each other, and her eyes narrowed. 'What is my son to you, girl?'

Sumael blinked, and her dark cheek coloured. 'I . . .' Yarvi had never seen her at a loss for words before.

'She is my friend,' he said. 'She risked her life for mine. She is my oarmate.' He paused for a moment. 'She is my family.'

'Is that so?' Yarvi's mother still glared at Sumael, who was now studying the floor with minute interest. 'Then she must be mine also.'

In truth Yarvi was far from sure what they were to each other, and less than keen to put it to the test before his mother. 'Things have changed here.' He nodded towards the window, the entreaties of the One God's priest coming faint from outside.

'Things lie in ruins here.' His mother's eyes came back to his, and angrier than ever. 'I had only just taken off my black for your death when an eagle came to Mother Gundring. An invitation to the High King's wedding in Skekenhouse.'

'Did you go?'

She snorted. 'I was, and am, reluctant to attend.'

'Why?'

'Because Grandmother Wexen has me in mind for the bride, Yarvi.'

Yarvi's eyes went wide. 'Oh.'

'Yes. Oh. They think to chain me to the key of that withered old remnant and have me spin them gold out of straw. Meanwhile your snake of an uncle and his worm of a daughter frustrate me at every turn, and do their damnedest to destroy all I have built here.'

'Isriun?' muttered Yarvi, with the slightest croak in his throat. He almost added, 'my betrothed,' but with a glance at Sumael thought it best to stop short.

'I know her name,' growled his mother. 'I choose not to use it. They break agreements years in the making, turn hard-won friends to enemies in a moment, seize the goods of foreign merchants and drive them from the market. If their aim was to ruin Gettland they could not have done a finer job. They have given my mint over as a temple to the High King's false god, you saw that?'

'Something of the kind—'

'One God standing above all others, just as one High King sits above all others.' She barked a joyless laugh that made Yarvi jump. 'I fight them, but I am losing ground. They do not understand the battlefield, but they have the Black Chair. They have the key to the treasury. I have fought them every day, with every weapon and strategy—'

'Except the sword,' grunted Nothing, without looking up.

Yarvi's mother turned her dagger gaze on him.

'That will be next. But Odem takes no chances with his safety, and has all the warriors of Gettland behind him. I have no more than two score men in my household. There is Hurik—'

'No,' said Yarvi. 'Hurik is Odem's man. He tried to kill me.'

His mother's eyes widened. 'Hurik is my Chosen Shield. He would never betray me—'

'He betrayed me easily enough.' Yarvi remembered Keimdal's blood speckling his face. 'Believe me. It is a moment I am not likely to forget.'

She bared her teeth and placed one trembling fist upon the table. 'I will see him drowned in the mire. But to beat Odem we will need an army.'

Yarvi licked his lips. 'I have one on the way.'

'Did I lose a son and gain a magician? From where?'

'Vansterland,' said Nothing.

There was a stony pause then. 'I see.' Yarvi's mother turned her glare on Sister Owd, who ventured an apologetic smile, then cleared her throat and looked down at the floor. Few looked elsewhere when his mother was in the room. 'You forged an alliance with Grom-gil-Gorm? The man who killed your father and sold you as a slave?'

'He did not kill my father. I am sure of that.' Three-quarters sure, at least. 'Odem killed your husband and your son, his own brother and nephew. And we must seize the allies the wind blows us.'

'What was Gorm's price?'

Yarvi worked his tongue around his dry mouth.

He should have known the Golden Queen would miss no detail of a deal. 'That I would kneel before him and be his vassal.' And from the corner of the room Nothing gave an angry grunt.

His mother's eye twitched. 'Their king kneeling before their most hated enemy? What will our people think of such a devil's bargain?'

'Once Odem is sunk in the midden they can think what they will. Better a king on my knees than a beggar on my feet. I can stand later.'

A smile touched the corner of her mouth. 'You are far more my son than your father's.'

'And proud to be so.'

'Still. Would you unleash that butcher in Thorlby? Make our city a slaughter-yard?'

'He'll only act as bait for the city's warriors,' said Yarvi. 'Lure them out so the citadel is lightly manned. We'll enter by the tunnels beneath the rock, seal the Screaming Gate, and take Odem while he's unguarded. Can you find enough good men for that?'

'Perhaps. I think so. But your uncle is no fool. What if he will not spring your trap? What if he keeps his men in the citadel and bides his time in safety?'

'And seem a coward while the Breaker of Swords mocks him from his very doorstep?' Yarvi sat forward, staring into his mother's eyes. 'No. I have sat where he sits and I know his mind. Odem is new to the Black Chair. He has no great victories to sing of. And he has the memory of my father, and the legend of my Uncle Uthil to contend with.' And Yarvi smiled, for he knew how it felt to lurk always in the shadow of a better brother. 'Odem will not give up a golden chance to do what his brothers never could. Defeat Grom-gil-Gorm and prove himself a mighty war leader.'

His mother's smile spread, and Yarvi wondered whether he had ever seen her look at him with admiration before. 'Your brother may have got more than his share of the fingers, but the gods kept all the wits for you. You have become a deep-cunning man, Yarvi.'

It seemed that empathy, properly used, could be a deadly weapon. 'My years training for the Ministry were not wasted. Still, help from someone close to Odem would only sweeten our chances. We could go to Mother Gundring—'

'No. She is Odem's minister.'

'She is my minister.'

Yarvi's mother shook her head. 'At best her loyalties would be split. Who knows what she would judge the greater good? There is already so much that could go wrong.'

'But so much to win. Great stakes mean great risks.'

'So they do.' She stood, shaking out her skirts, and looked down at him in wonder. 'When did my favourite son become a gambler?'

'When his uncle threw him into the sea and stole his birthright.'

'He underestimated you, Yarvi. And so did I. But

I am glad to learn my error.' Her smile faded and her voice took on a deadly edge. 'His will bring him a bloody reckoning. Send your bird to Grom-gil-Gorm, little sister. Tell him we most keenly await his arrival.'

Sister Owd bowed very low. 'I will, my queen, but . . . once I do, there can be no going back.'

Yarvi's mother barked a joyless laugh. 'Ask your mistress, Sister. I am not one for going back.' She reached across the table and placed her strong hand on Yarvi's weak. 'Nor is my son.'

IN DARKNESS

'This is a bastard of a risk,' whispered Rulf, his words deadened in the darkness.

'Life is a risk,' answered Nothing. 'All things, from birth on.'

'A man can still rush at the Last Door naked and screaming or tread softly the other way.'

'Death will usher us all through regardless,' said Nothing. 'I choose to face her.'

'Can I choose to be elsewhere the next time?'

'Enough of your squabbling!' hissed Yarvi. 'You're like old hounds over the last bone!'

'We can't all act like kings,' muttered Rulf, with more than a little irony. Perhaps when you've watched a man make soil every day in a bucket beside you, it is hard to accept he sits between gods and men.

Bolts squealed with the rust of years and in a shower of dust the gate swung open. One of his mother's Inglings was crammed into the narrow archway beyond, frowning down at them.

'Were you seen?' asked Yarvi.

The slave shook his head, turned, and plodded up the narrow stair, stooped under the low ceiling. Yarvi wondered if he could be trusted. His mother thought so. But then she had trusted Hurik. Yarvi had grown out of the childish notion that his parents knew everything.

He had grown out of all sorts of notions over the past few months.

The stair opened out into a great cave, the ragged rock of the ceiling crusted with teeth of lime, each hung with its own dewdrop, sparkling in the light of their torches.

'We're under the citadel?' asked Rulf, peering nervously up at the unimaginable weight of stone above their heads.

'The rock is riddled with passages,' said Yarvi. 'With ancient elf-tunnels and newer cellars. With hidden doors and spy-holes. Some kings, and all ministers, sometimes want to go unobserved. But no one knows these ways like me. I spent half my childhood in the shadows. Hiding from my father or my brother. Creeping from one place of solitude to another. Seeing while unseen, and pretending I was part of what I saw. Making up a life where I wasn't an outcast.'

'A sad story,' murmured Nothing.

'Wretched.' Yarvi thought of his younger self, weeping in the darkness, wishing someone would find him but knowing they did not care enough to look, and shook his head in disgust at his own past weakness. 'But it might still have a happy ending.'

'It might.' Nothing let one hand brush the wall beside them. A face of jointless elf-stone, thousands of years old and smooth as if it had been laid yesterday. 'This way your mother's men can enter the citadel unseen.'

'As Odem's file out above to face Grom-gil-Gorm.'

The Ingling held out his arm to stop them.

The passageway ended at a round shaft. Far above a little circle of light, far below the faint glimmer of water. A stair wound about it, a stair so narrow Yarvi had to edge up sideways, shoulder-blades scraping the smooth elf-stone, toes of his boots grazing the brink, sweat springing from his forehead. Halfway up there came a whirring from above and he flinched as something flashed past his face, might have toppled forward had Rulf not caught his arm.

'Wouldn't want your reign cut short by a bucket.'

It splashed down far below and Yarvi breathed a long sigh. The last thing he needed was another plunge into cold water.

Women's voices echoed around them, strangely loud.

'. . . she still says no.'

'Would you want to marry that old husk after you'd been wife to a man like Uthrik?'

'Her wants don't come into it. If a king sits between gods and men, the High King sits between kings and gods. No one says no to him forever . . .'

They shuffled on. More shadows, more steps, more shameful memories, walls of rough stone laid by the hands of men that seemed older but were thousands of years newer than the tunnels below, daylight winking through grated openings near the ceiling.

'How many men has the queen bought?' asked Rulf.

'Thirty-three,' said the Ingling over his shoulder. 'So far.'

'Good men?'

'Men.' The Ingling shrugged. 'They will kill or die according to their luck.'

'Of how many could Odem say the same?' asked Nothing.

'Many,' said the Ingling.

'This might be a quarter of them.' Yarvi went up on tiptoes to squint through a grate into the light.

Today's training square had been set out in the yard of the citadel, the ancient cedar at one corner. The warriors were at shield-practice, forming walls and wedges and breaking them apart, steel flashing in the thin sun, clattering against wood, the scrape of shuffling feet. The instructions of Master Hunnan came brittle on the cold air, to lock shields, to keep by the shoulder-man, to thrust low, the way they used to be barked at Yarvi, to precious little good.

'That is a great number of men,' said Nothing, prone to understate the case.

'Well-trained and battle-hardened men, on their own ground,' added Rulf.

'My ground,' Yarvi forced through his gritted teeth. He led them on, every step, stone, turning familiar. 'See there?' He drew Rulf next to him, pressing him against another narrow grate with a view of the citadel's one gateway. The doors of studded wood stood open, flanked by guards, but in the shadows at the top of the archway burnished copper gleamed.

'The Screaming Gate,' he whispered.

'Why that name?' asked Rulf. 'Because of the screams we'll make when this goes wrong?'

'Never mind the name. It drops from above to seal the citadel. Six ministers made the mechanism. A single silver pin holds it up. It's always guarded, but a hidden stair leads to the room. When the day comes, Nothing and I will take a dozen men and hold it. Rulf, you'll take archers to the roof, ready to make pincushions of my uncle's guards.'

'No doubt they'll make fine ones.'

'When the moment is ripe we pull the pin, the gate drops, and Odem is trapped inside.' Yarvi pictured the horror on his uncle's face as the Screaming Gate fell and he wished, not for the first time, that doing a thing was as simple as saying it.

'Odem is trapped . . .' Nothing's eyes glinted in the darkness. 'And so are we.'

There was cheering in the yard as the latest exercise came to its end. One side the winner, the other laid low.

Yarvi nodded towards the silent Ingling. 'My mother's slave will show you the ways. Learn them.'

'Where are you going?' asked Rulf, and then added uncertainly, 'My king.'

'There's something I have to do.'

★　★　★

Holding his breath lest the slightest sound betray him, Yarvi eased through the fusty darkness toward the hidden door between the legs of Father Peace, pressed himself to the spy-slot and peered through into the Godshall.

It was before noon and the King of Gettland was in his proper place – the Black Chair. Its back was toward Yarvi, so he could not see Odem's face, only the outline of his shoulders, the gleam of the King's Circle in his hair. Mother Gundring sat on her stool at his right hand, arm trembling with the effort of holding up her minister's staff.

Below the dais, making a sea of dim-lit faces, were the great and good of Gettland, or at least the mean and meagre, best buckles and keys polished, faces pressed into servile smiles. The same men and women who had wept as Yarvi's father was howed up, and wondered wherever they would find his like again. Not in his crippled joke of a younger son, that was sure.

And standing unbowed upon the steps below the chair with Hurik looming at her back, was Yarvi's mother.

He could not see Odem's face, but he heard the false king's voice echo in the hallowed space. As calm and reasoned as it had always been. As patient as winter, and Yarvi felt a wintry shiver at the sound of it. 'Might I enquire of our honoured sister when she intends to travel to Skekenhouse?'

'As soon as I am able, my king,' answered Yarvi's mother. 'I have pressing matters of business that—'

'I wear the key to the treasury now.'

Yarvi peered from the corner of the slot, and saw Isriun sitting on the other side of the Black Chair. His betrothed. Not to mention his brother's. She wore the key to the treasury around her neck, and by all appearances it weighed less heavily than she had once feared. 'I can resolve your business, Laithlin.'

She sounded little like the nervous girl who had sung her quavering promises to him in this very chamber. He remembered her eyes shining as she touched the Black Chair, and saw them shine now as she glanced at her father sitting in it.

It seemed Yarvi was not the only one changed since he sailed for Amwend.

'See to it soon,' came Odem's voice.

'That you may stand as High Queen over us all,' added Mother Gundring, lifting high her staff for just a moment, elf-metal darkly gleaming.

'Or kneel as Grandmother Wexen's book-keeper,' snapped Yarvi's mother.

There was a pause, then Odem said softly, 'There are worse fates, sister. We must do our duty. We must do what is best for Gettland. See to it.'

'My king,' she forced through gritted teeth as she bowed, and though Yarvi had often dreamed of it, he felt a burning anger at seeing her humbled.

'Now leave me with the gods,' said Odem, waving away his retainers. The doors were opened, the great men and women bowed their bottomless respect and filed out into the light. Yarvi's mother went among them, Hurik beside her, and Mother Gundring after them, and Isriun last of all, smiling back at her father in the doorway as she had once smiled back at Yarvi.

The doors were closed with an echoing boom, and a heavy silence settled, and with a groan Odem wrenched himself up from the Black Chair as though it burned him to sit in it. He turned, and Yarvi found the breath stopped in his chest.

His uncle's face was just as he remembered it. Strong, with hard lines in the cheeks and silver in the beard. So like Yarvi's father, but with a softness and a care not even his own son could ever find in King Uthrik's face.

The hate should have flooded in, and swept away all Yarvi's fears, and drowned his nagging doubts that ripping the Black Chair back from his uncle's clutches might not be worth the blood it would surely cost.

But instead, when he saw the face of his enemy, the killer of his family and thief of his kingdom, Yarvi's heart betrayed him, and he felt of all things a choking surge of love. For the only one in his family who had ever given him kindness. Had ever made him feel that he was liked. Had ever made him feel he was worth liking. Next came a choking sorrow at the loss of that man, and Yarvi felt tears in his eyes, and he ground his twisted knuckles into the cold stone beside him, hating himself for his weakness.

'Stop looking at me!'

Yarvi jerked back from the slot but Odem's gaze was fixed high above. He walked slowly, the taps of his footfalls echoing in the velvet dimness of that great space.

'Have you deserted me?' he called out. 'As I have deserted you?'

He was speaking to the amber statues set about the dome. He was speaking to the gods, and his cracking voice was anything but calm. Now he lifted off the King's Circle Yarvi had once worn and with a wince rubbed at the marks left on his forehead.

'What could I do?' he whispered, so quietly Yarvi could scarcely hear it. 'We all serve someone. For everything there is a price.'

And Yarvi thought of Odem's last words to him, sharp as knives in his memory.

You would have been a fine jester. But is my daughter really to have a one-handed weakling for a husband? A crippled puppet dangling on his mother's string?

And now the hate boiled up, hot and reassuring. Had he not sworn an oath? For his father. For his mother.

For himself.

With the faintest ringing, the point of Shadikshirram's sword left the sheath, and Yarvi pressed the knobbled fist of his left hand against the hidden door. One good shove would send it swinging, he knew. One shove, and three steps, and a thrust of the blade could end this. He licked his lips, and worked his hand about the grip, setting his shoulders for the effort, the blood surging at his temples—

'Enough!' roared Odem, the echoes ringing, and Yarvi froze again. His uncle had snatched up the King's Circle and twisted it back on. 'What's done is done!' He shook his fist towards the ceiling. 'If you wanted it otherwise, why did you not stop me?' And he spun on his heel and strode from the chamber.

'They have sent me to do it,' whispered Yarvi, sliding Shadikshirram's sword back into its sheath. Not now. Not yet. Not as easily as that. But his doubts were burned away.

Even if he had to sink Thorlby in blood.

Odem had to die.

A FRIEND'S FIGHT

Yarvi strained at the oar, knowing the whip was over him. He tugged and snarled, plucked even with the stub of finger on his useless hand, but how could he move it alone?

Mother Sea burst roaring into the hold of the *South Wind* and Yarvi fumbled desperately with the ladder, watched the men straining against their chains for a last breath as the water surged over their faces.

'Clever children drown just like stupid ones,' said Trigg, blood running from the neat split in his skull.

Yarvi took one more floundering step in the merciless snow, slipped and teetered on hot rock smooth as glass. However he ran the dogs were always snapping at his heels.

Grom-gil-Gorm's bared teeth were red and his face blood-dashed and Yarvi's fingers threaded on his necklace. 'I am coming,' he sang like the clanging of a bell. 'And Mother War comes with me!'

'Are you ready to kneel?' asked Mother Scaer, arms covered in flashing elf-bangles and the crows on her shoulders laughing, laughing.

'He is on his knees already,' said Odem, elbows upon the black arms of the Black Chair.

'He always has been,' said Isriun, smiling, smiling.

'We all serve someone,' said Grandmother Wexen, a hungry brightness in her eye.

'Enough!' hissed Yarvi. 'Enough!'

And he flung open the hidden door and lashed out with the curved sword. Ankran's eyes bulged as the blade slid through him. 'Steel is the answer,' he croaked.

Shadikshirram grunted and elbowed and Yarvi punched at her, and metal squelched in flesh, and she smiled at him over her shoulder.

'He is coming,' she whispered. 'He is coming.'

Yarvi woke wet with sweat, tangled with his blankets, stabbing at his mattress.

A devil's face loomed over him, made of flame and shadow and stinking of smoke. He shrank away, then gasped in relief as he realized it was Rulf, a torch in his hand against the darkness.

'Grom-gil-Gorm is coming,' he said.

Yarvi tore free of his blankets. Sounds echoed distorted through the shutters at the window. Crashing. Shouting. The clangour of bells.

'He's crossed the border with more than a thousand men. Might be a hundred thousand depending on what rumour you listen to.'

Yarvi tried to blink away his dream. 'Already?'

'He moves quick as fire and spreads as much chaos.

The messengers barely outrode him. He's only three days from the city. Thorlby's in uproar.'

Downstairs the faintest grey of dawn was leaking through the shutters and across pale faces. The faintest smell of smoke tickled Yarvi's nose. Smoke and fear. Faintly he could hear the priest outside calling in a broken voice for folk to kneel before the One God and be saved.

To kneel before the High King and be made slaves.

'Your crows fly swiftly, Sister Owd,' said Yarvi.

'I told you they would, my king.' Yarvi flinched at the word. It still sounded like a joke to him. It was a joke, and would be until Odem was dead.

He looked at the faces of his oarmates. Sumael and Jaud each nursing their own kind of fear. Nothing with hungry smile and polished sword both unsheathed.

'This is my fight,' said Yarvi. 'If any of you want to leave, I won't blame you.'

'I and my steel are sworn to the purpose.' Nothing rubbed a speck from his sword with a thumb-tip. 'The only door that will stop me is the Last.'

Yarvi nodded, and with his good hand clasped Nothing's arm. 'I don't pretend to understand your loyalty, but I'm grateful for it.'

The others were slower to the cause. 'I'd be lying if I said the odds didn't bother me,' said Rulf.

'They bothered you on the border,' said Nothing, 'and that ended with the burning bodies of our enemies.'

'And of our friend. And our capture by a crowd

of angry Vanstermen. Angry Vanstermen are again involved, and if this plan miscarries I doubt we'll be talking our way clear, however nimble-tongued the young king may be.'

Yarvi put his twisted palm on the pommel of Shadikshirram's sword. 'Then our steel must talk for us.'

'Easy to say before it's drawn.' Sumael frowned across to Jaud. 'I think we had better head south before the swords begin to speak.'

Jaud looked from Yarvi to Sumael and back, and his big shoulders slumped. *The wise wait for the moment. But never let it pass.*

'You can go with my blessing, but I'd rather have you at my side,' said Yarvi. 'Together we braved the *South Wind*. Together we escaped her. Together we faced the ice and came through. We'll come through this as well. Together. Only take one more stroke with me.'

Sumael blinked at Jaud, then leaned close to him. 'You're not a warrior, not a king. You're a baker.'

Jaud looked sidelong at Yarvi, and sighed. 'And an oarsman.'

'Not by choice.'

'Not much in life that matters is by choice. What kind of oarsman abandons his mate?'

'This isn't our fight!' hissed Sumael, low and urgent.

Jaud shrugged. 'My friend's fight is my fight.'

'What about the sweetest water in the world?'

'It will be just as sweet later. Sweeter still, maybe.' And Jaud gave Yarvi a weak smile. 'When you have a load to lift, you're better lifting than weeping.'

'We all might end up weeping.' Sumael took a slow step towards Yarvi, dark eyes fixed on his. She raised a hand to reach towards him, and the breath caught in his throat. 'Please, Yorv—'

'My name is Yarvi.' And though it hurt to do it he met her gaze with flinty hardness, the way his mother might have. He would have liked to take her hand. To hold it the way he had in the snow. To be pulled far away by it to the First of Cities, and be Yorv again, and the Black Chair be damned.

He would have loved to take her hand, but he could not afford to weaken. Not for anything. He had sworn an oath, and he needed his oarmates beside him. He needed Jaud. He needed her.

'What about you, Rulf?' he asked

Rulf worked his mouth, carefully rolled his tongue, and neatly spat out of the window. 'When the baker fights, what can the warrior do?' His broad face broke into a grin. 'My bow's yours.'

Sumael let her hand fall and stared at the floor, her scarred mouth twisted. 'Mother War rules, then. What can I do?'

'Nothing,' said Nothing, simply.

MOTHER WAR'S BARGAIN

The dovecote was still perched in the top of one of the citadel's highest towers, still streaked inside and out with centuries of droppings, and still through its many windows a chill wind blew. More chill than ever.

'Gods damn this cold,' muttered Yarvi.

Sumael kept looking through her eye-glass, mouth fixed in a hard line. 'You saying you haven't been colder?'

'You know I have.' They both had, out there in the crushing ice. But it seemed there had been a spark between the two of them to warm him. He had well and truly snuffed it out now.

'I'm sorry,' he said, though it came out a grudging grunt. She kept her silence, and he found himself meandering on. 'For what my mother said to you . . . for asking Jaud to stay . . . for not—'

Her jaw-muscles worked. 'Surely a king need never apologize.'

He winced at that. 'I'm the same man you slept beside on the *South Wind*. The same man you walked beside in the snow. The same man—'

'Are you?' She looked at him then, finally, but

302

there was no softness in it. 'Over the hill there.' She passed the eye-glass across. 'Smoke.'

'Smoke,' croaked one of the doves. 'Smoke.'

Sumael eyed it suspiciously, and from their cages ranged about the walls the doves eyed her unblinking back. All apart from the bronze eagle, huge and regal, which must have come from Grandmother Wexen with another offer – or demand – of marriage for Yarvi's mother. It poked proudly at its plumage and did not deign to look down.

'Smoke, smoke, smoke . . .'

'Can you stop them doing that?' asked Sumael.

'They echo bits of the messages they've been trained to say,' said Yarvi. 'Don't worry. They don't understand them.' Though as those dozens of eyes turned on him as one, heads attentively cocked, he was forced again to wonder whether they might understand more than he did. He turned back to the window and pressed the glass to his eye, saw the crooked thread of smoke against the sky.

'There is a steading that way.' The owner had been one among the procession of hand-wringing mourners at his father's howing up. Yarvi tried not to wonder whether that man had been on his farm when Grom-gil-Gorm came visiting. And if he had not, who had been there to greet the Vanstermen, and what had happened to them since . . .

A wise minister weighs the greater good, Mother Gundring always said, *and finds the lesser evil.* Surely a wise king could only do the same?

He jerked the eye-glass away from the burning

303

steading, scanning the jagged horizon, and caught the glint of sun on steel.

'Warriors.' Coming down the northern road, spilling from a cleft in the hills. Slow as treacle in winter they seemed to crawl from this distance, and Yarvi found he was chewing at his lip, wishing them on.

'The King of Gettland,' he muttered to himself. 'Urging an army of Vanstermen to Thorlby.'

'The gods cook strange recipes,' said Sumael.

Yarvi looked up at the domed ceiling, gods painted there as birds in flaking colours. He Who Carries the Message. She Who Stirs the Branches. She Who Spoke the First Word and Will Speak the Last. And painted with red wings at the centre, smiling blood, Mother War.

'I've rarely prayed to you, I know,' Yarvi whispered at her image. 'Father Peace always suited me better. But give me victory this day. Give me back the Black Chair. You've tested me and I stand ready. I'm not the fool I was, not the coward, not the child. I am the rightful King of Gettland.'

One of the doves chose that moment to loose a spatter of droppings onto the floor beside him. Mother War's answer, perhaps?

Yarvi ground his teeth. 'If you choose not to make me king . . . if you choose to send me through the Last Door today . . . at least let me keep my oath.' He clenched his fists, such as they were, knuckles white. 'Give me Odem's life. Give me revenge. Grant me that much, and I'll be satisfied.'

Not a nurturing prayer of the kind that ministers are taught. Not a giving or a making prayer. But giving and making are nothing to Mother War. She is the taker, the breaker, the widow-maker. She cares only for blood.

'The king must die,' he hissed.

'The king must die!' screeched the eagle, standing tall and spreading its wings so it filled its cage and seemed to darken the whole chamber. 'The king must die!'

'It's time,' said Yarvi.

'Good,' said Nothing. His voice, through the tall slot in a helmet that hid most of his face, rang with metal.

'Good,' said the two Inglings together, one of them spinning a great axe about in his fists as though it were a toy.

'Good,' murmured Jaud, but he looked far from happy. Uncomfortable in his borrowed war-gear, and more uncomfortable still at the sight of his brothers-in-arms, squatting in the deep shadows of the elf-tunnel.

Honestly, they inspired scant confidence in Yarvi. It was a company of horribles his mother's gold had brought to his cause. Every land about the Shattered Sea – and some much further flung – had contributed a couple of its worst sons. There were rogues and cut-throats, sea-raiders and convicts, some with their crimes tattooed on their foreheads. One with an always-weeping eye had a face scrawled blue with them. Men without king or honour. Men without conscience or cause. Not to mention three fearsome Shend women, bristling with blades and muscled like masons, who took great delight in baring teeth filed to wicked points at anyone who glanced their way.

'Not the first folk I'd pick to trust my life to,' murmured Rulf, carefully averting his eyes.

'What can you think about a cause,' muttered Jaud, 'when all the decent folk stand on the other side?'

'Many tasks call for decent folk.' Nothing twisted his helmet carefully back and forth. 'The murder of a king is not one such.'

'This is no murder,' growled Yarvi. 'And Odem no true king.'

'Shhh,' said Sumael, eyes rolling to the ceiling.

Faint sounds were leaking through the rock. Shouting, perhaps, the rattle of arms. The very faintest whiff of alarm.

'They know our friends have arrived.'

Yarvi swallowed a surge of nerves. 'To your places.'

Their plans were well rehearsed. Rulf took a dozen men skilled with bows. Each of the Inglings took a dozen more to hiding places from which they could quickly reach the yard. The dozen that remained crept up the winding stair after Yarvi and Nothing. Towards the chain room above the citadel's one entrance. Towards the Screaming Gate.

'Have care,' whispered Yarvi, pausing at the hidden door, though his throat was almost too tight to force words through. 'The men in there aren't our enemies—'

'They will do for today,' said Nothing. 'And Mother War hates care.' He kicked the door wide and ducked through.

'Damn it!' hissed Yarvi, scrambling after.

The chain room was dim, light leaking in from narrow windows, the rumble of thumping boots echoing loud from the passageway below. Two men sat at a table. One turned, smile vanishing as he saw Nothing's drawn sword.

'Who are—'

Steel flashed through a strip of light and his head came off with a wet click, spinning into a corner. Ridiculous, it seemed, a mummer's joke at a spring fair, but no children laughed now. Nothing stepped past the slumping body, caught the other man under his arm as he rose and slid the sword through his chest. He gave a ragged gasp, pawed towards the table where an axe lay.

Nothing pushed the table carefully out of reach with one boot, then pulled his sword free and lowered the man gently to sit against the wall, shuddering silently as Death eased open the Last Door for him.

'The chain room is ours.' Nothing peered through an archway at the far end, then dragged the door shut and slid the bolt.

Yarvi knelt beside the dying man. He knew him. Or had done. Ulvdem was his name. No friend of his, but not one of the worst. He had smiled once at a joke Yarvi made, and Yarvi had been glad of it.

'Did you have to kill them?'

'No.' Nothing carefully wiped clean his sword. 'We could have let Odem be king.'

The hirelings were spreading out, frowning towards the centrepiece of the room, and their plan, the Screaming Gate. Its bottom was sunken in the floor and its top in the ceiling, a wall of polished copper softly gleaming, engraved with a hundred faces which snarled, screeched, howled in pain or fear or rage, flowing into each other like reflections in a pool.

Sumael stood looking at it with hands on hips. 'I think I can guess now why it's called the Screaming Gate.'

'A hideous thing to hang our hopes on,' said Jaud.

Yarvi brushed the metal with his fingertips, cold and awfully solid. 'A hideous thing to have drop on your head, no doubt.' Beside the great slab, about a post carved with the names of fifteen gods, was a confusion of interlocking gears, inscribed wheels, coiled chains, that even with his minister's eye he could not begin to fathom the workings of. In its centre was a single silver pin. 'This is the mechanism.'

Jaud reached towards it. 'All you do is pull the pin?'

Yarvi slapped his hand away. 'At the right moment! The last moment. The more of Odem's men have gone to face Gorm the better our chances.'

'Your uncle speaks,' called Nothing from one of the narrow windows.

Yarvi eased open the shutters of another and

peered down into the yard. That familiar patch of green amongst the towering grey walls, the cedar spreading its branches at one side. Men were gathered there, many hurriedly arming, many already arrayed for battle. Yarvi's eyes widened as he took in the number. Three hundred at a guess, and he knew there would be far more making ready outside the citadel. Above them, upon the marble steps of the Godshall, in fur and silvered mail and with the King's Circle on his brow, stood Yarvi's uncle Odem.

'Who stands outside the walls of Thorlby now?' he was roaring at the gathered warriors. 'Grom-gil-Gorm, the Breaker of Swords!'

The men stamped their feet and let go a storm of curses and contempt. 'He who murdered Uthrik, your king, my brother!' Howls of anger at that, and Yarvi had to stop himself making one of his own at the lie.

'But in his arrogance he has brought few men with him!' called Odem. 'We have the right, we have the ground, we have the numbers and the quality! Will we let this army of scum stand a moment longer within sight of the howes of my brothers Uthrik and Uthil, the howe of my grandfather Angulf Clovenfoot, hammer of the Vanstermen?'

The warriors clattered weapons on shields and shields on armour and roared that they would not.

Odem reached out, his kneeling blade-bearer offered up his sword, and he drew it and held it high, the steel breaking from the shadows and flashing so brightly for an instant Yarvi had to look away. 'Then let us do honour to Mother War, and bring her a red day! Let us leave our walls at our backs and stride out, and before sunset see the heads of Grom-gil-Gorm and his Vanster dogs above our gates!'

'We'll see whose head sits on the walls tonight,' said Yarvi, words lost in the answering cheer of the warriors of Gettland. The warriors who should have been cheering for him.

'They go to fight,' said Nothing, as men began to file from the yard, called off in stretches of the shield-wall, each knowing his place, each ready to die for his shoulder-man. 'You guessed your uncle's mind correctly.'

'It was no guess,' said Yarvi.

'Your mother was right.' He saw Nothing's eyes glint in the darkness of his helmet's slot. 'You have become a deep-cunning man.'

The youngest warriors came first, some younger even than Yarvi, the older and more battle-worn were next. They tramped under the Screaming Gate, the clatter of harness echoing about the chain room, shadows shifting across the pitted faces of Yarvi's rogues as they peered through the slots in the floor to watch better men pass below. And with each one gone down that passageway Yarvi's happiness grew, for he knew their odds were so much the better, and his fear grew too, for he knew the moment was almost upon them.

The moment of his vengeance. Or the moment of his death.

'The king's moving,' said Sumael, pressed into the shadows beside another window. Odem was striding through his veterans towards the gate, shield-bearer, and blade-bearer, and standard-bearers at his back, clapping men on their shoulders as he went.

'The moment is not ripe,' murmured Nothing.

'I see that!' hissed Yarvi. The boots tramped on, men draining from the citadel, but there were far too many yet in the yard.

Had he endured all this, suffered all this, sacrificed all this so Odem could wriggle carefree from the hook at the last moment? He fussed with his stub of finger, the very tips of his thumbs sweating.

'Do I pull the pin?' called Jaud.

'Not yet!' squeaked Yarvi, terrified they would be heard through the slots in the floor. 'Not yet!'

Odem strode on, soon to be lost from view below the archway. Yarvi raised his hand to Jaud, ready to bring it down and all the weight of the Screaming Gate with it.

Even if it doomed them all.

'My king!' Yarvi's mother stood on the steps of the Godshall, Hurik huge at one shoulder, Mother Gundring bent over her staff at the other. 'My brother!'

Yarvi's uncle stopped, frowning, and turned.

'Odem, please, a word!'

Yarvi hardly dared breathe in case it somehow upset the delicate balance of the moment. Time crawled as Odem looked to the gate, then to Yarvi's

311

mother, then, cursing, strode back towards her, his closest retainers rattling after.

'Wait!' hissed Yarvi, and with wide eyes Jaud eased his fingers from the pin.

Yarvi strained towards the window, cool breeze kissing his sweat-sheened face, but could not hear what was said on the steps of the Godshall. His mother knelt at Odem's feet, pressed hands to her chest, humbly bowed her head. Perhaps she made abject apologies for her stubbornness, her ingratitude to her brother and the High King. Perhaps she swore obedience and begged forgiveness. Then she took Odem's hand in both of hers, and pressed her lips to it, and Yarvi's skin crawled.

His uncle looked at Mother Gundring, and gave the slightest nod. His minister looked back, and gave the slightest shrug. Then Odem touched Yarvi's mother on the cheek and strode away, back towards the gate, his servants and closest guards about him in an eager gaggle.

The last trickle of warriors were following their brothers out of the citadel, no more than three dozen left in the yard. Yarvi's mother clasped her hands, and looked up towards the gatehouse, and Yarvi fancied she might even have met his eye.

'Thank you, Mother,' he whispered. Once again he lifted his withered hand to Jaud. Once again he watched Odem approach the gate. But this time, instead of seeing the gods pull all his plans apart, he saw them offer him his chance.

'Wait,' he whispered, the hot breath of the word tickling at his lips.

'Wait.' Here was the day. Here the hour.

'Wait.' Here the moment.

'Now.'

He chopped down his crippled hand and, weak though it was, thanks to the ingenuity of six ministers of old, it fell with the weight of mountains. Jaud snatched free the pin, gears whirred, a chain snapped taut, and the reason for the name was suddenly made clear. With a shrieking like all the dead in hell and a blast of wind that tore Yarvi's helmet off and slammed him against the wall, the Screaming Gate plunged through the floor.

It struck the ground below with a crash that shook the citadel to its elf-tunnelled roots, sealing the entrance with a weight of metal Father Earth himself would have strained to lift.

The floor reeled, tipped, and Yarvi wondered for a moment if the very gatehouse was collapsing at that shattering impact.

He stumbled to a slot in the floor, trying to shake the dizziness from his head, the ringing from his ears. The passageway below was full of Odem's closest. Some were tottering with hands clasped to their heads. Some were fumbling out their weapons. Some clustered at the gate, silently shouting, silently, stupidly, uselessly beating against the screaming faces. The false king himself stood in their midst, staring up. His eyes met Yarvi's, and his face paled as though he saw a demon that had clawed its way back through the Last Door.

And Yarvi smiled.

Then he felt himself seized by the shoulder.

Nothing was dragging at him, shouting in his face, he could see his mouth moving in the slot in his helmet, but could hear only a vague burble.

He scrambled after, the floor settling to level, down a winding stair, bouncing from the walls, jostled by men behind. Nothing flung a door wide, a bright archway in the dark, and they burst into the open air.

THE LAST DOOR

In the yard of the citadel, chaos ruled.

Weapons swung and splinters flew, steel clashed and faces snarled, arrows flitted and bodies dropped, all in dream-like silence.

Just as Yarvi had planned his mother's hirelings had spilled from hidden doorways and taken Odem's veterans in their backs, hacked them down where they stood, driven them witless about the yard, left their scattered bodies bleeding.

But those that survived the first shock were fighting back fiercely, the battle broken up into ugly little struggles to the death. In blinking silence Yarvi watched one of the Shend women stabbing at a man while he opened gashes down her face with the rim of his shield.

Just as he had planned, Yarvi saw Rulf and his archers send a flight of arrows from the roofs. Silently they went up, silently rattled down, prickling the shields of Odem's closest guards, formed into a knot about their king. One man caught a shaft in the face and seemed hardly to notice, still pointing towards the Godshall with his sword, still bellowing silent words. Another went down, clutching at an

315

arrow in his side, clutching at the leg of the man beside him who kicked his hand away and shuffled on. Yarvi knew them both, honoured men who once stood guard at the entrance to the king's chamber.

Battle makes all men animals, Yarvi's father used to tell him. He saw a snarling thug with *sheep thief* written on his cheek cut down an unarmed slave, water jug flying from his hands and shattering against a wall.

Could this be what he had planned? What he had prayed for?

He had flung wide the door, and begged Mother War to be his guest. He could not stop this. No one could. Surviving it would be challenge enough.

He saw Nothing hack the legs from under one man, slash another across the back as he turned to run, shove another by the shield so he tottered into the low wall of the well and over, vanishing from sight into the depths.

In a deafened stupor he dragged Shadikshirram's sword from its sheath. That was what a man did in battle, wasn't it? Gods, it felt heavy of a sudden. Men jostled him as they ran past to join the madness, but he was rooted to the earth.

He saw the doors of the Godshall standing open, Odem's guards crouching behind arrow-bristled shields around the archway, shepherding the false king into the shadows.

Yarvi pointed his sword towards them, shouted, 'There!' The deafness was fading. Enough that he heard thudding footsteps in time to spin around.

But not to do much more.

Steel clashed on steel and the sword was wrenched in his fist, almost out of his hand. He caught a glimpse of Hurik's scarred face, heard a snatch of his low growl before his shield crashed into Yarvi's chest, lifted him from his feet and dumped him groaning on his back two strides away.

Hurik's eyes slid sideways and he twisted to catch an axe on his shield, splinters spinning from the force of the blow. Jaud, charging in with a roar, hacking away like a mad woodsman at a stump. Hurik gave ground, blocked the second blow, but the third was clumsy and he caught it in a ready crouch, steering it wide, the heavy blade missing his shoulder by a hand's breadth and thudding into the turf. He clubbed Jaud in the head with the rim of his shield as he stumbled past, knocking him off balance, then with a short chop of his sword ripped the axe from Jaud's hand.

It seemed a baker was no match for a queen's Chosen Shield, however good a man he was.

Hurik's bared teeth showed white in his black beard, his sword flashed as he stabbed, blade sinking into Jaud's ribs to the hilt.

'No,' croaked Yarvi, struggling to get up, but wanting a thing is not always enough.

Jaud dropped to his knees, face crushed up with pain, and Hurik planted one great boot on his shoulder, ripped his sword free, then kicked Jaud onto his back. He turned to Yarvi.

'Let us finish what we started in Amwend.'

He stepped forward, red sword raised. Yarvi would have liked to face Death smiling, but few have courage when the Last Door yawns before them, even kings. Kings least of all, perhaps. He slithered back, holding up his withered hand as though that might ward off the blade.

Hurik's lip twisted. 'What a king you would have made—'

'We shall see.'

Hurik's chin was jerked back and there was steel under his white-streaked beard. A dagger, polished to an icy gleam. The face of Yarvi's mother, eyes narrowed and jaw clenched, appeared beside his.

'Drop your sword, Hurik.'

He hesitated for a moment and she leaned closer and murmured in his ear. 'You know me. Few better. Can it really be . . .' and she twisted the blade until a line of blood ran down his thick neck, 'that you doubt my will?'

Hurik swallowed, wincing as the knobble on his stubbled throat squirmed against the steel, then let his blade clatter to the dirt. Yarvi scrambled up, clutching Shadikshirram's sword, levelling the point at Hurik's chest.

'Wait,' said his mother. 'First answer me this. For nineteen years you have been my Chosen Shield. Why break your oath?'

Hurik's eyes shifted to Yarvi. Sad they looked, now, and broken. 'Odem told me the boy must die, or you must.'

'And why not kill Odem where he stood?'

'Because the High King had decreed it!' Hurik hissed out. 'And the High King would not be denied. My oath was to protect you, Laithlin.' He pushed his shoulders back, and slowly closed his eyes. 'Not your crippled son.'

'Then consider your oath discharged.'

The smallest movement of the knife and Yarvi stumbled back as blood spotted his cheek. Hurik fell, and keeled on his face, and Yarvi stood with his sword slack in his hand, blinking down at the dark pool creeping through the grass.

His skin was flushed and prickling. The breath tore at his throat. Lights danced in his eyes, his limbs heavy, bruised chest throbbing. He wanted only to sit down. To sit in the darkness and cry.

The dead and wounded were scattered blade-slashed and arrow prickled across the grass where Yarvi had played as a child. Cherished swords and shields, heirlooms of noble houses, had fallen from lifeless fingers and lay shattered, filthy with blood. The doors of the Godshall were sealed, those of Yarvi's men still standing gathered about them, Rulf's face red streaked from a cut in his hair. The two big Inglings were pounding away with their axes but the heavy wood stayed firm.

And against the trunk of the spreading cedar, that Yarvi's brother used to mock him for being too scared to climb, Jaud sat still with head tipped back and hands limp in his bloody lap. Sumael knelt beside him, her head hanging and her lips curled from her teeth, clutching at one bloody fistful of his shirt, as though she might lift him up. As though she might carry him to safety, as he once carried her. But there was nowhere to take him, even had she had the strength.

Nowhere but through the Last Door.

And Yarvi realized then that Death does not bow to each person who passes her, does not sweep out her arm respectfully to show the way, speaks no profound words, unlocks no bolts. The key upon her chest is never needed, for the Last Door stands always open. She herds the dead through impatiently, heedless of rank or fame or quality. She has an ever-lengthening queue to get through. A blind procession, inexhaustible.

'What have I done?' whispered Yarvi, taking a halting step towards Jaud and Sumael.

'What you had to.' His mother's grip on his arm was iron. 'There is no time to mourn, now, my son. My king.' One side of her face was pale, the other dotted red, and she looked at that moment like Mother War indeed. 'Follow Odem.' She squeezed harder. 'Kill him, and take back the Black Chair.'

Yarvi clenched his jaw then, and nodded. There could be no going back.

'Stop that!' he called at the Inglings. 'There are better ways.' They lowered their axes to stare darkly at him. 'Mother, stay with them and watch the door. Make sure no one leaves.'

'Not until Odem is dead,' she said.

'Nothing, Rulf, gather a dozen men and follow me.'

Rulf stared at the carnage in the yard of the citadel,

breathing hard. The wounded and the dying, the hobbling and the bleeding. And Jaud, brave Jaud, who had stood by his oarmate, sitting with his back to the trunk of the cedar, no oar to pull, no load to lift, no encouragement to give any longer.

'Will I find a dozen still able?' he whispered.

Yarvi turned away. 'Get what there is.'

A LONELY SEAT

'**R**eady?' whispered Yarvi.

'Always,' said Nothing.

Rulf worked his head one way then the other, the blood that streaked his face black in the shadows. 'Don't see that I'll get any readier.'

Yarvi heaved in a great breath, and as he pushed it out drove the heel of his twisted hand into the catch, barged the hidden door open with his shoulder, and burst into the sacred vastness of the Godshall.

Empty at the top of its dais the Black Chair stood, in the sight of the Tall Gods, their jewelled eyes agleam. Above them, about the dome, the amber statues of the Small Gods observed the petty doings of humanity without comment, emotion or even much interest.

Odem had only ten men left and those in a sorry state, clustered about the doors as they shook faintly from blows outside. Two were trying to shore them up with spears. Two others had swept the holy offerings from a table shiny with age and were dragging it towards the entrance as a barricade. The rest sat bewildered or stood stunned, not knowing how their king could have been taken unawares by a company of rogues in the heart of his own citadel. Mother Gundring hunched beside Odem, tending to his standard-bearer's bleeding arm.

'To the king!' he shrieked as he saw Yarvi burst in, and Odem's men clustered about their master, raising their shields before him, weapons ready. The man with the arrow in his face had snapped it off, the bloody shaft poking from his cheek. He had been leaning groggily on his sword but now he pointed it, wobbling, towards Yarvi.

Nothing rushed up at his left shoulder, Rulf at his right, and those slaves and mercenaries who could still fight spread out about them, bristling with sharpened metal.

They edged around the Black Chair, down the steps of the dais, spitting and rasping curses in half a dozen languages. Odem urged his men forward, the space between them ten strides of stone, then eight, then six, the coming violence hanging heavy as a stormcloud in the still air of the Godshall.

Then Mother Gundring squinted towards Yarvi, and her eyes went wide. 'Wait!' she screamed, beating her elf-staff upon the ground and sending crashing echoes bouncing about the dome above. 'Wait!'

For a moment the men held, staring, snarling, hands tickling their weapons, and Yarvi leapt into the narrow gap of opportunity the old minister had opened for him.

'Men of Gettland!' he shouted. 'You know me!

I am Yarvi, son of Uthrik!' And he pointed at Odem with the one stubby finger of his left hand. 'This treacherous *thing* tried to steal the Black Chair, but the gods will not suffer a usurper to sit upon it for long!' He dug his thumb into his chest. 'The rightful King of Gettland has returned!'

'The woman's puppet?' spat Odem at him. 'The half-king? The king of cripples?'

Before Yarvi could shriek his reply he felt a strong hand on his shoulder, steering him aside. Nothing stepped past, unbuckling the strap on his helmet. 'No,' he said. 'The rightful king.' And he pulled it off and tossed it spinning across the floor of the Godshall with a steely clatter.

He had chopped his wild shag of hair to a short grey fuzz, shaved clean his thicket of a beard. The face revealed was all sharp angles and ruthless lines, bones broken and set harder, work- and weather-worn, beating- and battle-scarred. The beggar of twigs and string was gone, and in his place a warrior of oak and iron stood, but his eyes, deep set in hollow sockets, were the same.

Still burning with a fire at the brink of madness. Hotter than ever.

And suddenly Yarvi was no longer sure who this man was that he had travelled beside, fought beside, slept beside. No longer sure what he had brought with him into the citadel of Gettland, right to the Black Chair itself.

He blinked around him, suddenly full of doubt. The young warriors of Gettland still growled their defiance. But on the older men the sight of Nothing's face worked a strange transformation.

Jaws dropped, blades wavered, eyes widened, even brimmed with tears, breathed oaths drifted from quivering lips. Odem had turned paler even than when he saw Yarvi. The face of a man who looks upon the end of creation.

'What sorcery is this?' whispered Rulf, but Yarvi could not say.

The elf-metal staff slipped from Mother Gundring's limp fingers and clattered to the floor, the echoes fading into heavy silence.

'Uthil,' she whispered.

'Yes.' And Nothing turned his mad smile on Odem. 'Well met, brother.'

And now the name was spoken Yarvi saw how like the two men were, and felt a chill to the tips of his fingers.

His Uncle Uthil, whose matchless skill the warriors toasted before every training, whose drowned body had never been washed from the bitter sea, whose howe above the wind-blasted beach stood empty.

His Uncle Uthil had been standing at his side for months.

His Uncle Uthil stood before him now.

'Here is the reckoning,' said Nothing. Said Uthil. And he stepped forward, sword in hand.

'Blood cannot be shed in the Godshall!' shouted Mother Gundring.

Uthil only smiled. 'The gods love nothing better than blood, my minister. What better place to shed it?'

'Kill him!' shrieked Odem, no calm in his voice now, but no one rushed to obey. No one so much as spoke a word. 'I am your king!'

But power can be a brittle thing. Slowly, carefully, as though they thought with one mind, the warriors backed away from him to form a crescent.

'The Black Chair is a lonely seat indeed,' said Uthil, glancing up at it, empty on its dais.

The muscles in Odem's jaw worked as he gazed at the circle of grim faces ranged about him, at those of his guards and those of the hirelings, at Mother Gundring's and at Yarvi's, and finally at Uthil's, so like his own, but passed through twenty years of horrors. He snorted, and spat on the holy stones at his brother's feet.

'So be it, then.' And Odem snatched his shield from its bearer, gilded and with winking jewels set in its rim, and barged the man away.

Rulf offered out his shield but Nothing shook his head. 'Wood has its place, but here steel is the answer.' And he raised his blade, the same simple one he had carried through the wastes, plain steel polished to a frosty shine.

'You have been so long away, *brother.*' Odem lifted his sword, one forged for Yarvi's father, pommel of ivory and hilt of gold, runes of blessing worked into the mirror-bright blade. 'Let us embrace.'

He darted forward, so scorpion-quick that Yarvi gave a gasp and stumbled back a pace himself, twitching this way and that as he followed his uncles' movements. Odem thrust, and thrust again, hissed as he slashed high and low with blows to cleave a man in two. But fast and deadly as he was, his brother was faster. Like smoke on a mad wind Uthil drifted, twisted, reeled, while the bright steel carved the air but gave him not a kiss.

'Do you remember when we last saw each other?' Uthil asked as he danced away. 'In that storm, at the prow of our father's ship? Laughing into the gale with my brothers at my back?'

'You never cared for anything but your laughter!' Odem rushed in again, chopping left and right and making the watchful guards lurch back. But Uthil wheeled to safety, not even raising his sword.

'Is that why you and Uthrik together threw me into the bitter sea? Or was it so that he could steal my birthright? And you in turn could steal it from him?'

'The Black Chair is mine!' Odem's sword was a shining arc over his head. But Uthil caught it on his own with a ringing crash. He caught Odem's shield as well and for a moment Yarvi's two uncles were locked together, blades grating. Then Uthil dipped his shoulder and jerked the shield upwards, the rim cracking into Odem's jaw. He twisted his other shoulder and flung Odem away, heels kicking at the stones, falling in a tangle against the men behind him.

They pushed him off and Odem shrank behind his shield, but Uthil only stood his ground in the centre of the circle. 'Even though my empty howe stands above the beach, I did not drown. I was plucked from the sea by slavers, and made to fight in a pit. And in those years in the darkness, for the amusement of blood-drunk animals, I killed ninety-nine men.' Uthil pressed a finger to his ear, and for a moment looked like Nothing once again. 'I hear them whisper, sometimes. Can you hear them whisper, Odem?'

'You're mad!' spat Odem, blood on his lips.

But Uthil only smiled the wider. 'How could it be otherwise? They promise a hundredth victory will set you free, but I was tricked and sold again.' Odem circled him, stalking in a hunter's crouch, shield up, sweat across his forehead from the weight of his silvered mail. Uthil stood tall, sword swinging loose and easy in his hand, scarcely even breathing hard. 'I was a war-slave, then an oar-slave, then . . . nothing. A dozen bitter years I spent upon my knees. It is a good place to think.'

'Think on this!' Odem spat blood as he came again, feinted a thrust and made it into a hissing, angling cut. But Uthil steered it wide to crash into the stone of the floor, striking sparks and filling the Godshall with ear-splitting echoes.

Odem gasped, stumbled, shuddering with the impact, and Uthil stepped away and with a terrible precision slashed him across the arm, just above his shield's garnet-studded rim.

Odem gave a howl, the gaudy thing sliding from his limp left hand and the blood already tapping on it from his dangling fingertips. He looked up at Uthil, eyes wide. 'I was the best among the three of us! I should have been king! Uthrik was nothing but violence, you nothing but vanity!'

'So true.' Uthil frowned as he wiped both sides of his sword carefully on his sleeve. 'How the gods have punished me for it. The lessons they have taught me, Odem. And now they have sent me to teach one to you. They do not make the best man king, but the first-born.' He nodded towards Yarvi. 'And our nephew was right about one thing. They will not suffer a usurper to sit in the Black Chair for long.' He bared his teeth and hissed out the words. 'It is *mine.*'

He sprang forward and Odem met him snarling. Blades clashed, once, twice, faster than Yarvi could follow. The third blow Uthil slid beneath, slashing his brother's leg as he danced away and making him roar again. Odem winced, knee buckling, only staying upright by using his sword as a crutch.

'The Last Door opens for you,' said Uthil.

Odem found his balance, chest heaving, and Yarvi saw the silvered mail on his leg turned red, fast-flowing blood working its way out from his boot down the cracks between the stones.

'I know it.' Odem lifted his chin, and Yarvi saw a tear leak from the corner of his eye and streak his face. 'It has stood open at my shoulder all these years.' And with a sound between a snort and a sob, he tossed his sword down to clatter into the shadows. 'Ever since that day in the storm.'

The blood surged in Yarvi's ears as Uthil lifted

his sword high, blade catching the light and its edge glittering cold.

'Just answer me one question . . .' breathed Odem, eyes fixed above him on his death.

For a moment Uthil hesitated. The sword wavered, drifted down. One brow twitched up, questioning. 'Speak, brother.'

And Yarvi saw Odem's hand shifting, subtly shifting around his back, fingers curling towards the hilt of a dagger at his belt. A long dagger with a pommel of black jet. The same one he had showed to Yarvi on the roof of Amwend's tower.

We must do what is best for Gettland.

Yarvi sprang down the steps in one bound.

He might not have been the sharpest pupil in the training square, but he knew how to stab a man. He caught Odem under the arm and the curved blade of Shadikshirram's sword slid through his mail and out of his chest with hardly a sound.

'Whatever your question,' Yarvi hissed into his ear, 'steel is my answer!' And he stepped back, ripping the blade free.

Odem gave a bubbling gasp. He took one drunken step and dropped onto his knees. He slowly turned his head, and for a moment, over his shoulder, his disbelieving eye met Yarvi's. Then he toppled sideways. He lay still on the sacred stones, at the foot of the dais, in the sight of the gods, in the centre of that circle of men, and Yarvi and Uthil were left staring at one another over his body.

'It seems there is a question between us, nephew,'

said his one surviving uncle, that one brow still raised. 'Shall steel be our answer?'

Yarvi's eyes flickered up to the Black Chair, standing silent above them.

Hard it might be, but harder than the benches of the *South Wind*? Cold it might be, but colder than the snows of the utmost north? He did not fear it any more. But did he truly want it? He remembered his father sitting in it, tall and grim, his scarred hand never far from his sword. A doting son to Mother War, just as a king of Gettland should be. Just as Uthil was.

The statues of the Tall Gods gazed down, as though awaiting a decision, and Yarvi looked from one stony face to another, and took a long breath. Mother Gundring always said he had been touched by Father Peace, and he knew she was right.

He had never really wanted the Black Chair. Why fight for it? Why die for it? So Gettland could have half a king?

He made of his fist an open hand, and let Shadikshirram's sword drop rattling to the bloody stones.

'I have my vengeance,' he said. 'The Black Chair is yours.' And he slowly sank to his knees before Uthil, and bowed his head. 'My king.'

THE BLAME

Grom-gil-Gorm, King of Vansterland, bloodiest son of Mother War, Breaker of Swords and maker of orphans, strode into the Godshall with his minister and ten of his most battle-tested warriors at his back, huge left hand slack upon the pommel of his huge sword.

He had a new white fur about his heavy shoulders, Yarvi noticed, and a new jewel on one great forefinger, and the triple-looped chain about his neck had lengthened by a few pommels. Mementos of his bloody jaunt through Gettland, at Yarvi's invitation, stolen from the innocent along with their lives, no doubt.

But the hugest thing of all, as he stepped between the scarred doors and into the house of his enemy, was his smile. The smile of a conqueror, who sees all his plans ripen, all his adversaries brought low, all the dice come up his number. The smile of a man greatly favoured by the gods.

Then he saw Yarvi standing on the steps of the dais between his mother and Mother Gundring, and his smile buckled. And then he saw who sat in the Black Chair, and it crumpled entire. He came to an uncertain halt in the centre of that wide floor, on about the spot where Odem's blood still stained the cracks in the stones, surrounded on all sides by the glowering great of Gettland.

Then he scratched at one side of his head, and said, 'This is not the king we expected.'

'Many here might say so,' said Yarvi. 'But it is the rightful one, even so. King Uthil, my eldest uncle, has returned.'

'Uthil.' Mother Scaer gave a hiss through her teeth. 'The proud Gettlander. I thought I knew that face.'

'You might have mentioned it.' Gorm frowned around at the gathered warriors and wives, keys and cloak-buckles all aglitter in the shadows, and heaved up a weighty sigh. 'I've an unhappy sense you will not be kneeling before me as my vassal.'

'I have spent long enough on my knees.' Uthil stood, his sword still cradled in his arms. That same plain sword he had taken up from the listing deck of the *South Wind* and polished until the blade glittered like moonlight on the chill sea. 'If anyone kneels it should be you. You stand on my land, in my hall, before my chair.'

Gorm lifted the toes of his boots and peered down at them. 'So it would seem. But I have always been stiff in the joints. I must decline.'

'A shame. Perhaps I can unstiffen you with my sword when I visit you in Vulsgard in the summer.'

Gorm's face hardened. 'Oh, I can guarantee any Gettlander who crosses the border a warm welcome.'

'Why wait for summer, then?' Uthil took the steps one by one, until he stood on the lowest, so that he looked straight into Gorm's face on about a level footing. 'Fight me now.'

A twitch began at the corner of Gorm's eye and set his cheek to flutter. Yarvi saw his scarred knuckles white on the grip of his sword, the eyes of his warriors darting about the room, the gathered men of Gettland hardening their frowns. 'You should know that Mother War breathed upon me in my crib,' growled the King of Vansterland. 'It has been foreseen no man can kill me—'

'Then fight me, dog!' roared Uthil, the echoes crashing about the hall and every person holding their breath as if it would be their last. Yarvi wondered if they might see a second king die in the Godshall within a day, and he would not have cared to bet on which of these two it would be.

Then Mother Scaer rested her thin hand gently on Gorm's fist. 'The gods guard those who guard themselves,' she whispered.

The King of Vansterland took a long breath. His shoulders relaxed, and he peeled his fingers from his sword and gently combed them through his beard. 'This new king is very rude,' he said.

'He is,' said Mother Scaer. 'Did you not teach him diplomacy, Mother Gundring?'

The old minister gazed sternly at them from her place beside the Black Chair. 'I did. And who deserves it.'

'I believe she means we don't,' said Gorm.

'I take that to be the case,' answered Mother Scaer. 'And find her rude also.'

'Is this how you keep a bargain, Prince Yarvi?'

This hall full of worthies had once lined up to kiss Yarvi's hand. Now they looked as if they would happily queue to cut his throat. He shrugged. 'I am prince no longer, and I have kept what I could. No one foresaw this turn of events.'

'There's events for you,' said Mother Scaer. 'They never flow quite down the channel you dig for them.'

'You will not fight me, then?' asked Uthil.

'Why so very bloodthirsty?' Gorm pushed out his bottom lip. 'You are new in the job, but you will learn a king is more than just a killer. Let us give Father Peace his season, abide by the wishes of the High King in Skekenhouse and make of the fist an open hand. In summer, perhaps, on ground that suits me better, you can put Mother War's breath to the test.' He turned away, and followed by his minister and his warriors, strode for the door. 'I thank you for your winning hospitality, Gettlanders! You will hear from me!' He paused for a moment on the threshold, a great black outline against the daylight. 'And on that day, I shall speak in thunder.'

The doors of the Godshall were swung shut upon them.

'The time may come when we wish we had killed him here today,' murmured Yarvi's mother.

'Death waits for us all,' said Uthil, lowering

himself back into the Black Chair, sword still cradled in his arms. He had a way of sitting in it, slouched and easy, that Yarvi never could have managed. 'And we have other matters to attend to.' The king's eyes drifted across to Yarvi's, bright as the day they met upon the *South Wind*. 'My nephew. Once prince, once king, now—'

'Nothing,' said Yarvi, lifting his chin.

Uthil gave the faintest sad smile at that. A glimpse of the man Yarvi had slogged through the ice with, shared his last crust with, faced death beside. A glimpse, then the king's face was sword-sharp and axe-hard once again.

'You made a pact with Grom-gil-Gorm,' he said, and angry mutterings broke out about the hall. *A wise king always has someone to blame*, Mother Gundring used to say. 'You invited our most bitter enemy to spread fire and murder across Gettland.' Yarvi could hardly deny it, even if denials could have been heard above the mounting anger in the Godshall. 'Good people died. What price does the law demand for that, Mother Gundring?'

The minister looked from her new king to her old apprentice, and Yarvi felt his mother's hand grip tight at his arm, for they both knew the answer. 'Death, my king,' croaked Mother Gundring, seeming to slump against her staff. 'Or exile, at the least.'

'Death!' screeched a woman's voice from somewhere in the darkness, and the harsh echoes faded into a quiet stony as a tomb's.

Yarvi had faced Death before. Many times, now,

she had eased open the Last Door for him, and he was still casting a shadow. Though he was far from comfortable in her chill presence, as with many things he had improved with practice. This time at least, though his heart pounded and his mouth was sour, he faced her standing, and let his voice ring out clear.

'I made a mistake!' called Yarvi. 'I made many. I know it. But I swore an oath! Before the gods I swore it. A sun-oath and a moon-oath. And I saw no other way to keep it. To avenge the killing of my father and brother. To turn the traitor Odem out of the Black Chair. And, though I am sorry for the blood that was spilled, thanks to the favour of the gods . . .' Yarvi gazed up towards them, then humbly down at the floor, spreading his arms in submission. 'The rightful king has returned.'

Uthil frowned towards his hand, fingers resting upon the metal of the Black Chair. A small reminder that he owed it to Yarvi's plans could do no harm. The angry muttering began again, mounted, swelled, until Uthil raised his hand to bring silence.

'It is true that Odem set you on the path,' he said. 'His crimes were greater by far than yours, and you have already delivered his just punishment. You had reasons for what you did, and there has been enough death here, I think. Yours would be no justice.'

Yarvi kept his head bowed, and swallowed his relief. In spite of the hardships of the last few months, he liked being alive. He liked it more than ever.

'But there must be a reckoning.' And it seemed

there was a sadness in Uthil's eyes. 'I am sorry, truly I am. But your sentence must be exile, for a man who has sat once in the Black Chair will always seek to reclaim it.'

'I didn't think it so very comfortable.' Yarvi took one step up the dais. He knew what he had to do. He had known ever since Odem lay dead at his feet and he saw the face of Father Peace above him. Exile was not without some appeal. To owe nothing. To be anything. But he had wandered long enough. This was his home, and he was going nowhere.

'I never wanted the Black Chair. I never expected it.' Yarvi lifted his left hand and shook it so the one finger flopped back and forth. 'I am no one's notion of a king, least of all my own.' In silence he knelt. 'I offer another solution.'

Uthil's eyes narrowed, and Yarvi prayed to Father Peace that his uncle was looking for a way to pardon him. 'Speak, then.'

'Let me do what is best for Gettland. Let me give up all claim to your chair forever. Let me take the Minister's Test, as I was to do before my father's death. Let me surrender all title and inheritance, and let my family be the Ministry. I belong here, in the Godshall. Not in the Black Chair, but beside it. Show your greatness through your mercy, my king, and let me atone for my mistakes through loyal service to you and to the land.'

Uthil slowly sat back, frowning, while the silence stretched out. Finally the king leaned towards his minister.

'What think you to this, Mother Gundring?'

'A solution Father Peace will smile upon,' she murmured. 'I always believed Yarvi would make a fine minister. I still believe it. He has proved himself a deep-cunning man.'

'That much I believe.' But Uthil still hesitated, rubbing at his sharp jaw in consideration.

Then his mother let go Yarvi's arm and swept up towards the Black Chair, the train of her red dress spilling down the steps as she knelt at Uthil's feet. 'A great king is merciful,' she murmured. 'Please, my king. Let me have my only son.'

Uthil stirred, and his mouth opened but no words came. He might have been fearless before Grom-gil-Gorm, but faced with Yarvi's mother he trembled.

'We were once promised to each other,' she said. One hard breath would have sounded like thunder in the Godshall, then, but every breath was held. 'You were thought dead . . . but the gods have brought you back to your rightful place . . .' She put her hand gently upon the scarred back of his, where it rested on the arm of the Black Chair, and Uthil's eyes were fixed on her face. 'My dearest wish is to see that promise fulfilled.'

Mother Gundring shuffled closer, speaking low. 'The High King has proposed marriage to Laithlin more than once, he will take it very ill—'

Uthil did not look at her. His voice was rough. 'Our promise is older than the High King's suit by twenty years.'

'But only today Grandmother Wexen sent another eagle to—'

'Does Grandmother Wexen sit in the Black Chair, or do I?' Uthil finally turned his bright eyes on his minister.

'You do.' Mother Gundring turned hers to the floor. The wise minister coaxes, wheedles, argues, advises, and the wise minister obeys.

'Then send Grandmother Wexen's bird back to her with an invitation to our wedding.' Uthil turned over his hand so that he held Yarvi's mother's in his calloused palm, worn to the shape of a scrubbing block. 'You will wear the key to my treasury, Laithlin, and manage those affairs at which you have proved yourself so very able.'

'Gladly,' said Yarvi's mother. 'And my son?'

King Uthil looked at Yarvi for a long moment. Then he nodded. 'He shall take back his place as Mother Gundring's apprentice.' And at a stroke he made himself look stern and merciful both at once.

Yarvi breathed out. 'At last Gettland has a king to be proud of,' he said. 'I will thank Mother Sea every day for sending you back from the depths.'

And he stood and followed Grom-gil-Gorm towards the doors. He smiled through the taunts, and the jeering, and the mutters, and rather than hide his withered hand up his sleeve as his old habit had been, he let it proudly dangle. Compared to the slave pens of Vulsgard, and the torments of Trigg's whip, and the cold and hunger of the trackless ice, the scorn of fools was not so very difficult to endure.

With a little help from his two mothers, each no doubt with her own reasons, Yarvi walked from the Godshall alive. A crippled outcast once again, and bound for the Ministry. Where he belonged.

He had come full circle. But he had left a boy, and returned a man.

The dead were laid out on chill slabs in a chill cellar beneath the rock. Yarvi did not want to count them. Enough. That was their number. The harvest of his carefully-sown plans. The consequences of his rash oath sworn. No faces, only shrouds peaked at the nose, the chin, the feet. There was no way to tell his mother's hired killers from the honoured warriors of Gettland. Perhaps, once they had passed through the Last Door, there was no difference.

Yarvi knew which body was Jaud's, though. His friend's. His oarmate's. The man who had forged a path through the snow for him to follow. Whose soft voice had murmured 'one stroke at a time' as he whimpered over the oar. Who had taken Yarvi's fight as his own, even though he had been no fighter. It was the one Sumael stood beside, her clenched fists on the slab, dark face lit down one side by the flame of a single flickering taper.

'Your mother's found a place for me on a ship,' she said, without looking up, her voice with a softness he was not used to hearing there.

'Good navigators are always in demand,' said Yarvi.

341

The gods knew, he could have done with someone to point out the path for him.

'We leave at first light for Skekenhouse, then on.'

'Home?' he asked.

Sumael closed her eyes, and nodded, the faintest smile at the corner of her scarred mouth. 'Home.' When he first saw her he had not thought of her as fine-looking, but she seemed beautiful now. So much he could not look away.

'Have you thought that, maybe . . . you could stay?' Yarvi hated himself even for asking. For making her turn him down. He was bound for the Ministry anyway. He had nothing to offer her. And Jaud's body lay between them, a barrier there was no crossing.

'I have to go,' she said. 'I can barely remember who I used to be.'

He could have said the same. 'Surely all that matters is who you are now.'

'I barely know that either. Besides, Jaud carried me, in the snow.' Her hand twitched towards the shroud, but much to Yarvi's relief she let it lie. 'The least I can do is carry his ashes. I'll leave them at his village. Maybe I'll even drink from that well of his. Drink for both of us.' She swallowed, and all the while for some reason Yarvi felt a cold anger growing in him. 'Why miss the sweetest water in the—'

'He chose to stay,' snapped Yarvi.

Sumael slowly nodded, not looking up. 'We all did.'

'I didn't force him.'

'No.'

'You could have left, and taken him, if you'd fought harder.'

Now she looked up, but with none of the anger he knew he deserved, only her own share of the guilt. 'You're right. That will be my weight to carry.'

Yarvi looked away, and suddenly his eyes swam with tears. A set of things done, and choices made, and each had seemed the lesser evil but had somehow led him here. Could this really be anyone's greater good?

'You don't hate me?' he whispered.

'I've lost one friend, I don't mean to throw away another.' And she put one hand gently on his shoulder. 'I'm not much good at making new ones.'

He pressed his own on top of it, wishing he could hold it there. Strange, how you never see how much you want a thing until you know you cannot have it.

'You don't blame me?' he whispered.

'Why would I?' She gave him a last parting squeeze, then let him go. 'It's better if you do it.'

SOME ARE SAVED

'I'm glad you came,' said Yarvi. 'I'm fast running out of friends.'

'Happy to do it,' said Rulf. 'For you and for Ankran. Can't say I loved the skinny bastard when he was storekeeper, but I warmed to him in the end.' He grinned at Yarvi, the big scab above his eye shifting. 'Some men you stick to right off, but it's those that take time to stick as stick longest. Shall we get some slaves?'

There was a muttering, and a grunting, and a clattering of chains as the wares got to their feet for inspection, each pair of eyes with its own mixture of shame, and fear, and hope, and hopelessness, and Yarvi found himself rubbing gently at the faint scars on his throat where his own collar used to sit. The stink of the place smothered him with memories he would much rather have forgotten. Strange, how quickly he had grown used to free air again.

'Prince Yarvi!' The proprietor hurried from the shadows at the back, a big man with a soft, pale face, faintly familiar. One of the procession who had grovelled before Yarvi at his father's howing up. Now he would have a chance to grovel again.

'I'm a prince no longer,' said Yarvi, 'but, otherwise, yes. You're Yoverfell?'

The flesh-dealer puffed up with pride at being known. 'Indeed I am, and deeply honoured by your visit! Might I ask what sort of slave you are—'

'Does the name Ankran mean much to you?'

The merchant's eyes flickered to Rulf, standing grim and solid with his thumbs in his silver-buckled sword-belt. 'Ankran?'

'Let me sharpen your memory as the reek of your shop has sharpened mine. You sold a man called Ankran, then extorted money from him to keep his wife and child safe.'

Yoverfell cleared his throat. 'I have broken no law—'

'And nor will I when I call in your debts.'

The merchant's face had drained of colour. 'I owe you nothing . . .'

Yarvi chuckled. 'Me? No. But my mother, Laithlin, soon to be once again the Golden Queen of Gettland and holder of the key to the treasury . . . I understand you do owe her a trifling debt?'

The knobble on the merchant's scrawny throat bobbed as he swallowed. 'I am my queen's most humble servant—'

'Her slave, I'd call you. If you sold all you own it wouldn't come close to covering what you owe her.'

'Her slave, then, why not?' Yoverfell gave a bitter snort. 'Since you concern yourself with my business, it was because of the interest on her loans that I had to squeeze what I could from Ankran. I did not want to do it—'

'But you put your wishes aside,' said Yarvi. 'How noble.'

'What do you want?'

'Let us begin with the woman and her child.'

'Very well.' Eyes on the ground, the merchant scraped away into the shadows. Yarvi looked across at Rulf, and the old warrior raised his brows, and about them the slaves looked on in silence. Yarvi thought one might be smiling.

He was not sure what he had been expecting. Outstanding beauty, or stunning grace, or something that struck him instantly to the heart. But Ankran's family were an ordinary-looking pair. Most people are, of course, to those that don't know them. The mother was small and slight with a defiant set to her jaw. The son was sandy-headed, as his father had been, and kept his eyes down.

Yoverfell ushered them forward, then plucked nervously at one of his hands with the other. 'Healthy and well cared for, as promised. They are yours, of course, gifts, with my compliments.'

'Your compliments you can keep,' said Yarvi. 'Now you will pack up here, and move your business to Vulsgard.'

'Vulsgard?'

'Yes. They have many flesh-dealers there, you will feel very much at home.'

'But why?'

'So you can keep an eye on the business of Grom-gil-Gorm. Know your enemy's house better than your own, I've heard it said.'

Rulf gave an approving grunt, puffed out his chest a little and shifted his thumbs in his sword-belt.

'It's that,' said Yarvi, 'or find yourself being sold in your own shop. What price would you fetch, do you think?'

Yoverfell cleared his throat. 'I will make the arrangements.'

'Quickly,' said Yarvi, and strode from the stink of that place to stand in the air and breathe, eyes closed.

'You . . . are our new owner, then?'

Ankran's wife stood beside him, one finger wedged inside her collar.

'No. My name is Yarvi, this is Rulf.'

'We were friends of your husband,' said Rulf, ruffling the boy's hair and causing him some discomfort.

'Were?' she asked. 'Where is Ankran?'

Yarvi swallowed, wondering how to break that news, searching for the proper words—

'Dead,' said Rulf, simply.

'I'm sorry,' added Yarvi. 'He died saving my life, which strikes even me as a poor trade. But you are free.'

'Free?' she muttered.

'Yes.'

'I don't want to be free, I want to be safe.'

Yarvi blinked at that, then felt his mouth twitch into a sad smile. He had never wanted much more himself. 'I daresay I could use a servant, if you're willing to work.'

'I always have been that,' she said.

Yarvi stopped beside a smith's shop, and flicked a coin over a trestle covered with boat-maker's tools. One of the first coins of the new kind – round and perfect, and stamped on one side with his own mother's frowning face.

'Strike their collars,' he said.

Ankran's family gave no thanks for their freedom, but the ringing of hammer on chisel was thanks enough for Yarvi. Rulf watched with one foot up on a low wall and his forearms crossed upon his knee.

'I'm no high judge of righteousness.'

'Who is?'

'But I find this to be a good thing.'

'Don't let anyone know, it might ruin my reputation.' Yarvi saw an old woman glaring at him from across the square, and he smiled back, and waved, and watched her scuttle muttering away. 'It seems I've become the villain of this piece.'

'If life has taught me one thing, it's that there are no villains. Only people, doing their best.'

'My best has proved disastrous.'

'Could've been far worse.' Rulf curled his tongue and spat. 'And you're young. Try again. Might be you'll improve.'

Yarvi narrowed his eyes at the old warrior. 'When did you become wise?'

'I've always been uncommonly insightful, but you were blinded by your own cleverness.'

'A common fault with kings. Hopefully I'm young enough to learn humility too.'

'It's well one of us is.'

'And what will you do with your twilight years?' asked Yarvi.

'As it happens, the great King Uthil has offered me a place with his guard.'

'The stench of honour! You'll accept?'

'I said no.'

'You did?'

'Honour's a fool's prize, and I've a feeling Uthil is the sort of master who'll always have dead servants about him.'

'Wiser and wiser,' said Yarvi.

'Until recently I thought my life done, but now that it begins again I find I've no pressing desire to cut it short.' Yarvi looked sideways, and saw Rulf looking sideways back. 'Thought maybe you could use an oarmate.'

'Me?'

'What could a one-handed minister and a rogue fifteen years past his best not achieve together?'

At a final blow the collar sprang open and Ankran's son stood, blinking, and rubbing at his neck, and his mother took him in her arms and kissed his hair.

'I'm not alone,' murmured Yarvi.

Rulf put an arm around him and hugged him crushing tight. 'Not while I'm alive, oarmate.'

It was a great affair.

Many powerful families in the far reaches of Gettland would be angered that news of King

Uthil's return had barely reached them before he was married, denying them the chance to have their importance noted at an event that would live so long in the memory.

No doubt the all-powerful High King on his high chair in Skekenhouse, not to mention the all-knowing Grandmother Wexen at his elbow, would be far from delighted at the news, as Mother Gundring was keen to point out.

But Yarvi's mother brushed all objections away with an airy wave and said, 'Their anger is dust to me.' She was the Golden Queen again. Once she had spoken it was as a thing already done.

And so in the Godshall the statues were garlanded with the first flowers of spring, and the wedding gifts were heaped about the Black Chair in gaudy abundance, and the people were packed beneath the dome tight as sheep in winter quarters until the very air was misty with their breath.

The blessed couple sang promises to one another in the sight of gods and men, shafts of light from the dome above striking fire from the king's burnished armour and the queen's daunting jewels, and all applauded though Uthil's singing voice was, in Yarvi's opinion, not up to much and his mother's little better. Then Brinyolf droned out the most elaborate blessing even that hallowed place had ever witnessed, while beside him Mother Gundring slumped ever more impatiently around her staff and every bell in the city sent up a merry clangour from below.

Oh, happy day!

How could Uthil not be pleased? He had the Black Chair and the best wife any man could ask for, coveted by the High King himself. How could Laithlin not be delighted? She had the jewelled key to the treasury of Gettland once again upon her chain and the priests of the One God dragged from her mint and whipped through Thorlby into the sea. How could the people of Gettland not rejoice? They had a king of iron and a queen of gold, rulers to trust in and be proud of. Rulers with poor singing voices, possibly, but two hands each.

In spite of all that happiness, though – or more likely because of it – Yarvi scarcely enjoyed the marriage of his mother more than he had the burning of his father. That event Yarvi had been unable to avoid. If anyone noticed him steal away from this one, no doubt they were not sad to see it.

The weather outside better suited his mood than the petal-scented warmth within. There was a seeking wind off the grey sea that day, and it moaned among the battlements of the citadel and cut at him with a salt rain as he wandered up the worn steps and along the empty walkways.

He saw her from far off, on the roof of the Godshall, clothes far too thin plastered to her with the rain, hair furiously whipping in the wind. He saw her in good time. He could have walked on and found another place to frown at the sky. But his feet led him towards her.

'Prince Yarvi,' she said as he came close, tearing a scrap from her bitten-down thumbnail with her teeth and spitting it into the wind. 'What an honour.'

Yarvi sighed. There was a wearying pattern to the last few days. 'I'm not a prince any more, Isriun.'

'No? Your mother is queen again, isn't she? She has the key to the treasury of Gettland on her chain?' Her white hand strayed to her chest, where there was no key, no chain, nothing any more. 'What's a queen's son, if not a prince?'

'A crippled fool?' he muttered.

'You were that when we met, and no doubt always will be. Not to mention the child of a traitor.'

'Then we have more in common than ever,' snapped Yarvi, and saw her pale face twitch, and instantly regretted it. Had things been only a little different, it might have been the two of them raised up in glory down below. He in the Black Chair, she upon the stool beside him, eyes shining as she gently held his withered hand, as they shared that better kiss she had asked for on his return . . .

But things were as they were. There would be no kisses today. Not today, not ever. He turned to look at the heaving sea, his fists bunched on the parapet. 'I didn't come to argue.'

'Why did you come?'

'I thought I should tell you, since . . .' He gritted his teeth, and looked down at his twisted hand, white on the wet stone. Since what? *Since we were promised? Since we once meant something to each other?* He could not bring himself to say the words. 'I'm leaving for Skekenhouse. I'm taking the Minister's Test. I'll have no family, no birthright, and . . . no wife.'

She laughed into the wind. 'And more in common yet. I've no friends, no dowry, and no father.' She turned to look at him then, and the hatred in her eyes made him feel sick. 'They sank his body in the midden.'

Perhaps that should have made Yarvi glad. He had dreamed of it often enough, bent all his prayers and all his will towards it. Broken everything, and sacrificed his friend and his friendships for it. But looking into Isriun's face, red eyes sunken in shadowed sockets, he felt no triumph.

'I'm sorry. Not for him, but for you.'

Her mouth twisted with contempt. 'What do you think that's worth to me?'

'Nothing. But I'm sorry still.' And he took his hands from the parapet, and turned his back on his betrothed, and walked towards the steps.

'I've sworn an oath!'

Yarvi paused. He wanted very much to leave that blasted roof and never return, but now the skin on his neck prickled, and he turned back despite himself. 'Oh?'

'A sun-oath and a moon-oath.' Isriun's eyes burned in her white face and her wet hair lashed at her. 'I swore it before She Who Judges, and He Who Remembers, and She Who Makes Fast the Knot. My ancestors buried above the beach bore witness. He Who Watches and She Who Writes bore witness. Now you bear witness, Yarvi. It will be a chain upon me and a goad within me. I will be revenged upon the killers of my father. I have sworn it!'

She smiled a twisted smile, then. A mockery of the one she gave him when she left the Godshall on the day they were promised. 'So you see, a woman can swear the same oath as a man.'

'If she's fool enough,' said Yarvi, as he turned away.

THE LESSER EVIL

Mother Sun smiled even as she sank beneath the world on the evening Brother Yarvi came home.

The first day of summer, the Gettlanders had declared it, with cats basking on the hot roofs of Thorlby, the sea-birds calling lazy to one another, the slightest breeze carrying a salt tang up the steep lanes and through the open windows of the city.

Through the door to Mother Gundring's chambers too, when Yarvi finally managed to wrestle the heavy latch open with his crippled hand.

'The wanderer returns,' said the old minister, putting aside her book in a puff of dust.

'Mother Gundring.' Yarvi bowed low, and presented her with the cup.

'And you have brought me tea.' She closed her eyes, and sniffed the steam, then sipped, and swallowed. Her lined face broke into the smile which Yarvi had always felt so proud to see. 'Things have not been the same without you.'

'You need never want for tea again, at least.'

'Then you passed the test?'

'Did you ever doubt?'

'Not I, Brother Yarvi, not I. And yet you wear a sword.' She frowned towards Shadikshirram's blade, sheathed at his waist. 'A kind word parries most blows.'

'I carry this for the others. It reminds me where I've come from. A minister stands for Father Peace, but a good one is no stranger to Mother War.'

'Hah! True enough.' Mother Gundring held out her hand to the stool on the other side of the firepit. The one where Yarvi had so often sat, following the old minister's stories with rapt attention, learning tongues, and history, and the lore of plants, and the proper way to speak to a king. Could it really be only a few months since he last sat there? It seemed he had done so in a different world. In a dream.

And now he had woken.

'I am glad you are back,' said Mother Gundring, 'and not just because of your tea. We have much to do in Thorlby.'

'I don't think people love me here.'

Mother Gundring shrugged it off. 'Already they forget. Folk have short memories.'

'The minister's task is to remember.'

'And to advise, to heal, to speak truth and know the secret ways, to find the lesser evil and weigh the greater good, to smooth the path for Father Peace in every tongue, to spin tales—'

'Shall I spin a tale for you?'

'What manner of tale, Brother Yarvi?'

'A tale of blood and deceit, of money and murder, of treachery and power.'

Mother Gundring laughed, and took another sip from her cup. 'The only sort I enjoy. Has it elves in it? Dragons? Trolls?'

Yarvi shook his head. 'People can do all the evil we'll need.'

'True again. Is it something you heard in Skekenhouse?'

'Partly. I've been working at this tale for a long time. Ever since that night my father died. But I think I have it now from start to end.'

'Knowing your talents it must be a fine tale indeed.'

'You will thrill to it, Mother Gundring.'

'Then begin!'

Yarvi sat forward, looking into the flames, rubbing at his twisted palm with his thumb. He had been rehearsing it ever since he passed the test, gave up his birthright and was accepted into the Ministry. Ever since he kissed the cheek of Grandmother Wexen, looked into her eyes, found them brighter and hungrier than ever, and knew the truth. 'I find I hardly know where to begin.'

'Set it up. Let's have the background.'

'Good advice,' said Yarvi. 'But yours always has been. So . . . a High King well past his youth, and a grandmother of the Ministry no closer to hers, most jealous of their power, as the powerful often are, looked to the north from Skekenhouse, and saw a threat to their majesty. Not a great man wielding iron and steel, but a great woman wielding gold and silver. A golden queen, with a plan to stamp coins all of one weight, so that every trade about the Shattered Sea would be made with her face.'

Mother Gundring sat back, the many lines on her forehead deepening as she considered. 'This story has the smack of truth.'

'The best ones do. You taught me that.' Now that he was begun the words spilled out easily. 'The High King and his minister saw the merchants leave their wharves for those of this northern queen, and their revenues shrivelling month upon month, and their power shrivelling with them. They had to act. But kill a woman who could spin gold from the air? No. Her husband was too proud and wrathful to be dealt with. Kill him, then, and topple the queen from her lofty perch and take her for their own, so she could spin gold for them. That was their plan.'

'Kill a king?' muttered Mother Gundring, staring hard at Yarvi over the rim of her cup.

He shrugged. 'It's how these stories often start.'

'But kings are cautious and well-guarded.'

'This one especially. They needed the help of someone he trusted.' Yarvi sat forward, the fire warm on his face. 'And so they taught a bronze-feathered eagle a message. The king must die. And they sent it to his minister.'

Mother Gundring blinked, and very slowly swallowed another mouthful of tea. 'A heavy task to give a minister, killing the man she was sworn to serve.'

'But was she not sworn to serve the High King and her grandmother too?'

'We all are,' whispered Mother Gundring. 'You among us, Brother Yarvi.'

'Oh, I'm forever swearing oaths: I hardly know which ones to honour. This minister had the same trouble, but if a king sits between gods and men, the High King sits between gods and kings, and has been thinking himself higher yet, of late. She knew he would not be denied. So she fashioned a plan. Replace her king with a more reasonable brother. Trim away any troublesome heir. Blame some old enemy from the utmost north where even the thoughts of civilized men rarely stray. Say that a dove came from another minister with an offer of peace, and drew this rash king into an ambush . . .'

'Perhaps that was the lesser evil,' said Mother Gundring. 'Perhaps it was that or see Mother War spread her bloody wings across the whole Shattered Sea.'

'The lesser evil and the greater good.' Yarvi took a long breath, and it seemed to hurt deep in his chest, and he thought of the black birds blinking in Sister Owd's cage. 'Only the minister given the blame never used doves. Only crows.'

Mother Gundring paused with the cup halfway to her mouth. 'Crows?'

'It is so often the small things overlooked which leave our schemes in ruins.'

'Oh, troublesome detail.' Mother Gundring's eye twitched as she looked down at her tea and took a longer swallow, and for a while they sat in silence, only the happy crackle of the fire and the odd floating spark between them. 'I thought you might untangle it in time,' she said. 'But not so soon.'

Yarvi snorted. 'Not before I died at Amwend.'

'That was never my choice,' said the old minister. She who had always been like a mother to him. 'You were to take the test, and give up your birthright, and in time take my place as we had always planned. But Odem did not trust me. He moved too soon. I could not stop your mother putting you in the Black Chair.' She gave a bitter sigh. 'And Grandmother Wexen would by no means have been satisfied with that result.'

'So you let me flounder into Odem's trap.'

'With the deepest regret. I judged it the lesser evil.' She set her empty cup down beside her. 'How does this story end, Brother Yarvi?'

'It already has. With the deepest regret.' He looked up from the flames and into her eyes. 'And it is Father Yarvi, now.'

The old minister frowned, first at him, then down at the cup he had brought her. 'Black-tongue root?'

'I swore an oath, Mother Gundring, to be avenged on the killers of my father. I may be half a man, but I swore a whole oath.'

The flames in the firepit flickered then, their reflections dancing orange in the glass jars on the shelves.

'Your father and your brother,' croaked Mother Gundring. 'Odem and his men. So many others. And now the Last Door opens for me. All . . . because of coins.'

She blinked then, and swayed towards the fire, and Yarvi started up and caught her gently with his left arm, and slipped the cushion behind her with his right, and eased her with great care back into her chair. 'It seems coins can be most deadly.'

'I am sorry,' whispered Mother Gundring, her breath coming short.

'So am I. You will not find a sorrier man in all of Gettland.'

'I do not think so.' She gave the faintest smile. 'You will make a fine minister, Father Yarvi.'

'I will try,' he said.

She did not answer.

Yarvi took a ragged breath, and brushed her eyelids closed, and crossed her withered hands in her lap, and slumped back sick and weary on his stool. He was still sitting there when the door banged wide and a figure blundered up the steps, setting the bunches of drying plants swinging like hanged men behind him.

One of the youngest warriors, newly past his tests. Younger even than Yarvi, firelight shifting on his beardless face as he loitered in the archway.

'King Uthil seeks an audience with his minister,' he said.

'Does he indeed?' Yarvi tossed the half-drunk tea hissing into the firepit, then wrapped the fingers of his good hand about Mother Gundring's staff. His staff, the elf-metal cold against his skin.

He stood. 'Tell the king I am on my way.'